Guardian's Circle: Book 1

Lost and Found

J.M. Beal

Golden Fleece Press
PO Box 1464,
Centreville, VA 20122
www.goldenfleecepress.com

Special discounts are available on quantity purchases by corporations, associations, and others. For details, contact the publisher at the address above.
U.S. trade bookstores and wholesalers please contact Ingram Content Group at customerservice@ingramcontent.com or by telephone at 800.973.8000(option 3).

Epub ISBN 13:   978-1-942195-15-3
Mobi ISBN 13:   978-1-942195-17-7
Print ISBN 13:   978-1-942195-14-6
Pdf ISBN 13:   978-1-942195-18-4

Printed in the United States of America

First Edition

10 9 8 7 6 5 4 3 2 1

DEDICATION

To Julie, who looked at me and said something to the effect of 'you're not doing it because you're afraid' and convinced me to shut up and write it.

To all my lovely editors, who suffered through a strange morass of ellipses and conjoined-words. I cannot tell you how thankful I am for all your help and patience.

And of course, as always, to my husband and son. I love you both, and I owe you more than I could ever repay for all your support and encouragement.

Bestiary:

Noun
A treatise on various kinds of real ~~or mythical~~ animals.

PROLOGUE

Fall, twenty-five years ago.
Rural Kentucky

Nate Carter was six when his dad was killed by some
thing in their barn.

They'd only been living there for a year, in a rickety
old farmhouse with a couple of acres of pasture and a barn
that was older than his parents. Nate's dad bought it from
his mom's great-aunt. They were happy. They had an old
gray nag that tried to bite anybody but his dad, and plans
for more horses. Half the barn housed his dad's classic
Charger and when Nate was being good—when he'd done
his homework and helped his mom with the dishes—he
got to help with the car. His mom said his dad loved the
car more than he loved them.

It was a joke. His dad could never love anything more
than he loved them.

Nate wasn't sure how he felt about first grade. He
knew his dad expected him to do good. He said he wanted
his son to be able to do more than work as a handyman
until he made his dreams happen. He liked his teacher
okay, and there was a boy at his table named Michael that
promised Nate could come over the next weekend and
play with his action figures. He was sitting at the old

dinged-up kitchen table, drawing a picture of his favorite hero—his name was CentaurMan, and he carried a magical lasso he used to round up the bad guys—while his mom sang along with the radio and made silly faces. She was making his favorite for supper; macaroni and cheese out of the box, with hamburger.

There was a noise from the barn, loud and strange. They heard the high agitated whinny of the mare, too. His mom pulled everything off the burners, switching them off, and took his hand. She worried a lot. She worried when Dad was working on the car alone, or had to go out at night, or worked late. She worried when he wasn't right there with them.

The sun was hanging low over the fields, making everything warm and orange. It was that perfect week when fall started to get cold and Nate kicked at the leaves crunching under their feet while they hurried across the yard. He couldn't wait to carve pumpkins soon; Dad said he could even have his own.

His mom pushed the old barn door open, face pale. "Ben, are you…"

The *thing* at the back of the barn didn't even look up. Nate couldn't see it clearly, not really. Teeth and claws and blood. His Mom pushed him into the corner and grabbed the gun they kept by the door. He remembered the noise, the rattle and boom of the shotgun, more than the sight or the smell. It echoed in his ears over the way the thing screamed, slammed against the back doorway of the barn, and ran off into the fields.

Everything after that was sort of a blur. His mom crying, making him stay back when all he wanted was his dad. His mom stayed next to his dad for a long time, yelling and begging until her words spilled over each other and Nate couldn't understand anything. Until it was so still he couldn't even hear the ringing in his ears from the shotgun anymore.

Eventually she called the police, and frantically explained to Nate they could not tell them about the monster.

Nate didn't have to lie. No one asked him any questions anyway.

At the funeral everyone told them how sorry they were. How sad they were. How wonderful his dad had been. Nate had never seen so many people in his life, tear stained faces and sad frowns. Everyone wanted to hug him, or pat him on the head. He spent half the day hiding in the bathroom. The Sheriff said he thought it was a rabid wolf-hound someone ditched on the highway. It had been after the Nag and his dad just...got in the way.

That part was probably true.

He didn't talk about it, growing up. Just told people how old he was, and that his mom didn't handle it well. In her defense, there probably wasn't a good way to handle your husband being ripped apart by some creature on a random Thursday in October. He had clearer memories of her then, than any other time.

It was three years before she started hunting the junk thumping along behind the human race in the night. Before she threw them into a long succession of changing schools, and family that's probably not family, and increasingly elaborate lies. It was seven more years before she plunked a GED book down in front of him because she was tired of planning things around his school life.

Nate was six when his dad was killed by some thing in their barn, and it was years before the moving and the monsters and the family that's not family, but in his head one came right after the other. After that random Thursday in October nothing ever felt stable again.

Prologue II

August, year before last.
Galesburg, Illinois

Grace Cleary stepped out of the library, dragging her bag further up her shoulder, and waving to Mr. Jenkins. He'd been watching her uncomfortably for the last half hour, since closing, because he wanted to turn the lights off. The computer system updates she was doing for them were important, but she could have been ready to leave sooner. He just needed to ask.

Miss Anderson was standing on her porch on the corner next to the library, watching Grace walk by. Grace had moved to Galesburg after college. It was quiet and small, and therefore safe enough that her best friend didn't panic about her being alone. The rent was cheap, which helped. She'd known when she started college making enough money as a copy-editor to survive was going to be difficult.

It'd been a lot easier than she'd planned. She picked up extra local jobs for the newspaper or the library when she could. Grace had never figured it was her skills that were lacking, more the ability to find something that paid in her field.

The walk home from the library wasn't long, and it was that part of fall where the nights were just cool enough to be comfortable. The grass was still crunchy and dry under her feet. They'd had a pretty harsh summer. Grace had happily spent a large chunk of it holed up in her house with the air-conditioning, enjoying the fact she did a job that allowed her to be as antisocial as she liked.

That was possibly part of the reason people in town didn't really consider her less of a stranger after six years.

Grace wasn't the sort of antisocial that couldn't or didn't talk to people. She was socially capable; college had taught her that, as much to her own surprise as anybody else's. She'd just always liked books more than she liked people.

Galesburg was as quiet as always at night. She'd gotten used to the normal sounds rattling around after dark; a car, a couple of streets over, and a barking dog. But it was a strange bark, and she could hear pounding feet.

A kid came tearing out of the park across Main Street, running as fast as he could, skateboard clattering to the ground behind him. She didn't know his name. He'd been told off the week before for bringing his skateboard in the library. Mr. Jenkins had called him a 'middle-school troublemaker' but Grace pegged him as a new sixth-grader.

Being chased by the largest dog she'd ever seen.

It growled low and dark, despite the running, and its eyes stayed completely fixed on the boy. An animal that large prompted a fight or flight response—how could it not in an unarmed person—and if she'd been on the street alone Grace would have probably miraculously managed to climb to the top of the nearest tree.

There was no way that kid was going to outrun it much longer.

Grace dropped her bag off her shoulder and got between them. She didn't actually think it was a dog anymore, as it ran under the street-lamp—it was too big, and the curve of its shoulder was wrong—but she still swung her bag at its head. Hard enough she could feel the *thump* when it connected. Hard enough to throw it off its feet.

It was fast though. An aborted roll, strange white eyes fastening on Grace instead of its earlier prey, and her brain couldn't process the lunge before it was on her, knocking her to the ground. Grace's hand landed on a helpful rock, and she managed a good solid hit to the snout. Its claws caught on her side, pain erupting on her thigh when it bit down and pulled.

She was grabbing the rock again, slippery in her bloody fingers, when a gunshot rang out in the dark.

There was a high-pitched whine, and then it thumped on the ground next to her.

Grace blinked, swallowing.

"Miss?" Strong hands clamped over the bloody portion of her leg, pressing down. "Hey."

Grace looked away from the figure on the concrete next to her, mind rebelling at the switch from rabid dog-thing to the lowlife who worked at the gas station across town. "Wha—"

"Don't start screaming now." He pulled off his belt and cinched in around her leg, tight.

Grace didn't think she was bleeding that badly, but she didn't really want to look. She laid her head back on the ground as he checked her side, and stared at the dark trees swaying in the breeze.

"Hey, don't go into shock." He shook her slightly and looked at her side, eyes dark. "You're losing enough blood as it is."

Grace didn't know him, which in a town as small as Galesburg was almost disturbing. He seemed normal, like he'd have fit in better than she would have with his ratty flannel shirt, close-cropped salt and pepper hair, and double-barreled shotgun.

He might have had a point about the shock.

"Those don't look too deep," he said, motioning to her side. He swallowed, grabbing her securely. "Small place like this, I imagine you'll do better I just take you to the hospital."

"It's over on—"

"I know where it is." He huffed, helping her stand on her uninjured leg.

"What…"

He glanced at her, quickly shuffling across the street. "Concentrate on staying up, questions can wait."

She frowned, because questions or not, she was actually concentrating on hobbling wherever he was taking her and not on the sickly slick feel of the blood still oozing down her leg, or out of her side. He was right about the blood-loss though. Her head had that strange, floaty quality that came with the attendant low-blood-pressure.

Her leg probably wouldn't end up with a scar that matched the one on her elbow though. That was a simple line, because she'd fallen off a ladder in the stacks at the University library.

"Don't float off on me there sugar," her new friend grumbled, throwing the shotgun in the backseat of a rusting white truck. "Scoot back there against the seat and pull yourself in. There ain't exactly anywhere I can grab and lift."

Grace managed to squiggle herself onto the high bench seat, and swing her legs in the cab. "I'm gonna bleed in your truck."

She watched him jog around the front of the truck, after he'd shut her door.

"It's happened before." He slammed his door, starting the engine.

"What about…um…him?"

The truck jerked as he threw it in drive, the first real pain shooting up her leg.

"Rule number one, always take care of the living first."

~~~~~~

It was three, nearly four hours before Grace was in anything that resembled a *room*. They'd been light on the pain meds so far, giving her small short-term doses, but it was an even trade. She was still in pain, so the doctor and the night nurse had been pretty adamant about Animal Control being able to wait a bit to talk to her. And since she didn't know what to say to them, that was good.

It was nearly an hour and a half before anybody thought to ask about the guy who came in with her.

They'd have probably made him leave, but then some other poor sod started coding, and the harried nurse just thrust the paperwork at him and ordered him to fill it out.

Grace wasn't sure how she felt about spilling out her entire life in next-of-kin questionnaires for a complete stranger, but he had just saved her life. He was good at them, re-asked whether she had any drug allergies or special conditions three times, until he was sure she was coherent enough to have answered right.

She was in a triage room that should have had more people in it, but county hospital or not it wasn't the sort of night that brought in a lot of emergency cases. The walls were that sort of mauvey-green scheme she thought every hospital on the planet must be painted. Complete with the hotel duck-print hanging on the wall.

She heard footsteps, and a quiet hello, and tried to deal with the half-dose of morphine swimming around in her head and focus on something. On a half dose she could *almost* make sense of the world around her.

"We've got the films back." The doctor stood at the side of her gurney, looking ridiculously young in the middle of the night with his surgery scrubs and his white coat and his perfect hair.

She was in shock. That was why she felt old enough the doctor looked young. Realistically he had to be nearly her age unless he was a child prodigy.

10

"Nothing broken bone wise." He showed her the x-rays, sighing. "You've got a lot of potential muscle damage though."

Grace swallowed.

"Still, I'm confident we'll get you all patched up. We're scrubbing a surgery theater now, we'll give you a dose of the good stuff—that'll knock you under—and when you wake up we'll have that all cleaned and stitched up."

"'Kay."

It wasn't as if she had much of a choice.

"Good. And then we'll be keeping you overnight for observation, just because it's so late, providing we don't find anything worrying." He turned to her rescuer. "Family is allowed to stay in this circumstance."

"Thank you."

Grace looked over at him while the doctor left. She should probably have been shouting something about the fact he wasn't family.

"He seems like a good doctor," he said.

Her lips twitched, head falling back on the pillow. "I don't even know your name."

"Curt." He pushed an uneasy hand through his hair. "Curt Jacobs."

"Pleasure to meet you, Mr. Jacobs," Grace deadpanned.

"Just Curt. I do my best to avoid being mister to anybody." He shifted uncomfortably. "If I'm making you uncomfortable, I can go. Thought once you weren't so..." He died off, not bothering with a descriptor.

She didn't really know what she was either.

"...you might have some questions for me."

Grace almost smiled, closing her eyes. "Some."

She opened her eyes again as he looked outside the room. "Nobody around. Now's probably as good a time as any."

"The thing that bit me." Grace swallowed. "Is my overactive imagination going the right place with that?"

"It is."

"Because unless I missed something, tonight wasn't a full moon."

"It wasn't." He rubbed the back of his neck, trying to pat his hair down self-consciously. "This stuff don't exactly have a manual." He gave her a tired, avuncular smile. "Been at this job more than twenty years, there are still days it's new."

"Job?" Grace frowned, her head swimming. The drugs had started to kick in."So you...hunt monsters? Or is it just werewolves?"

Curt was watching her, face troubled. "Not just those. And yeah, something like that. You know most people are trying to reclaim some sort of normal reality about now."

Grace was asleep before she could tell him that she'd never held much stock in normal.

It was morning before she woke up again.

"Look who's rejoined the land of the living."

Her mind was utterly and completely blank for three very long seconds, before she remembered his name. "Curt."

He nodded, arms crossed over his chest. "I wondered if you'd remember any of that."

Grace scoffed. "Kind of hard to forget." She struggled up a bit, moving up the bed, back protesting. Her leg was covered in stiff bandages, and the kind of numb anybody with sense left alone.

He pawed at his hair, sighing. "The Doctor should be here in a minute—the new one anyway, that kid from last night went home at some point." He shrugged. "Once they're done with you for a bit, we'll talk."

She winced, watching him carefully. "Alright. Have you been here all night?"

He shifted in obvious discomfort. "I left for a bit to take care of...things." He forced a smile. "They were kicking me out anyway, while you were getting patched up."

Things. She wasn't going to ask what *things* meant. She'd been attacked by a werewolf. She was under no obligation to feel sorry for him. "How worried should I be about..." she gestured to her leg.

He didn't want to answer. At all. She could see it in his face.

Of course he got lucky and didn't have to then. The morning-shift doctor popped up. This one looked old enough to vote—or she was done with being in shock— and muttered to himself while he checked the chart at the end of the bed. Looked at her dressings and checked her side.

"Right, I think we're going to send you home." He beamed easily. "The nurse will bring an appointment card, when she brings your paperwork. Sometime next week, and we'll look at how those stitches are doing."

"Yay."

The doctor huffed lightly, amused. "She'll give you a sheet about wound care and dressing changes too. If it feels unusually hot, or hurts more than the drugs can handle, don't hesitate to come back in." He cleaned his hands with sterilizer, and gave her his best bed-side smile. "And no bending that knee until we see you again. The nurse will be in in a bit with a crutch, and she'll do a dressing change with you before you go home, so we're sure you can manage it." He frowned. "Do you have a ride?"

"I'll take her," Curt offered.

"Might want to keep an eye on her for a couple of days, just to be safe."

"I'd planned on it."

"Then she's in good hands." The doctor smiled benignly at Curt, as he swept from the room.

Grace was relatively sure he hadn't meant his assurance the way the doctor took it.

~~~~~~

Grace hobbled her way up the front steps, unlocking the door. There was something positive to be said for the fact her little house was only one level. No dealing with stairs just to go to the bathroom, or bed.

"Make yourself at home." She glanced back at her strange houseguest. Ignored the shotgun he was carrying, and the small black duffle. "I'm not sure I'd trust my ability to do much right now."

Curt narrowed his eyes at her. "Why don't you sit down? I can find my way around anything I need."

"Sure."

He didn't though. He waited until she was down, and then lowered himself into the chair across from her. "I don't know for sure what's going to happen to you."

Grace cocked a brow. Talk about jumping right in. "If I were on slightly fewer drugs right now I'd probably be panicking about that."

He almost smiled. "The guy who bit you, he wasn't normally a werewolf."

"Just having a bad day?"

"Something like that." He nodded. "Near as we can tell, some people are a little further away from this crap. His granddad was, or something like that." He watched her carefully. "Means they're human, and then they get just the right cocktail of chemicals in 'em, and they're not anymore. I can't even tell you for sure if he'd have turned next full moon."

Grace had questions, sure. How did people normally wind up werewolves? Were there vampires around somewhere? Witches?

But none of that was relevant to right then. "So what do we do here then?"

Curt tapped his hand on his knee. "I stay and keep an eye on you for the next couple of days. Make sure you don't develop an unusual taste for rabbit in the middle of the night."

Grace swallowed, stomach turning. It wasn't just the pain and the general looking down the barrel of a giant unknown. She didn't want to hurt someone. Not to mention figuring out how to live with something like that.

"And then I come back at the full for a couple of days, or send somebody else if I'm busy, and..." He frowned. "You're supposed to be freaking out by now, you realize that?"

She drew a deep breath, forcing her muscles to relax, ignoring the numb tingling in her leg. "Would it help any?"

"Might make me worry about you a little less."

She shrugged. "I'll save the worry and the questions for when I've got fewer drugs," she relaxed back suddenly, sighing. "Do you have something to protect yourself with, just in case?"

Curt stood the shotgun up against his leg, eyes serious. "Always."

Chapter 1

August
Somewhere in Wisconsin

Nate feels some level of bad, killing about half this shit. Uninterested about self-reflection or whatever the hell you want to call it, he knows he's not that broken. Even the nasty shit—the ones that haven't ever been even a little human—he feels bad about.

Curt said once he was a like a game warden who had to put down a park animal. He's got to, because it's trying to eat the tourists, but that's not the bear's fault.

Curt was a little more interested in reflection than Nate was.

All that aside, that doesn't happen with water demons. Ever.

Four days he'd followed this thing. Sure, for three of those he thought it was a ghost—not the easy answer by any means—what with the sucking the local assholes into the lake and drowning them mercilessly. It had looked like a pattern, like they'd done something, even odds involving water, and they were being punished for it. He forgets sometimes that people in small towns can seem connected just because it's small and they are.

Finding himself face to face with a Scandinavian water demon was exactly the way his life went.

He should have figured. He was in Wisconsin, and half the shit in town had those little red Swedish Dala horses on it, and that was usually a dead give-away that the place was a little more connected to its history than most of the country was. It was a cute little town, sure, and most of the people seemed nice.

They just had a giant pest problem.

Most of the time this stuff was just bad news after bad news. If he was prepared for a ghost it was a water demon. If it was a water demon, it was one of the bastards that shot boiling oil—the only reason he was happy about how cold the water was in Wisconsin—out its nostrils and had stupid boney protrusions protecting its neck. Not that he'd wanted to try jumping in the water to cut its head off. He wasn't generally that stupid.

He knew what he was doing. He needed to haul the bastard out of the water and cut its heart out. He set up the trap as far in the shallows as he could manage, and attached the net to a sturdy, healthy tree. Made sure he had a wrist strap on his knife in case things went sideways.

It pulled him under anyway. Grabbed him with one giant gnarly hand before he even got it fully in the trap and damn near drown him. Nate kept one hand wrapped around the net, because it was probably the only thing keeping the damn thing from pulling him deep. He ignored the panic, and the desire to breathe, and managed to loop the net around it a couple of times. He struggled away, surfacing long enough for a gulp of air, and to hit the control on the winch and reel the net in.

Just as a scaly, clawed hand grabbed him by the arm and hauled him with it.

It wasn't nice about dying. Spitting slightly less than boiling oil at him—that apparently didn't work as well outside the water, and he'd have to make sure he told Curt that—and clawing at him with jagged fingers. Nate had a sturdy fishing knife in his hand, and he was good at ignoring the gush of blood that mixed in with all the other stuff he was covered in. He dug the knife into its chest, pulling the heart out with his bare hand and throwing it on the bank, watching it dry hard almost instantly in the sun.

He rolled off to the side, staring up at the bright blue sky, dotted with fluffy little clouds, just breathing. He really, desperately hated water demons.

Now you're messin' with a son of a bitch...

The familiar strains of one of his favorite songs echoed from his hip. Nate dug around in his sodden pocket for the waterproof phone he'd gotten from Deke—this damn job was Deke's idea, bastard—last Christmas.

"Yeah?" He held the phone up to his ear without bothering to check the ID, wincing as the stretch of his arm made his side burn.

Silence crackled on the line for a long beat.

He knew who it was. Curt was the only person who called him, and then had to take a minute to decide how to start the conversation. Probably because he was freakishly good at telling what Nate was doing at the exact moment he called.

"Damn it, boy," Curt started, "getting your ass kicked by whatever it is you're after right now is about the *only* time it's okay to not answer your phone."

Nate watched the trees sway in the breeze, ignoring the fact he'd been laying there a little longer than he'd really want to admit to. "No, we're past that part."

"Nate..."

"Jesus Curt, you were just telling me last week I'm not getting any younger. It's dead, I'm just..."

"Getting a little slow to get up after, are ya? I told you the other side of thirty was a bitch."

"Yeah? How's the other side of fifty-five feeling?" Nate grumbled, pinching the bridge of his nose as he sat up slowly. "Did you need something?"

"You."

"Aww, I'm flattered."

"For a job, dipshit," Curt replied, unimpressed.

Nate smiled. "Yeah yeah, spoil my fun." He pushed himself to his feet, glancing around to make sure he was alone. It was a beautiful late-summer day, and maybe if it weren't for the surety this place was fucking *Baggiennik* central—just because he doesn't use the name doesn't mean he doesn't know it—he'd have been more interested in that. "Let me clean up here, and I'll head your way." He frowned. "Or am I meeting you somewhere?"

"No, here is fine," Curt answered. "Then you can sleep the last bit of the drive. We're not going far."

He wasn't far from Curt anyway, which he appreciated when he had to drive in wet clothes. It was only a couple hours from small-town southern Wisconsin to small-town northern Iowa, even if it felt like a different planet. "Sure. See you in a few."

Nate hung the phone up, staring at his morning's work. It was always a bit of a shock, when the thing was on the bank and he could see all of it that it hadn't managed to snap his neck. The Scandinavian ones were big; it was all long splayed legs and big barrel chest, long arms and a flat face with big nostrils, and gills between the ridges on its neck.

Nate sighed, stripping off his sopping over-shirt. As if killing the thing wasn't enough, he couldn't exactly just leave it on the bank.

"You and I have a date first though." He huffed, grabbing the thing by its horned legs and tugging toward the forest. "Not that kind of date. You, my friend, are *grotesque.*"

~~~~~~

Jacobs Storage and Repair had been home, more or less, since Nate was ten. Since he and his mom had pitched up there after she'd gotten hurt on a job. He drove past the line of old cars and appliances Curt was always threatening to fix, and the ones he'd set aside for Nate to fix. There were worse ways to finance a life on the road, and once in a while when things got a little rough Nate actually liked rebuilding a car from scratch or stripping down a washing machine and retooling it. He pulled to a stop in front of the house, and cut the engine.

Well. House might have been a little grand. Curt built the place as a temporary stay back in the stone ages, while he and the Misses were designing their dream house on the back of the property, before the Misses decided she didn't really want to be married to a man who hunted monsters. Mostly it was an office for the business with a bathroom and a couple of bedrooms. Half a kitchen with a table crammed in it. It had a 'living room' with a ratty old couch and a book collection any university would envy. An old root cellar Curt had somehow turned into a 'library' when Nate was in his teens.

Still, after a few months of cheap hotels and run down crap, it looked pretty nice.

Not that I'm staying, he reminded himself as he grabbed his bag from the back.

Curt hauled the door open, shaving cream over half his face, eyes narrowed. "What in the name of all that's holy are you *covered* in?"

"You don't want to know." Nate dropped his keys on the hall table, cocking a brow at the shaving. "Finally start to bother you, or are we trying to impress someone?"

Curt huffed. "Go get cleaned up, we're taking my car and I'm not letting you in it smelling like that if I don't have to."

Nate rolled his eyes and took the stairs up to the second floor, stepping over the random salt-traps and the occasional giant silver cross—he wasn't sure that was actually good for anything—before he ducked into the spare room to grab some fresh clothes.

"And next time you can do your own laundry," Curt hollered. "I'm not your goddamn maid!"

Nate stopped, pausing before the bathroom door. "You're gonna have to give me more than a day between jobs, if you want that. Can't do it when I'm not here."

"You could *take* time between jobs," Curt muttered. "Not this time, but—"

Nate rolled his eyes and shut the door, turning on the shower. Grouching and shit aside, he was pretty happy at the prospect of getting clean. He pulled the shirt over his head and inspected the stains on it, debating whether it was worth the bitching if he left it here for Curt to wash. He sighed, and threw it in the trash. Oil based crap and blood, mixed together, tended to permanently adhere to cotton.

He lifted his arm over his head and checked the scratch on his ribs. He hadn't thought it was deep enough to need stitches, but it was always better to check it again. Curt took the whole *family* bullshit seriously, and got more than a little cross with him when he didn't take care of bleeding injuries.

Rule number one, always take care of the living first.

Twenty minutes later he was downstairs digging through the fridge, clean and ready to go, when Curt thumped the rest of the supplies on the table.

"So what are we doing?" Nate asked around a mouthful of cold chicken.

Curt glanced up, glared at him and threw him a paper napkin off the table. "I'll explain on the way, let's go."

He shrugged, and dragged his stuff out to the car—with a couple extra chicken legs—and settled into the passenger seat. He glanced over at his car, because he'd been pretty sure Curt had put the cover on the Charger, but he always checked.

"Thanks for getting the cover for me."

"We drive off with it uncovered and your Momma shows up I sure don't wanna deal with her."

Nate rolled his eyes. "It's my car."

"Uh huh." Curt looked at him, putting the truck in gear. "That work?"

"No," he muttered, laying his head back and closing his eyes. "Wake me up when you need to talk, or before we get there, whatever."

Curt ignored him and turned the radio up slightly.

Nate never slept well in the car, just dozed lightly, his dreams weaving in with the songs on the radio and the sunlight spilling through the windows. He'd probably been dozing for nearly an hour when Curt hit the brakes and started cursing at someone who'd cut him off.

"Sorry." Curt glanced at him. "Didn't mean to wake you."

Nate sat up in the seat, rubbing his face tiredly. "That's fine. Just been a long morning."

"What was it?"

"Baggien...whatever the crap you call it," he muttered, stretching. "Scandinavian water-bastard."

"Badge-ee-ay-neek." Curt shook his head. "You're lucky it didn't drown you."

He shrugged. "It tried, as they do." He watched Curt pulled off the highway, the normal green city welcome sign—*Welcome to Galesburg*—next to the exit. One further up the block said *Greetings from Galesburg, Illinois.* "So, this job..."

Curt glanced at him, turning on to a sleepy little side street. "Remember that werewolf I tracked, on the off cycle about two years ago?"

"Sure." Nate frowned, nodding. "The one that wasn't actually a were. You said it bit somebody." He looked around them as they pulled up to the curb.

Curt cut the engine, crawling out of the truck, and Nate followed. Waited patiently while Curt locked the truck and walked over to stand next to him in front of a cute little one-story house.

"If we're after a were I'm going to need—"

"No." Curt rolled his eyes at him. "No, her name's Grace. He bit her, but she's...fine." He stashed his gun behind his back, under his jacket. "Bout six months ago they had a ghost in town, and I was a little busy with your Momma so I just gave her the incantation and said I'd be here when I could. She managed it herself."

Nate rose a brow, and followed him up toward the house. "Boss."

Curt scoffed. "Yeah well, I sent her a crash course book and a talisman, but she called me early this morning to say they had another one, but the thing laughed at my Latin and tried to choke her."

"Laughed?" Nate asked. "That's—"

"Strange." Curt nodded. "I don't like doing strange by myself. And useful as Grace will probably be, I ain't planning for that." He reached out and rapped on the doorframe smartly, glancing around him.

The inner door swung open, and Nate blinked in shock. "Oh. She's pretty," he muttered, thankfully too low for her to hear.

Curt turned, glaring at him for a second, before he looked back at the woman in the door. "Hi, Grace."

Maybe it was the name, but when Curt had described her he'd pictured someone older. Grace was probably younger than he was, maybe just under thirty, with brown-gold hair, wide brown eyes, and a heart-shaped face. Answering her door in an old t-shirt and jeans, with an armful of books and a serious black eye.

Curt pulled the screen open, frowning. "That from the ghost?"

She scoffed, stepping back from the door. "No, the freaking deputy sheriff panicked." She rolled her eyes. "I caught an elbow."

"You should avoid those," Curt said wryly.

Grace stuck her tongue out at him. "This must be Nate."

Nate smiled, holding a hand out. "Nate Carter. Whatever he said, it wasn't true."

She shook his hand easily, juggling the books. "Nothing but nice stuff. Grace Cleary."

Curt huffed at them. "What are those for?"

"Work." Grace tilted her head toward the kitchen, and started that way.

She walked with a slight limp, but it wasn't too pronounced. Nate watched, because a person down for the count because of an injury ran the risk of getting someone killed, least of all themselves.

They followed her into a decent sized, bright kitchen. An old table took up most of the room, papers and pens strewn all over it, and she thumped the books down on the edge.

"How is it?" Curt asked, nodding to her leg.

Grace shrugged. "Spent too much time sitting this morning, after the action yesterday. When I move around a bit it'll loosen back up. Smith promised to call me if he heard anything. I've been trying to keep myself occupied." She pointed them toward the other chairs. "Can I get you a cup of coffee or something?"

Curt pushed him into a chair. "Coffee for him, he slept most of the way here."

Nate glared at him. "You called me three seconds after I finished a job."

She chuckled softly, and poured him a cup of coffee. "The way he usually tells it, you wouldn't be disappointed about that."

Curt dropped into a chair next to him, taking a cup of coffee. "Haven't heard from you in a couple of weeks. Other than this bit, how's life?"

"Alright," she answered. "Work, mostly."

Curt took a swallow. "I'd ask how your social life was, but it sounds like you usually get enough of that."

"I do." She glared at him slightly. "Thanks for that, by the way, took me nearly an hour to get out of that conversation."

"Weren't you telling people I was a cousin?"

Nate watched them, the easy camaraderie, and amended his tally because it wasn't just that Curt had decided he was responsible for Grace, he liked her.

She gave Curt a droll look. "Jamie and I have been best friends since I was eight. Claiming you were my cousin would *not* have made that better," she said. "For a start because he wouldn't have believed me."

He glanced at Nate, catching his curious gaze, and shrugged. "I called last month and Grace's not-boyfriend answered her phone."

"Not-boyfriend?" Nate looked between them, waiting.

"Hell if I know. Pretty sure friends aren't usually that involved in each other's lives," Curt answered.

"I'm the first to admit we're weirdly co-dependent, or as much as you can be when you live nearly four hours apart," Grace said, clearing her papers up a bit. "We're not sleeping together. I'm pretty sure that makes us just friends."

Nate blinked. "Be my guess. Four hours?"

She looked up at him, blinking for a second, like she'd lost track of the conversation. "He teaches Sociology at Northwestern."

"I don't know where that is."

"Evansville." Grace lowered herself into a chair, and stretched her leg out on the extra. "North of Chicago."

Curt sipped his coffee. "So this ghost."

"I got nothin'." Grace shifted. "Started a couple of days ago. Local drunk tried to jump off the top of the bar, which would be easily explained except he doesn't remember anything after getting to the bar, and the door upstairs is normally locked. Tom's not exactly the lock-picking sort, even when he's lucent."

"But he's still alive?" Nate asked.

"Caught his pants-leg on the drainage spout. Hit his head pretty hard on the side of the building, but just hung there until the fire department got him down." She blew out a breath. "Then the night security guy at the library got crushed under a bookshelf. He didn't make it."

Curt winced.

"That sounds like it's pretty explainable too, though," Nate said carefully.

Grace shook her head no. "The shelves are those giant metal ones that bolt to the floor. Something unscrewed the bolts and then pushed it over on him. And even unscrewed, from ground level it would have been hard to shift."

"And last night?" Curt prompted.

"Deputy Smith finally decided something strange was going on, and showed up here. Said I was the only person he knew who wouldn't commit him for asking questions. I told you he was around for that one I called you about in February, didn't I?"

Curt nodded.

"So, anyway, he wanted to know if I could tell him if there was a ghost."

Nate rose a brow.

"Oh, he didn't want there to be. He's your average un-imaginative law-man. But when something's unexplainable enough you'll take what you can get, and Jenkins was sort of a fixture in town. The library didn't need security so much as he'd needed a job. Anyway." She frowned. "I wasn't exactly poking around. New to all this or not, I'm not about to start poking shit with a stick."

"That's because you have sense," Curt said.

"But I said I'd look for him," she continued. "And we were in the building for about ten seconds and some bitch I've never seen before shows up out of nowhere, and I started the incantation you sent me." Grace shot him a dark smile. "She laughed in my face and tried to choke me."

"How did you stop her?" Curt asked.

"I didn't. Smith took a shot at her, and she screamed at him and disappeared." She blew out a breath. "But she's not gone, just lying low, and obviously *I'm* not equipped to deal with her." She flashed them a smile. "I'll introduce you to Smith."

"Be weird working with law-enforcement, rather than avoiding them like the plague," Nate muttered.

"Yeah, it usually is." Curt agreed. "Only happens when somebody with standing introduces me."

"Wow, thanks," Grace said, standing. "I'll try not to let that go to my head. Make yourselves at home, you can fight to the death over who gets the attic room."

~~~~~~

Nate liked libraries. Even aside from the fact that if a case got strange enough he could usually find some kind of clue in any library he could find. Also, it seemed like the smaller the town or the county was, the better their local genealogy section was. When you were trying to figure out where a restless spirit had come from that could be helpful.

He preferred the grant ones from the turn of the century that had elaborate limestone outsides and strange shoe-horned rooms. According to the plaque at the curb, Galesburg used to have one of those. About a block away, that burnt to the ground in the fifties.

"Well, I think we can rule out a displeased former librarian," he said to Curt, tapping the plaque.

Curt read it quickly, shrugging. "I don't think librarians do that."

"I don't know, if somebody made noise they might."

"Grace," Curt looked up at her, as she was unlocking the building for them. "Do librarians come back to haunt a library?"

"How the hell would I know?"

"You work here."

"I help with their computer system once in a great while."

"I thought you graduated with some sort of library degree?"

"No." She glanced back at them, shrugging. "I started one, as a backup plan." She wrinkled her nose. "And,

27

alright, I worked at the university library most of the way through college. I'm a copy-editor, not a librarian."

Nate walked up to the library, and started to come up with some sort of snappy comeback when a flashlight beam hit him square in the face.

"Who is that? Identify yourself!"

"It's alright John, they're with me," Grace said, stepping back out of the doorway.

The flashlight lowered, and Nate blinked until he could see something other than green and yellow dots. The guy's name was really John Smith? Nate wasn't stupid enough to say that out loud. He didn't have any actual reason to be uneasy about law enforcement—other than the fact that sometimes he shot things that could make themselves look like people—but he didn't chance it.

Deputy John Smith had one hand on his service weapon, the other wrapped around the chunky flashlight he'd just been blinding Nate with, and a look on his face that said he was wildly out of his depth. "Evening Grace." He looked at them uneasily. "Are you sure about this? I'm letting unauthorized people into a crime scene."

"We're here to help," Curt said reassuringly.

Reassuring was something Nate hadn't ever gotten the hang of. That, or his smart-ass mouth always got in the way.

"Something hard enough Grace couldn't make a dent in it, you want all the help you can get," Curt continued.

Grace scoffed. "You say that like I've got any clue what I'm doing." She looked at the deputy, sighing. "He's the only reason I'm not dog chow," she pointed to Curt. "So I'd say they're trustworthy."

When he didn't have anything else to say, Grace went back to unlocking the library.

They were three steps in the door when Smith finally found his voice again. "Grace..." his voice cracked and he had to stop and swallow. "The thing that attacked you, that was just a dog right?"

She flipped on the low-level lighting. "Don't ask questions you don't want the answers to, John."

He swallowed, face going pale. "Are you…are you…"

"*I am the terror that flaps in the night,*" Grace said wryly. "*I am the smoke that smokes smoked oysters…*"

Nate choked back a laugh. "I don't think either of them are going to get that."

She sighed, popping her head in the office right inside the door. "Darkwing Duck is vastly under appreciated." She looked at Smith, forcing a smile. "Aside from the mess it made of my leg I'm perfectly fine." She turned to Nate and Curt. "I don't know why you're all watching me look, because I've got no clue what I'm looking for."

Curt pulled out his extra weapon and held it out for Grace. "Special shot, it'll probably make her back off if she finds you, but it won't get rid of her. At this stage there are a few different possibilities. You go with Nate, he knows what to look for." He waved them across the building. "Deputy Smith and I can check this side."

"You use fire-arms on a ghost?" Smith asked, confused.

Curt bodily steered Smith across the building. "We use fire-arms on most things."

Nate watched them go, and then rose a brow at her. "You know the library, so show me where someone could hide stuff."

"What size stuff, and how well hidden?"

He blinked.

"Because if it's just little or flat, there are a few thousand places between books."

Nate blew out a breath. "Crash course? If someone's called it up then we're looking for either a little packet of…um…stuff they've had to hide somewhere, or a little doll or…" He shrugged. "You obviously watch TV, or you did once, so just assume we're stuck in an episode of whatever and guess."

Grace nodded seriously. "Well, probably better check the large places first. Under a desk in the computer rooms wouldn't get noticed."

Nate followed her to the computer rooms in the back. Small library or not, he was feeling a little uneasy.

He supposed, now that he'd met Grace, the fact she'd been worried enough about this to call Curt told him it was something serious. She was, so far, the least jumpy or hysterical person he'd ever met.

Nate looked back as she silently pushed the door to the glass-walled room open.

"Should we just stick our heads under?" She asked, and waved under the desks.

"Let's assume she is actually a problem and not both get under there together." Nate grinned darkly. "See if you see anything out of the ordinary, and I'll keep an eye out for anything that's going to try and jump you when you're not looking."

Grace dropped down to look under the desks. "Nope, nothing." She'd stood, and they were about to leave the room again, when Curt called.

"We found something," he hollered across the building. "Over here by the old catalog."

"Catalog?" Nate asked.

Grace dusted her hands off. "Yeah, they still have the old card catalog."

"Seriously?"

He hung back and let her lead again, detouring past the section of shelf toppled in the middle of the building, a giant blood stain on the floor. She walked past it without a glance. But if she'd worked at the library for long, and she lived here, she'd probably known the old man that worked security.

Curt watched them walk over. He was standing careful, the way he did when he felt like talking about Nate's dad. "Everything good?"

"Yeah." Grace looked at him, confused. "I'm fine. What?"

30

Curt puffed out a breath and pointed at a strange shadow against the wall, right across from the fallen shelving.

"Shit." Nate blinked at it. "Is that—"

"A Revenant." Curt looked at the shadow, shuddering.

"What's a…" Smith died off, like he didn't know what the word was.

"A Revenant. It's like a ghost on crack," Nate answered. "They start off nasty, sure, but the more blood they spill the stronger they get. Eventually they get to a point they can body-snatch."

"Wonderful." Grace cocked her head at it. "So where did it come from?"

"No telling." Curt shrugged. "It's in town now though. And these things are nasty. You don't just exorcise them." He frowned. "Actually, I'm kind of surprised she just laughed at the Latin."

"So how do we get it out of the library?" Smith asked carefully.

"Oh, it's gone already." Nate stepped closer to the stain, frowning. "Not sure why it was even here when you were here the other night."

"Looking for fresh blood?" Curt offered. "If the bar's been closed since what's-his-face dove off the roof. There aren't a lot of other places in town to find people. Houses are off limits unless the door's opened. Sounds like it's been too cold this week for much of that."

Nate looked over at the town map on the wall. "Yeah, so where'd it—"

Smith's radio crackled to life, loud in the dim stillness of the empty library.

"Deputy Smith, where the hell are you?" a dark male voice sounded from the speaker.

"Looking over the scene at the library, Sir." He frowned, looking at his radio strangely and Nate felt his stomach drop.

"We've had shots fired on second and Chester. The old convenience store."

~~~~~~~

Grace wrapped her palm securely around the handle of the pistol Curt had handed her earlier and tried to calm her racing heart. She stared up at the decrepit peeling white storefront, aware of the utterly silent and empty street around them.

"Got that?" Nate asked, watching her carefully through clear green eyes. He smoothed his short, spiky brown hair and tugged his shirt down.

He didn't look anything like she'd expected. Curt described him like a kind of scruffy man-child. And maybe his jeans were stained and his boots were scuffed but he'd been presentable and mature so far.

"Yep." She looked up at the building, nose twitching. "Why does this feel like a trap?"

Nate scoffed tellingly, as Curt came up beside her.

"Because, as we've discussed, you have sense," Curt answered. "Smith went around back. He seems pretty sure the Chief was supposed to be out of town today, and the switchboard said she hadn't had any reports at all, but the Chief sent her on break for ten minutes."

"Fun." Nate grabbed a double-barreled shotgun. "So we're assuming our Revenant is wearing the Chief of Police?"

Curt adjusted his sawed-off shotgun. "We are."

"What's the guy's name?" Nate asked.

"Anderson." Grace swallowed. "George Anderson."

Anderson had been nice to her. He wasn't exactly part of the welcome wagon, but he seemed good at his job. Like the sort of guy who kept a little town like this even. And now he was being possessed by some bloodthirsty ghost.

A Revenant. If she was doing this she needed to start learning the names. "So how sure are you it won't help to shoot it?" Grace asked.

"Might slow it down," Curt offered. "Which we should do if it gets a hold of somebody else."

The last ghost had just liked to throw plates and things around. Grace had done what Curt told her to and it'd been taken care of. And she'd absolutely do that again. Anderson would still be dead if they shot him though.

"He's pretty much dead already," Nate said softly, stopping in front of the building. "These things aren't nice when they crawl in your head."

Grace shuddered, and didn't ask if he was psychic. "Sure."

Curt lead the way. "Job at hand. Just remember, always—"

"Take care of the living first," she and Nate said at exactly the same time.

Curt glared at them.

"Am I allowed to be disturbed that you've said that to me enough in two years that I'm already there?"

"You so are," Nate muttered, nodding her into the dilapidated old store.

Somewhere in the 1960's Sycamore Convenience had been the place to be, in town. It'd been bigger then. The town had been bigger, she wasn't sure the store had changed since it opened as a five-and-dime in the thirties. Now it was a strangely eerie collection of old shelves with boxes and odds and ends crammed on them, everything surrounded by a truly epic layer of dust and mouse droppings.

I feel like I've stepped into some ridiculous zombie movie.

She didn't say it out loud. Curt and Nate were making hand signals at each other. Nate grabbed her by the back of the shirt and physically moved her to a specific spot, pointing at the door he wanted her to watch. Grace made sure the shelf she was steadying her arm on was sturdy enough to hold the pressure.

Smith came through the back carefully, freezing at the sight of them, but not saying anything. Curt motioned

33

him up the stairs, because between them coming in the front and Smith coming in the back they knew the place was clear on the ground level.

"Chief?" Smith called out, hesitating by the stairs.

"Coming down."

Smith waved them back, mouthing *hide* exaggeratedly. Curt ducked behind a shelf, and Grace was about behind the next one when Nate folded his arms over his chest, frowning at them.

Curt shot him a furious glare, and Grace reached out and physically pulled him over behind the ice-cream case. He glared at her, and she just lifted a brow at him. What the hell were they supposed to do?

Footsteps shuffled down the stairs, and Smith took two giant steps back, going pale and grabbing his stomach.

Grace leaned her head back against the counter, rolling her eyes. Clearly they should have left someone out there who could act. Or who'd had some clue of what to expect. Not that that would have been her.

Grace chanced a peek around the corner, and had to withhold the urge to vomit. If the giant hole in his chest was anything to go by, Anderson wouldn't be making it home that night. She could see why Smith was a little poleaxed though, because Anderson probably shouldn't have still been walking.

"S...sir. You're injured."

"How astute of you, Deputy."

Does he usually talk like that? Nate mouthed at her, forehead wrinkling.

Grace shook her head no, tightening her hands on her weapon.

"I'll call—"

"You won't." Anderson held a hand out, and Smith's radio made a popping noise, then a high squeal before it emitted a small curl of smoke. "I am sorry, Deputy, but I rather needed you here."

"What? W...why?"

"The others can come out." The thing riding around in Anderson looked over at where Curt was hidden. "It's rather obvious he didn't come in alone. He wouldn't."

Curt stepped out, gun leveled at It's head. "I'd be quite interested to hear where you got that injury from."

It laughed. "Hobo upstairs." It looked down at Anderson's chest, touching a gruesome spot. "He was stronger than I thought, wasn't dead yet when I jumped for greener pastures." It grinned. "No issue. If you were at the library, then I'm guessing she's here." It looked around the room. "And I think she'll make a better...vessel."

Grace started to stand, and Nate grabbed her elbow, shaking his head.

She tugged slightly.

No. Give him a minute, Nate mouthed.

"What good's that gonna do you? Smith and I are armed, and even if he won't shoot you, I will."

"All shooting me does is get me out of the body. You still have to deal with me. I can tell she's in here. Can practically smell her." It laughed. "Do come out dear, you aren't doing anyone any good."

Can I go now? she mouthed at Nate, waiting.

He nodded, and let her stand.

"I don't know what good you think I'm going to do now." Grace edged around the counter, gun loose in the hand hidden by the shelf. She stole a half glance at Curt, and decided he must have had some sort of plan for getting rid of this thing.

She'd like to think she knew him well enough; they wouldn't be here if he didn't. The only plan she had required... Well, it wasn't an ideal plan. Screw whether or not she wanted to, she wasn't sure she *could*. Self-defense target practice was gun safety and a way to make Jamie shut up about her living alone. It wasn't supposed to be practical.

Granted, in the last year that particular line had gotten a little fuzzy.

The thing riding Anderson drew a deep, faintly sickening breath that caused blood to bubble and gush from his chest, and stepped toward Grace. "Oh...oh I almost didn't believe it at the library." It grinned, stepping forward again. "Unprotected and everything."

Curt cocked his shotgun ominously. "Unprotected?"

It ignored Curt, eyes only for Grace. "Yes, just a little more blood..."

Grace had half a second, to see the gun leveling at Smith and make a decision. Which ended up not being a decision. It was a reaction. *Breathe, aim, steady, fire.*

Anderson dropped to the ground, silver mist smoking out of the hole in his chest and assuming the blurry form of a woman.

"That won't slow me down much," it breathed, claw-like fingers reaching for Grace.

Chapter 2

It'd grabbed her around the neck once already, the night before at the library.

Well, it'd started to. Right then, with bony fingers that weren't fingers wrapped tight around her trachea Grace didn't know what she'd expected. It looked filmy and insubstantial, but it clearly wasn't.

It had a proper hold this time, pushing Grace back against the wall and nearly taking her off her feet, squeezing ice-cold around her throat. She felt like she'd never be properly warm again, like something was pushing ice-water into her veins, and sinking into her bones.

Once, when she was ten, she'd gone sledding with Jamie. It hadn't really been sledding weather. Sure, they'd had snow, but it was nearly forty degrees out and everything was already starting to melt. They'd spent all day sledding, two kids just out enjoying the snow. Gone and gone and gone, until their legs were sore and tired, until Jamie was tired of his wet ski-pants.

Until Grace couldn't make her fingers work to pick up the sled. If Jamie'd let her go home alone that day she'd probably have died of hypothermia.

She was starting to feel about that cold.

It slammed her back again, frustrated by its inability to do *something*.

"Nate!" Curt shouted, voice coming through the fog.

Grace felt a peppering of something thrown at her, and it started screaming. Curt was yelling in Latin, and it turned to hiss at him, clearly unhappy about that. She didn't know what she was doing, but anything that made the damn thing unhappy was a good place to start.

"Quicúmque vult salvus esse, ante ómnia," She joined in with Curt, voice raspy, trying to push past the obstruction around her throat. "Opus est, ut téneat cathólicam fidem: Quam…"

It dropped her back against the wall, moving to the middle of the room, trying to strike out at whatever it could.

"Quam nisi quisqui íntegram inviolatámq…" they continued.

The scream sounded louder, and suddenly everything in the room went bright magnesium white and Grace felt like her ears were about to burst.

Grace slid to the floor, swallowing, wincing at the taste of blood in her mouth. She prodded her split lip carefully, just trying to breathe.

Nate got to her before Curt did, she wasn't sure if that was because Curt didn't think she was a civilian anymore—he was busy checking over Smith—or if Nate had just been closest.

"Holy shit." He checked her over, shaking his head. "All right there?"

"Relative." Grace managed, using his offered hand to pull herself to her feet. "Since I just shot the chief of police in the head."

Curt winced. "I'll help Smith take care of…that." He died off. "Nate'll stay with you, just to be safe."

Grace frowned. "That's the same rite I did before."

"Shouldn't have worked now either." Curt winced. "And in the honest column, that amulet I gave you shouldn't have kept her out, either."

She blinked, pulling it out of the place she'd hidden it under her shirt, frowning.

Curt squeezed her shoulder. "Don't worry about it right now. If you knew what was going on, you'd have told me."

Which she would have, absolutely.

"It was after you," Smith said, clearly just starting to get a handle on the situation.

"Oops." Nate grabbed her by the shoulder, steering her toward the door. "Johnny Law's starting to come back down to earth," he muttered. "That's our cue to get you out of here."

"But—"

"Curt can deal with him."

~~~~~~

Nate's got no framework for how you're supposed to deal with this shit taking over your life when you're an adult. He'd been dropped in the deep end at nine, six if you asked Curt, and never seen the sun again.

He was pretty sure you were supposed to complain.

By the time he heard the rumble of Curt's truck in the front—and really, how long did it take to get rid of a body or two, they'd been *hours*—he'd nearly called the man four times. He didn't know what was going through Grace's head, and he didn't feel comfortable asking given he'd known her for slightly more than a day.

She was packing.

It wasn't flurry packing, wasn't panic and adrenaline. He could probably have dealt with that. It was calm, *I need this, this and this but not that* packing.

Yes, he realized he lived the sort of life where a woman calmly packing scared the shit out of him.

And then Curt was coming through the door and Nate still didn't say anything, because Smith was still with him. Of course it was Curt, so he didn't have to. Curt looked down at the little box in the hall, duffel bag next to it, and back up at Nate.

"Yeah." Nate swallowed. "I got nothing."

"Grace." Curt looked up as she came down the stairs. Nate watched Curt's eyes flick over her, reading the way he always did that Nate was seriously not good at.

Curt kept telling him he'd get there someday. That feeling a bit old for the job or whatever was just because he'd started so young, and at thirty-one he was a goddamn baby.

Grace sat another slightly larger box next to the first one.

"Are you coming with us?" Curt asked. "I ain't trying to talk you out of this, but are you sure?"

She nodded once. "If it was actually looking for me—I've got no clue why but that's...whatever—I should...go."

Smith frowned. "But if it wasn't?"

"I still..." Grace stopped and shifted, folding her arms over her chest. "I didn't know Anderson, probably not even really enough to say 'hello' on the street." She looked Smith dead in the eyes. "It's better if I go."

Smith swallowed. "What about your house?"

Grace held out a set of keys. "I called Kelly, told her my cousin was having health problems and I was going to stay with him for a while. I'll pay for her to have someone clean the house, and then put it up for rent." She smiled sadly. "Told her I thought you were a safe person to leave the keys with, rather than the night box she doesn't have."

He took them carefully. "Okay. But—"

"I'll leave you my contact information," Curt said easily. "Case something else happens to find its way to you."

"And I'll still have the same cell number," Grace offered. "I'm not trying to drop off the map."

"Yeah." Smith swallowed. "Sure. You'll take care of yourself?" He gave her a serious smile. "Don't be surprised if I call in a couple of days, convinced I imagined the whole thing."

Grace lifted a box, nodding Nate toward the other one as Curt grabbed the bag. "The seventy-two hour mark is the hardest, for convincing yourself you aren't crazy. Or at least it was for me. Once you're past that it's easy."

Nate didn't hear the rest of the conversation. He shouldered the bag from Curt, and carried everything he had out to the truck, putting it under the tarp in the back. He knew how that was going to go. Curt was going to tell him he didn't want Grace driving by herself right then— not that he blamed him, because he wouldn't be real easy about that either—and he was going to get roped into being the one who rode with her.

Curt had never really been above a little low-level emotional manipulation. If Nate pushed him, he'd make some comment about wanting them to get to know each other, since clearly he had absolutely every intention of Grace being around a while.

"—you're only like an hour away," Grace insisted, as they walked over to the curb. "I can come back and get more if I want it. I'm just sort of inviting myself home with you."

"Sugar, there was no way this visit wasn't ending without my at least threatening to kidnap you." He flicked a sideways glance at her. "And if you are…"

"Special?"

Curt nodded. "Well, at least if you're there we can keep an eye on you."

Grace dropped the last box in the back of her old Cherokee. "Were you slipping into the royal we, or did you just rope Nate into that?"

"Curt's the king of Texas, and Oklahoma too, wasn't it?" Nate said, brow cocked. "Hey, mind if I ride with you?

If I have to listen to another hour of Hank Williams Junior I'll hurt myself."

"No, that's fine." Grace frowned at him. "You don't mind?"

Nate shrugged. "Eh, rule number one. And you're not useless in a fight, never know when that'll come in handy."

He wasn't sure Grace believed that, but she didn't question it. Went to make sure the house was all locked up one more time, and left he and Curt standing on the curb.

"Nice save, ex-lax," Curt muttered.

"Well, did you want me to tell her you were worried about her emotional stability?"

Curt looked away innocently, checking to make sure Grace was still out of sight.

"Yeah, I didn't think so." Nate sighed. "Listen—"

"Not sure if you noticed in there, but—"

"She's got absolutely no family pictures?" Nate had been about to ask that. He'd noticed. He just hadn't felt comfortable saying anything. "Is there a reason why?"

"Hell if I know," Curt answered. "Been my experience in life, people who have a good relationship with their family, they tell you why they ain't around. People ask about your Daddy, you may not go into detail, but you don't change the goddamn subject like a professional. I can tell you everything you'd want to know about Jamie the best friend, and I've never had to ask more than about one question. The family is just...blank."

"Right. Well, it's not like I'm gonna bring it up tonight." Nate muttered. "It's an hour to yours. We'll talk about Latin Rites or shit. Whatever."

"I wouldn't worry about it," Curt said softly. "She doesn't seem sensitive, she just doesn't talk about it."

Grace came back over then, fishing out the keys. "Following you?"

Curt nodded, squeezing her shoulder. "And I figure Nate can find his way there stinking drunk, so—"

"That was once," Nate defended. "And I was twenty-one and having a *really* bad week."

Grace laughed. "I know my way to Milton," she said, sliding into the car. "But that's useful."

Nate crawled in the front of the old rusty white Cherokee, glancing around him. It was a clean car, and in decent shape. "This thing still run decently?"

Grace laughed, starting the engine up easily. "Only if you're nice to it."

Nate rose a brow.

"She goes through oil like it's going out of style, and brake fluid anymore." She shifted into drive, as Curt pulled his truck away from the curb. "And I think I've replaced damn near everything at least once." She shrugged. "It still drives, and the cost of gas doesn't make me want to deal with having a car payment for the first time since I was sixteen and I bought it off a neighbor."

"My mom drives an old Ram-Charger, that's basically this with fewer seats and more space in the back."

"And you got the classic Charger?"

Nate blinked. "Yeah. It was my Dad's, he restored it and everything." He swallowed. Because he wasn't going to go searching for information, but he liked to get over the "my dad's dead" conversation as fast as possible. "Curt mentioned?"

"Your dad," She glanced at him, merging onto the highway. "And you being overly attached to your car."

Nate rolled his eyes, and left it there.

"Which I could kind of see. Jamie had an old Monte Carlo for like twelve seconds."

He laughed, shaking his head. "That long?"

"He wrapped it around a tree," she answered. "Wasn't even drunk, just…"

"Young and stupid?"

Grace's voice was low and reminiscent. Perfectly comfortable talking about her friend. "No one should ever tell a teenage boy how well their car corners."

Nate choked out a laugh. "I can guess. I'd probably have been stupider with mine…"

"But?"

He glanced at her. "Let's just say the concept of teenage rebellion doesn't hold water when your mother owns an impressive collection of guns and knows people who would shoot you for money."

"No," Grace agreed. "I imagine not."

"Was the Monte Carlo his attempt at teenage rebellion?"

"A little." She nodded. "Jamie liked to do things just to prove he could. They weren't always bad things." Her lips twitched. "He read War and Peace cover to cover in sixth grade because someone said he wasn't smart enough to do it."

"Jesus."

She shifted lanes around a slow moving mini-van, grumbling. "I'm relatively sure your car wouldn't fall apart if you went the speed limit and GOT OFF YOUR PHONE."

Nate chuckled, waiting until she was back in a lane and had huffed out a breath. "You tell 'em, sister."

Grace grumbled. "Common courtesy used to be a thing." She paused then, pushing a hand through her hair. "Jesus, I'm turning into Aunt Rhoda."

"Delayed adrenaline reaction probably," Nate offered. "Happens to all of us. Curt get's all existential."

She choked out a laugh. "You?"

"Honestly? Depends on how bad the job was. One like this is pretty standard." He shifted. "Well, usually it's just me, and I avoid the law."

"You said."

He glanced at her, shrugging. "The bad ones, I have a tendency to drink a little more than I should. I mean pretty much everybody in this job drinks."

44

Hell, his mom's answer to a bad job had been to sit him down and hand him a beer and teach him about suppressing his emotions to get on with the next job. Wasn't really any wonder he was messed up. Most days he agreed with Curt, it was sort of a miracle he wasn't more messed up than he was.

Nate understood himself perfectly well, even the bits he didn't necessarily like. He wasn't always so clear on other people. Even Curt. The man took Nate in, gave him a roof over his head as soon as he couldn't stand kicking around with his Mom all the time, and helped him keep enough money at hand to get by.

Curt worried about him, and tried to get him to settle into some sort of life that wasn't spending so much time alone on the road.

And sure, Nate helped him out where he could, went on jobs with him when he needed an extra hand. He wouldn't call it anywhere near even.

He blinked suddenly, looking over at Grace. She was driving relaxed and easy, watching the road. He suspected she was tuned out, but her eyeballs were moving around enough he figured she was still present.

But he'd stopped talking, in the middle of a freaking conversation, probably a good ten minutes ago and she hadn't done anything.

"Sorry." Nate pawed at his hair, glancing over at her before looking back at the tail-lights of Curt's truck.

Grace frowned at him, confused. "Hm?"

"I kind of floated off on you."

She shrugged, like it hadn't bothered her, and went back to driving.

Nate had about half a dozen questions. And he'd never been good with silence, but something said it was a bad time to start asking what she was going to do now. Everything else he had was sort of stupidly personal, and not his business whether Curt had decided to drag this girl home as family or not.

"Mind if I turn the radio on?"

"No, go ahead. If you can find something that's not Hank Williams or some other version of country, good luck."

He groaned. "Swedish house pop? Teen rock? Just about anything would be better."

"I think there might be an old CCR tape in the glove box."

He fiddled with the radio for a moment, but the only rock station that might have been acceptable was staticky. Nate popped open the glove box and grabbed the tapes he found shoved between old road maps and piles of napkins. And a rubber duck.

"You have a…" He stopped. "Why…"

Grace looked over at him, eyes snagging on the duck, and burst out laughing.

"You know what, I don't want to know." He shoved it back in the glove box and shook it off. "That's just…seriously. I've seen some weird shit in my time, that's just creepy."

She didn't try to explain it, which probably just made it stranger. Nate forced himself to look at the tapes in his hand. CCR, which he was alright with, but it wasn't really a favorite. Jim Croche which was sort of the same. He flipped the third one over, trying to read the scratched labels.

"Dude." He looked at her, eyes wide. "Pearl Jam? You have a Pearl Jam mix tape in your car?" He paused halfway to putting it in. "Is that…"

"Fine with me." She nodded.

Nate turned the volume up, leaning back and singing along with the music, watching the evening landscape slip past the window. It wasn't long before they made it to Milton, and Curt led them right through the center of town, before the turned down the dusty drive and pulled up to the house.

"Place is kind of a mess," Curt said, almost shy, as they stepped out of the cars.

"It's a storage yard, Curt." Grace shook her head at him. "It's fine."

Curt clapped her on the shoulder, and shook his head. "Well, we're low on space but I don't want to hear about it. You stay until we're sure you've got your feet."

"Might be stuck with me for a while," Grace muttered, grabbing her box.

~~~~~~

Nate shifted around, checking the tubing and connectors. Half the time Curt said he only came back because Nate couldn't exactly carry around all the tools he'd need to keep his car running as well as he wanted it.

Working on the Charger calmed him. Gave him something to do with his hands. Something to think about that wasn't wondering when he could take a job and not feel like he was abandoning Curt and the new girl. He wasn't, no part of her coming back with them had been his decision. But Curt wouldn't appreciate him leaving just to leave. If a job came in he could probably squeak away.

Nate finished up, and dropped the hood easily. He wiped his hands, and washed them as well as he could before he strapped the watch back on his wrist. He slipped his over-shirt back on, and headed back for the house.

He stopped halfway up the path, swallowing. He hadn't heard Grace come outside, but that wasn't surprising. She moved quiet, and after a week he and Curt were about to put a bell on her just so they could keep track of where she was.

"No." Grace was folded sideways somehow, a ridiculous pile of limbs inside the old swing next to the door. She glanced up at him, forcing a bit of a smile. "It's not that simple, Jamie."

He winced, nodding, and slipped inside the house, careful to close the door quietly. They'd been back four days, and Nate wasn't sure if he'd call her settled, or trying to, or what.

47

"Wondered when you were gonna come back in," Curt asked, looking up from the pile of books strewn all over his living room/office/whatever.

He'd gone on a tear, looking for anything he could find about Revenants. Because clearly he cared about this girl and he wanted to know why their last critter had thought she was special.

"How many times' he called now?"

Curt huffed, looking back down at his books. "It's a fair few." He flipped pages, brow furrowed. "How would you feel in his place though? It ain't like she's givin' him much by way of answers."

Nate couldn't imagine how any answer was managing that. If they were close the half answers and lies couldn't hold up long.

"So far she's managed to convince him she's fine, and he doesn't need to come..." He grimaced, pausing as he flipped pages, muttering to himself.

"Doesn't need to come?"

Curt looked up at him, blinking. "I imagine, from what I've heard her say, he's not entirely sure about her upping stakes in the middle of the night to move in with people he's never met," he said. "And when I say it out loud I'm sort of surprised she's managed it with just phone calls so far."

"Okay," Nate replied. It wasn't like he had anything constructive to add there.

"Fair warning," Curt said, before he turned away. "Grace is cooking tonight, and I didn't have the balls to ask if she's a decent cook so—"

"I'm a perfectly fine cook."

Nate jumped, spinning around, hand naturally going for the silver knife he kept in his belt. He fell back against the door frame, cursing softly. Grace winced, and he looked over at Curt surreptitiously slipping the shotgun back under his desk.

"Sorry."

"Goddamn it," Curt muttered under his breath. "Make more noise when you move, woman."

"Sorry." She winced, curling her hands in her shirt sleeves. "It's a habit."

Curt frowned, eyes distant and sad. Nate knew that look, and usually it happened just before they had another conversation about Nate's Dad. Only Curt had already said he wasn't poking at Grace, and Nate decided he needed to find something to say before the silence got any more uncomfortable. "What'cha makin?"

"Cheeseburger mac, probably. Everything's in the kitchen."

He grinned. "I'll go get cleaned up, sounds good."

"Made his day with that," Curt said. "It's about the only thing he eats without poking at it first."

"Everybody has a childhood comfort food," Nate said, seriously. "What about you and cobbler?"

"Point," Curt admitted. "What about you, Sugar."

Grace shrugged, leaned against the door frame. "Aunt Rhoda used to make us chicken and dumplings and raspberry pie when we visited in the summer."

"We?" Nate asked. He sort of felt like if she'd had a sibling this wouldn't have been the first he heard about it.

"Jamie," she answered. "It's his Aunt Rhoda. I tried calling her Miss for like a week, but she threatened me with a marble rolling pin." She stretched slightly. "Should I start food?"

Curt nodded. "I'll be done with this in a bit, and that bum needs to go clean up before he comes to the table."

"I'm goin." He stopped at the doorway. "Oh, hey, Grace?"

She stopped, halfway in the kitchen. "Yeah?"

"While I've got all the tools out, you want me to give the Cherokee a once over? I can check the seals for you, make sure that's not why it's gobbling oil."

"Thanks." She smiled, eyes light. "Yes please."

"Sure." Nate flushed, and ignored Curt's pointed look before he thumped up the stairs for the shower.

It wasn't a big deal. He was just being nice. Nate wasn't stupid, and at this point he figured whether Revenant smack-talk meant anything or not, Grace was a permanent fixture. He rushed through his shower, scrubbing off a day's worth of engine grease and dirt, before he dried off and dressed. He grabbed his dirty clothes and started a load of wash in the downstairs hallway.

"You might tell Grace to get her stuff out of the dryer before it's time for you to switch over," Curt offered, walking into the hallway, squeezing past toward the kitchen.

Nate thumped his bag down by the washer. "Sure."

He walked into the kitchen, watching as Curt put plates and silverware out.

"Figured we're all here, we can have a meal like real people."

"As opposed to?"

"Koalas," Grace offered, face straight, as she put the pan of food on the table. "Or, if you don't like Eucalyptus or Australia, buffalo."

Nate grinned, opening his mouth—

"Sit down." Curt threw a napkin at him. "She doesn't know what a drop-bear is and she doesn't need to."

Nate held his hands up in surrender, and slid into a chair.

Drop-bear? Grace mouthed.

"It's a giant Koala, they drop out of trees on people."

"He killed one." Curt rolled his eyes. "He'll show you the picture I'm sure."

"You keep a picture?" Grace asked, sitting down.

Nate held his plate out for her, when she started dishing up. "Only because they're pretty rare anywhere, particularly outside of Australia, and no one ever believes me."

"Was it doing something?"

Nate pulled his plate back, grinning at it. "I don't hunt. Not animals for fun anyway. Bambi never did anything to anyone, and I'm not starving," he answered. "Usually they're pets? Witches, that sort of thing. But they're *big*. Like slightly smaller than a normal sort of bear, and omnivores."

"Nate made friends with that one because it started eating random campers," Curt offered.

"I did seriously think about calling Animal Control and convincing them I'd seen a giant Koala in the woods."

"But?"

Nate took another bite of his food. "This is good, by the way." He shrugged. "It'd have them for breakfast. Mythical animals are always smarter. Better at hiding, obviously."

"I can see that. Otherwise they'd be all over the place, and no longer mythical."

They ate in easy silence, occasionally Curt would bring up a point about something he'd read during the course of the day. It was simple. Nate caught himself looking at the empty chair and kicked himself. His mother would *hate* something like this.

For a start, she hadn't looked at a plate of Macaroni and Cheese since he was six years old.

The wall phone rang, and Nate stood up to start clearing the table while Curt answered it, maneuvered around Grace dumping the leftovers into some old containers.

"That's special, why you callin' me?"

Nate scoffed. "That'll be Richards."

"Richards?" Grace glanced back over her shoulder, before cocking a brow at him.

"He's a...um...friend? Sort of. Fellow hunter, and..." Nate died off, looking for a good way to say Richards was a train-wreck waiting to happen. His last three jobs had gone inexplicably *seriously* wrong and they were relatively sure he'd shot the wrong person at least once.

"Dedicated?" Grace offered.

"Crazy," Curt said, hanging the phone up with a clunk. "Bastard's crazy." He huffed. "And his shit keeps going wrong for reasons he ain't doing a real good job of explaining."

"Did he get arrested again?" Nate asked wryly.

"Not yet." Curt sighed. "But he's got a job." He looked expectantly at Nate. "You're getting antsy, you want this one?"

"I'm not..." Nate started to defend, but gave up and held his hands up. "Whatever. Yeah, sure."

Curt handed him the hastily scribbled paper. "He's got no clue what it is, but it's something." He clapped Nate on the shoulder. "Go get yourself packed, I'll finish with the dishes."

Nate nodded, and headed off to grab his clothes. He kept most of the weapons and everything he'd need in the car, which sounded less secure than it was. He thumped back down the stairs a couple minutes later, stuffing a long-sleeved shirt into his bag, and almost ran into Grace in the hallway.

"Hey." He swallowed, stopping, while she pulled her things out of the laundry.

"Hey." She glanced at him. "You want me to throw your stuff in the dryer?"

"Nah, I can do it real quick." He shifted uncomfortably. "Supper was good, in case I forgot to say."

"You didn't." Grace stopped, turning to lean her hip against the dryer. "Hey, you want some help?"

Nate froze, blinking. "What... With the job?"

"Yeah." She shrugged.

He stalled, casting around for a way to ask why without being rude about it.

"Just..." Grace tugged on her sleeves. "It sounded like you didn't really know what was going on, and Curt mentioned the ones that needed research worked better with two people." She smiled. "I even promise to follow directions."

He rubbed a hand through his hair. "Means traveling light. One hotel room and basically no personal space."

"Long as you knock on the bathroom door, I'm good."

"Can you pack in less than half an hour?"

Grace grabbed her bag. "I can pack in five minutes."

"I'm timing you," Nate called, watching her walk up the stairs before he threw his stuff in the dryer.

"Did I hear that right?" Curt asked, lounging in the doorway.

Nate glanced back at him, frowning. "That okay with you?"

"Not for me to say," the older man answered. "You're both adults."

Nate blinked at him.

"Grace isn't useless in a fight, like you said." Curt looked over toward the stairs. "Wouldn't hurt you to have somebody watching your back for a bit." Curt turned around, heading for his books. "You get in over your head, you call."

"Yes sir," Nate answered, sarcastic. He hefted the bag on his shoulder and walked out to put it in the car.

He'd barely managed to get the tarp folded up and the back secured the way he liked it when Grace came out the door silently—he was watching for her this time—cheeks a bit pink, staring at the zip on her bag.

He wasn't surprised Curt had said something embarrassing. The first time Nate'd left here for a job on his own the bastard had nearly made him *cry* with his "you're important to me, be careful with yourself" speech. Because along with all the other ways Curt did the job like nobody else he'd ever seen, he'd apparently missed the part about burying your emotions so deep you couldn't find them with a team of submariners and a diving license or a crate of whiskey.

She was halfway to the car when her phone rang. "Son of a bitch," Grace muttered.

Nate blinked as she practically threw her bag in the back seat.

"Jamie…" She huffed. "No. Yes. No, I'm…" She grumbled, rubbing her forehead. "Well, you can't now because I won't be here."

Nate leaned on the side of the car, curious as to how she was going to get out of the conversation this time.

"No, I'm not," she grumbled. "Will you *let me finish*?" She swallowed, flushing. "Sorry, just I get that you're worried and I'm sorry I'm not… I obviously seriously suck at lying to you, which is why I'm not really trying. I'm helping Nate with a job so I'm gone most likely at least for the weekend."

She looked at him, rolling her eyes. "Yes, Mother. I have my phone and I promise not to get shot."

Nate smothered a laugh, turning away.

"No, I won't give Nate the phone."

He looked back, waiting.

"Because I'm an adult and I'm capable of making my own decisions and taking care of myself. He's not my keeper any more than you are."

Grace drew a deep breath, and pulled the phone away from her ear, hitting speaker. "Fine, there."

"See, it's not that hard." A deep male voice echoed from the phone, perturbed. "Hello person I've never met who's taking my best friend to do something involving guns she's doing a very bad job of lying about."

Nate choked, laughing again. "Hi. Jamie. Heard a lot about you."

Jamie sighed. "I'd say Grace lies, but if she did she'd be better at it. Just…" he paused, serious. "Promise you won't get her shot? Obnoxious and secretive as she is, I still love her."

Nate looked up at Grace and winced. "I'll…do my best not to get her shot."

"Seriously?"

"Well. I'm not as crappy at lying as she is, so I could probably manage it." Nate flushed. "But I figure you care, I should be as honest as I can be."

Jamie huffed softly. "Alright. Well… Thanks."

"Are we done?" Grace asked darkly. "You have class in the morning, and a court hearing this weekend, and—"

"I'm *worried about you*," Jamie interrupted.

"I know." Grace pulled the phone back to her ear, turning the speaker off as he crawled in the car. "Just...take care of your own life, alright? I'm better than the lying would make you believe." She smiled, sitting in the car and shutting the door carefully. "I love you too."

She settled in the seat, looking around her, and whispered evilly into the phone just before she hung up. "I'm sitting in a 1969 Charger."

Nate laughed, starting the engine. "Poke the bear, why don't you."

She flushed, fastening her seatbelt. "Sorry. He's...um..."

"Freaked out because you upped stakes in the middle of the night and you're lying to him? I get that. In his place I'd be going nuts."

"Yeah," Grace agreed. "I told him you were a bounty hunter, just so you know. I figure the first time I fail to answer the phone we'll have like two hours to hide all the shit that doesn't look normal."

"I thought Northwestern was like three hours away?"

"Yep," she bit off. "So, where are we going?"

Chapter 3

One job turned into two. And then there was an emergency werewolf issue, and then a false alarm, and a Nisse—a kind of elf that generally helped people—who'd had a falling out with an unknowing farmer in Texas.

Nate dumped his bag out on the hotel bed. They'd left Curt's for a 'weekend gig' nearly three and a half weeks ago. He always packed more than he thought he was going to need, because this generally happened to him. He never seemed to short the number of other supplies he needed, bullets and holy oil or whatever.

He shook the mostly empty can of shaving cream, and tossed it in the trash. "I think we probably need to go shopping."

"Sure." Grace came out of the bathroom, waving a mostly empty tube of toothpaste at him.

He blinked, almost wincing. Her shirt was some sort of coral color, the closest she'd gotten to pink in the entire time, and against the ridiculous red floral wallpaper in their room it was almost sickening.

There'd been a room in Texas that was alien vomit green, with some unidentifiable stain on the ceiling and mirror mounts. The last one had been desert-themed with a whirlpool bath they'd neither of them been too sure about.

He'd offered to take her back to Curt's. Twice. Not this last time, because they'd been in freaking Arizona, and the next job was Oklahoma, and if she wasn't going to crack he wasn't driving her all the way back to Iowa.

Each time she'd said it was fine, and she'd go with him. She'd used a computer at a library for a few minutes between jobs two and three, and gotten the stuff she was supposed to be doing for the day job she was miraculously keeping up on, despite rattling around the country with him.

Curt had prefaced his last two conversations with "are you two about to kill each other yet?"

It should have been a valid question.

He checked the meager state of his finances, sighing. "Might want to pick up some cheap meals, too."

Grace leaned against the rickety oriental style table, arms crossed over her chest. "You realize there's a point I'm going to start paying for stuff without asking, right?"

Nate grumbled, and didn't touch that. "So, we need shaving... Well. I need shaving cream," he muttered, watching her move back over by her bag on the other bed. "Your toiletries are your own business."

She laughed. "Nice save."

Nate threw a pillow at her, unsurprised when she wasn't anywhere near where he'd thought she was. The moving quiet didn't just happen at Curt's. He wasn't complaining about that because it'd kept them out of shit twice already. He knew better than to look a gift horse in the mouth, even if he kept wondering where it came from.

She was like a goddamn Ninja. People didn't learn that shit by accident.

"Do we have any concept what we're looking for?"

Nate glanced back at her, shrugging. "Not yet. Curt got the ping from a local boy, there are a couple hunters in this area." He dug through his clothes, making sure he hadn't had to junk too much to get through the next week. Or that they didn't need to go to the Laundromat.

"They're both on other jobs, so it's just us."

"Alright." Grace wrinkled her nose. "Well, I don't need anything girly from the store, do you want to stick me with library duty?"

Nate stared at his stuff and balanced doing the shopping—ugh—with wading through a few dozen years of town death records for anything that fit the profile their latest friend was concocting.

He could do the library, but then he'd have to leave the car with Grace.

"You're thinking about this entirely too hard," she muttered, grabbing her jacket.

Nate sighed. "Give me your list."

She scribbled it quickly, and Nate bit back his comment on her hand-writing. Half-asleep upside down, it was still more legible than his. Which was part of the reason she was doing the library. When he did it they ended up having half an argument about neither of them being able to read his handwriting well enough for the research to have done them any good. Also, cracks about Grace being a librarian aside, he'd already figured he could throw her at any library in the country and she'd find what the needed with more success, faster, than Nate would.

"I don't know what you think I'm going to do to your car."

Nate grabbed the keys, holding the door open for her.

He wasn't good with women. Sure, he was passable at picking up a girl at a bar. And once in a while when he was working the sort of job that required more finesse than he normally needed he'd pulled the male version of a honey-trap. He didn't have female friends.

Well, with the exception of Deke, he didn't really have friends so that probably wasn't the issue. He was learning how to talk to women you weren't sleeping with. Some questions you didn't answer.

They rode to the little town library in silence. Nate was a little watchful, always. He didn't doubt Grace was capable of taking care of herself in the normal run, but he wasn't sure she'd realized yet how far out of the normal run she was. Even bouncing along behind him, she hadn't been doing a lot of the physical part of the job.

His mom was the kind of woman who could shoot someone or something from two paces and not think twice about it. And as uncomfortable as it made him, he didn't think her willingness to do that was just the job. Grace was more like Curt, only violent when the job made her be.

That was a fine way to be. Probably better, all told. That gave her a better chance of living without developing the truckload of issues the rest of them struggled with.

Not that she was a candidate for some of that anyway. Grace didn't drink.

In fact, so far, the most uncomfortable he'd seen Grace was in the bar after their first job when he'd been about half-way to toasted.

He could drink less and get by, and he thought when you got along with people you were supposed to make some sort of concessions for them. Play fair and adjust where you could. The best answer he had, for how to deal with Grace, was to treat her the same way he treated Deke.

There was something pathetic about that, given the fact she was young and attractive, but that was the best option he had that wasn't going to be awkward. And it didn't fit. He wasn't sure what was going on with them, but he didn't really feel like Grace fit in the normal friend category.

Even after knowing her for less than a month.

~~~~~~

Nate looked up from the printed papers, as Grace slid a beer bottle at him. He was relaxed here, in his element. Reading strange paranormal crap at a tiny, sticky table surrounded by drunken cowboys. Completely oblivious to the stares. And she had eyes. She understood why they were staring. Nate occupied his space with loose muscle and steady masculine grace.

And he was obviously not from around there, and new blood was special in a place like this. They didn't either of them fit here, but Grace probably came closer.

"Thanks." Nate swallowed, snagging his bottle, eyes catching on her root beer.

He hadn't commented on her not drinking yet. Or on her inability to make noise when she moved around a room. Or the fact she woke up if he got within three feet of her sleeping space—in a hotel room, one of the smaller ones, he'd pretty much always been within three feet.

But a few weeks into this, Grace was starting to get a feel for the way Nate did things. He was seemingly one of those rare people who let you be whatever or whoever you were. At least so far.

He was much brighter than she'd first figured. It wasn't book-smart, but as far as she could tell that was just because he'd never had the chance. There was a faintly ridiculous breadth of knowledge someone needed to have, to wander into this job blind and have any chance of dealing with it. He was smooth and charming when he wanted to be, when he felt like it was warranted.

Curt had complained, on more than one occasion that most of the other hunters out there just sort of started hacking at things until they found the right combination that killed whatever they were up against. Apparently he'd taught Nate better than that.

Still, the concept of Curt—or even Nate who was young and capable—doing this job alone was enough to give her its own set of nightmares. He did research, and he planned, and all of that. She could tell by the way he moved, and talked, that things had been quiet the last few weeks she'd been with him. That he'd expected it to be a little more violent than it was being right then. So far things had been pretty easy, which was sort of freaky all on its own.

And yeah, they were eating Asian noodles and peanut butter but still going out for beer. Next time she'd insist on taking store duty, it was the only way he'd let her pay for anything.

He looked up at the guy who'd been hitting on her at the bar—yes, she'd noticed, no she wasn't interested—and frowned. "If you wanted to…um…"

"If I wanted to?" She offered, wondering how he was going to finish that.

"You know...um," he stumbled. "Just…It's been nearly four weeks."

Grace cocked a brow at him. "You aren't giving me permission." It took nearly every single ounce of self-control she had not to mention the six different women—really. Six—who were watching the back of Nate's head, trying to figure out if they were together and they could approach without causing a cat-fight.

They'd already suffered through the conversation about how he didn't pick women up while he was actually working, usually.

"Nope." He looked back down at the papers, face flushing. "I was looking for a tactful way to say if you were interested I could hang out here for a few hours."

She laughed outright, and hoisted herself onto the stool. "Thanks for the offer, but no."

Nate looked over her shoulder. "He's interested, obviously, so?"

She ignored that and nodded at the paper in his hands. "What do you think?"

He sighed, because he wasn't stupid and Grace knew that had been about as subtle as a pink elephant.

Nate had an odd unwillingness to push the way most people did, even with the best of intentions, when Grace tried to avoid things. He was careful with her, probably more than he needed to be. She'd nearly had a panic attack in the bar after their first job and Nate hadn't gotten drunk since. Never mind it hadn't been about him—there was an old man on his third bottle who'd looked disturbingly like her father.

"I think you're right, and we're going to have fun figuring out where she's buried."

Grace fingered the edge of the top paper, after he'd flipped it over to start the next one. Her name was Rachel. According to the local paper she'd been killed in an auto accident with a friend, driving out by the town water reservoir. In 1921. But there was no mention of a funeral, and she'd already checked the grave-yard listings.

She looked up, watching him twitch as Hank Williams came over the speakers. Nate didn't seem to have a problem with country music in general, there were just certain corners of it that made him twitch.

The bar was busy, one of those 'only place in town' numbers that probably used to look old west, but now looked a little more new-age cowboy. A tiny little dance floor in the corner—only place in town meant it was the only place for the ladies to go too—under neon lights, jukebox, pool tables, everything wreathed in a fine coating of cigarette smoke.

If she'd been a different person, she might have met someone and fallen in love in a place like this.

"But yeah, it fits. They've just started doing work on the reservoir, and about half the town, so there's no telling what's kicked her up." He sighed. "But it fits the witness tally, the bloody woman on the side of the road, and…"

"You said something earlier about a Lady in White." He'd grumbled it, while they were checking into the hotel and both of them trying too hard not to comment on the "we're not together" vibe that kept springing up.

He nodded. "You've heard of a Lady in White?"

"Yeah. I'm not sure it's possible to avoid hearing that one." Grace was pretty sure every state in the union had at least one story about the ethereal girl on the side of the highway in a white nightgown creeping out drunk country boys.

"Well, for as prevalent as it is, it nearly never actually happens." He took a swig of his beer. "I've seen like...two of them? In fifteen years, that's saying something."

She wasn't going to say anything about the fact doing the math meant he'd been doing this shit since he was fifteen. Though given what she'd heard from Curt over the last two years, she thought fifteen years was probably a conservative number. Rounded down.

"Well." She sighed, leaning her elbows on the table. "Nothing like a little grave-robbing to round out the month."

He snorted. "Not grave-robbing."

"We're not?"

"We're not taking anything. I've got no use for the bones of an already uneasy spirit." He pushed the papers to her. "We're *settling*, not taking."

"Have you tried explaining that to someone who caught you?"

"No." Nate pulled his phone out, frowning as it vibrated in his hand. "But I've never been caught." He blinked at it, but answered.

Grace started to stand, to give him a little privacy. Even if it was for her own piece of mind, she felt like there needed to be some lines somewhere. Not that she had any clue where to put them.

"Hello?" He scoffed, looking up at her. "Your best friend is stalking me."

Grace froze.

"He says he weaseled my number out of Curt, and if you're following me around like some lame band he's allowed."

She opened her mouth, about to...

"Hey, Jamie." Nate grinned, pleased. "Why did she laugh at me when I suggested she could pull a guy at the bar?" *It's fine*, he mouthed.

It was, because if Nate wasn't uncomfortable with it, talking to him might slightly get Jamie off her back. That didn't mean she wanted to be around for the conversation.

She trusted Nate not to give anything away. He understood as well as she did keeping Jamie in the dark about what all was going on was probably temporary at best. Nate being supportive was super flattering, in a way she wouldn't have expected it to be.

She looked in the smoky mirror, sighing, and adjusted her hair. Shoved off the urge to call Aunt Rhoda and ask when she was allowed to stop learning new things about herself.

When she wandered back out to the table a moment later Nate was fiddling with his coaster, face serious. It was a little comforting to know Jamie could rocket other people between conversational extremes. That that wasn't just her.

"Yeah." Nate glanced up at her. "I get that, and you're right." He frowned. "Just... Curt and I aren't the reason for the new weird. You aren't getting an explanation from me, but it's the other way around. And Curt's fond of her. I'm not stupid enough to be careless."

"You're not stupid at all," Grace huffed. "And Jamie needs to go back to his own life."

Nate laughed softly. "Yeah, I'll tell her." He hung up the phone, and sat it on the table, spinning it idly. "He said you were part of his life, and he was worried." He slipped his phone in his pocket. "I'm not sure if I helped that or not."

Grace sighed. "Sorry, we're..." She didn't exactly know how to finish that without potentially over-sharing.

Nate chuckled, nodding. "Yeah. A bit. I get it though. You're a package deal." He bit his lip, watching her for a long moment. "And I'm...I'm staying out of your business, but you might want to prepare yourself for the fact he's only going to take the half answers and made up job titles for me for so long."

She pushed negligently at a mar on the table top, swallowing. "Yeah. I know."

He was watching her, and she could feel all the normal questions gearing up. All the things she didn't like to deal with. This was why she didn't make new friends. With Jamie, she never had to mess with it. He just knew. Not that he never pushed, she'd just learned how to deal with it.

"So." Nate finished his beer, pushing the bottle aside. "Any idea's where we should start looking for this woman?"

Grace blinked, thrown. "No?"

"Was that supposed to come out a question?"

"Sorry. I thought..." She frowned, stopping. *Over-sharing again.* "Nope. Nevermind." Grace cleared her throat and tried not to blush. "No. But it sounded like the cemetery was just for town, and they had land and a big set-up. At the house maybe?"

Nate stood, stretching. "Worth a try. Should probably call it a night, tomorrow'll be long."

"Sure." She got up slowly, nodding.

Nate Carter was one strange man.

~~~~~~

Grace stepped out of the car, leaning back against the side. Grass blew in the fields around them, a wide cloud-dotted blue sky stretching overhead. A couple of trees swaying next to the house gave the wind something to make noise in. She hadn't liked Arizona. Never mind the weather, everything was some shade of brown and scrubby. It was dry and white. Like even the sunlight had forgotten half its colors.

Oklahoma wasn't like where she'd grown up. It was *drier*. Cattle country, mostly, and the soil smelled different. Grittier. She didn't notice it so much when they were in town. Towns were towns. The world always looked different in the country. Not always for the better, but that was by the by. Dirt was only just dirt when it wasn't yours.

Right now, miles and days away, Grace could remember the exact smell of an Illinois rain, or the color gray of the winter sky.

The fact it wasn't the part of Illinois she'd grown up in was beside the point. She wasn't homesick. She didn't get homesick. She was maybe starting to miss Jamie a little, nearly daily phone calls notwithstanding.

"So what's the plan here?" Grace glanced through the window as Nate packed a bag of supplies.

He shrugged, cramming an EMF reader and some other stuff in, then stopped to check the ketchup bottle of holy oil he was adding last. "No clue. You got any suggestions?"

Nate didn't plan things. Not generally, that she'd seen. He planned when it was time to deal with whatever they were after. When there was an obvious, forthcoming possibility someone could get hurt, he had a step-by-step plan worked out with some sort of nebulous backup in mind.

When it came to talking to people, not so much.

And it wasn't that she was concerned about just waltzing in and trusting their collective brain cells to save the day. They'd done plenty of that in the last couple of weeks. She just didn't like to tempt fate.

"Place like this, Water Quality's probably a decent cover story. That or a sociology project on old grave sites."

Nate blinked. "Aren't we a little old for college kids?"

Grace cocked a brow. "If you're implying I look to old to reliably pass for twenty-six—"

"Point," he headed her off, flushing. "Do they do that?"

"They do everything. Jamie dug through other people's trash for fourteen months." Grace paused, frowning. "Well. I say Jamie…"

He chuckled. "Right. Well, I'll never pull college doctorate."

She shrugged, stepping away from the car. "You can be the suckery friend."

It was a somehow typical white clapboard Oklahoma house. The danger to traversing three-quarters of the mid-west in less than a month was turning out to be over-generalizing places.

She knocked smartly on the door and thirty minutes of talking later—Grace wasn't even entirely sure what she'd said—they were standing in a barn with a shovel and verbal permission to dig whatever they wanted, so long as they picked up after themselves.

"So apparently I missed a lucrative profession as a con artist." She felt maybe a little bad about lying to the nice old man in the house, who'd been tickled to have visitors and talked their ears off about his grand-kids for more than she needed to have let him.

Just because she didn't like people didn't mean she relished being mean to them.

Nate scoffed, and sunk the shovel in the packed dirt floor. "You're still young."

It took her a second to realize that had been about the 'con artist' crack, and not about her internal musings about being mean.

Grace watched him dig for a moment. He was trying to put her at ease. The entire time they'd been inside she could practically hear Curt lecturing her on ghosts. *Once these things are up, they just get worse until they're back down. Lying to him is better than his winding up dead.* All the other things he'd said to her over and over since they'd met.

Fighting with the junk as it came at you at home was a vastly different animal to tracking it down. She wasn't sure how she felt about the fact this was swiftly becoming her life.

But it wouldn't do any good to pretend. "Either let me dig, or give me something else to do. I'll go buggy standing here watching you work."

Nate paused, tossing her the EMF reader he'd shoved in his pocket at the house. "Might get a little advanced warning when she shows up."

She'd give him crap about 'when' but being slightly paranoid was probably at least half the reason Nate was still breathing.

I'm standing in a barn, holding an EMF reader that looks like it was made out of toilet paper rolls and string, while someone digs up a body.

Occasionally the new level of strange hit her all at once. Grace hadn't ever, that she could figure, been normal, but this was new even for her.

And not as disturbing as it should have been.

They'd been quiet jobs so far, and she knew that. A Finnish house-spirit that got left behind when the family moved. Some sort of shape-shifter Grace hadn't seen as anything other than human until he'd screamed at them and disappeared when she started the exorcism Nate told her to do. A hag. A werewolf that had brought its own hunter, and she was still trying to process that particular bag of fun.

It'd all been weird. Maybe not quite as weird as the night she'd been walking home from the library and kept a dog from chewing on some kid only to find herself on the under-side of a werewolf, but still weird.

She was honest enough with herself to admit she probably wasn't ever going to freak out, even if she wasn't dealing, per se.

Nate wasn't anywhere near six feet down when he hit the coffin. More like three. Grace had the sudden, slightly hysterical thought that they were going to have to report human remains buried too close to the water table. Was there a way to do that, that wouldn't cause problems? She understood completely how hard he worked to stay away from the police. Nate had never said that he hadn't ever accidentally shot the wrong person, and he moved and thought through things like it was a constant concern.

But so did Curt, and he'd made that claim for both of them.

He cleared off the coffin, and then grabbed a crowbar to pry the lid off. The instant he touched the crowbar to the lid, the EMF in her hand crackled and made noise.

"Nate."

He froze, poised over the coffin. "Beeped?"

"Yep."

He tightened his shoulders, hands twisting on the bar. "Right. Back up a step. She'll probably come out swinging."

Grace took a careful step back, and glanced around for something iron.

Nate cracked the lid off and opened the container of oil to pour over the bones, before the gray form slammed him back against the side of the grave. She screamed, and pinned Nate back, knocking the crowbar out of his hands.

The EMF screeched, falling onto the bag next to her feet with a soft thump, little lights blinking crazily, almost brighter in the sudden cold of the room around them.

Grace grabbed a wrench off the tool stand, throwing it at the ghost. "Hey, over here!"

Chapter 4

Nate felt the tool hit him in the chest, through the ghost.

And normally he'd have said something about the fact someone just threw a freaking wrench at him, but it had the wanted effect. Or at least Grace's wanted effect. Their less than friendly spirit let go of him, and lunged at her.

Nate collapsed back against the edge of the grave, just trying to breathe for a second. People always heard "ghost" and thought filmy little insubstantial things. It never occurred to them that by the time these things were capable of trucking with the outside world they were generally capable of serious damage.

Like the one that was currently throwing Grace back against the tool table, pinning her down before she could reach for another wrench.

Nate was halfway out of the pit, intent on helping, when Grace managed to find something small and metal under the table and edge it off a bit.

"Take care of that," she panted, throwing something else small at the spirit.

He wasn't sure if Grace realized she was just pissing it off or not, but she had a point. He could try to protect her, or he could take care of the spirit so protecting Grace wasn't an issue. He scrambled around for the crowbar, and the oil. He popped the cap open, pushing the lid of the coffin off and dumping oil over it.

The ghost started to turn on him, but Grace managed to get its attention again.

It threw her across the room, slamming her back into a wall, and Nate froze for a second, concerned.

Grace coughed, slow to move. "That all you've got? My grandma Mary could hit harder than that."

It turned, lunging back at Grace. Whatever amount of intelligence you credited a ghost with, most spirits—particularly the vengeful ones—were ridiculously prone to smack-talk.

Nate pulled a cheap lighter out of the bag, flicking it on and lighting a bit of reed twisted into the shape of a cross as a wick. He dropped it on the corpse. She turned then, lunging across the room and slamming into Nate again. He'd probably have been in a lot worse shape except she'd barely gotten him pinned when she was burning up and…gone.

They sat quietly for a long moment, neither of them particularly quick to move.

Nate swallowed, pushing himself to a sitting position on the edge of the grave, and then swinging out to go help Grace to her feet. "Grandma Mary?" he asked, hauling her up.

Grace snorted, wiping her face, her lip bleeding slightly. "My grandma Mary was a hardass."

Nate looked at the smoldering pile they were going to have to bury again. "Must run in the family," he said, the words popping out before he could think them through.

He winced, glancing up at her sharply, because for a start he didn't imagine women generally liked to be called a hard-ass, and also because there hadn't really been any sort of affection in her tone about Grandma Mary, so maybe she wouldn't appreciate being compared to her.

Grace smiled, small and genuine, and knocked their shoulders together, grabbing the shovel. "I'll start. Your throat okay?"

Nate blinked at her. "Is my..." He huffed. "Yes, my throat's okay. How about your ribs?"

She shifted slightly, shrugging. "I might be a bit sore tomorrow. I'll live."

He watched as Grace worked at refilling the hole, and got about half the soil put back into it, before he took over. Even shoveling the dirt back in, and patting it down, he couldn't stop watching her.

She should have been freaked out, right? She'd just had a ghost try and ring her bell. Even with all the other jobs—they'd been dangerous but they hadn't really been hands on—and what had happened in Galesburg before they met it should have cracked the surface.

Nate was all about the job. Absolutely. He'd never had any choice not to be. Once he'd passed the GED and his mom had taken him with her all the time chickening out had never been an option.

Well, that wasn't fair. He could have freaked out and told Curt he just couldn't truck it and Curt would have done *something*. The older man had gotten between Nate and his mother plenty of other times. So yeah, if Nate had been slightly less concerned with his mom's good opinion he could have gotten out.

But if a frog had wings it wouldn't bump its butt, and out certainly wasn't an option now. He'd tried it once. There were days where he wasn't happy about his life. He didn't have much by way of marketable life skills, he'd drank more than he didn't, and when his mom showed up and needed help on a job he'd gone back out without a second thought.

He remembered what that first year actually full on hunting was like. The blinding terror the first time he found himself face to face with a werewolf. Shaking and vomiting the first time he'd had to shoot something that looked human. All of that.

Maybe Grace wasn't going to be like that. Probably she wasn't going to be like that. She was older, for a start, and not him, and that was fine.

Nate hung back while she explained things to the old man, about the grave they'd found, and how they'd put it back where it was and said a few words in remembrance. He'd have never thought of that, but in a place like this it helped. She thanked him for his time and made some crack about being a klutz to excuse the obvious bruise forming on her mouth.

He wasn't sure that should have worked, but the guy was deaf as could be, and obviously he hadn't heard anything from the house. Even then, pretty frequently he had civilians wonder up while he was in the middle of a haunting, and they always looked at him funny but it generally didn't take a whole lot of work to convince them to go away again. People didn't question. He was never sure how much of that was because they didn't really want to know.

Grace jogged back out to the car, sliding in with him and fastening her belt. She waved easily at the old man as they pulled down the gravel drive and headed back for the hotel. Grace called Curt, checking in and telling him that for the moment they were headed back to him in the morning. She seemed fine.

He was starting to worry, maybe a little, that the panic was just delayed. That someday they were going to be in the middle of a job and he'd turn around and she'd be curled up in a little ball on the floor.

Which was stupid, obviously, because as soon as they finished with this she was going to...do something. Go back to her work, or stay with Curt or hell if he knew what.

Nate shut the door to the hotel room carefully, watching as she unzipped her hoodie and dropped it with the rest of the dirty clothes, arching her back slightly.

"Flip a coin for the first shower?" Grace asked, glancing back at him, brow cocked.

"No." Nate cleared his throat. "No, go ahead."

She nodded and grabbed her things, humming along with the music coming through the wall.

Or maybe Grace just didn't scare.

~~~~~~

They didn't make it back to Curt's.

Which is no real kind of surprise at all. It's even starting to push at Nate a little, the number of jobs they've done back to back. The number of hours on the road between them. Today was an all time high, and apparently their mutual max for the number of hours they could spend in a car in one day.

Nineteen.

He'd even let Grace drive for a while. Mostly because he was going to break something if he had to cling to the steering wheel any longer.

"Where are we again?" Grace asked, sprawled back on the teal bed-cover like an obscene, coat wearing star-fish. "And why the hell is it so cold here?"

Nate flopped face first on his bed, and wrapped his arms around the pillow, eyes closing already. He was working on a headache of epic proportions, and looking down the barrel of talking their way into the morgue tomorrow. "I'm pretty sure the answer to both is 'end of the universe Minnesota' because if we passed border patrol I'm sure one of us would have noticed," he mumbled into the lumpy hotel pillow.

"Do we cross borders? I would think Canada's ghosts would be Canada's problem."

"Isolationist."

Grace laughed softly. "No. Just trying to avoid Curt talking us into going to Canada."

"Don't think they have ghosts in Canada." Nate managed to lift his arm, intent on getting up and…doing something. Taking a shower, or getting food, or wallpapering the shower. It was all about the same level of effort right then.

"What's their secret?"

He collapsed back, sighing. "State medical care and medicinal marijuana probably," he choked, falling into easy laughter. Fuck he was punch-drunk.

Grace laughed too, burying her head under a pillow. "Alright, is there any reason this whatever the shit it is can't wait until tomorrow? Cause I'm seriously too tired to even care that I'm hungry."

"No." Nate shook his head. "Can't do anything before tomorrow anyway. Sleep. Or find food, whatever. If you—"

Grace's phone went off, and she groaned and dug around for it. "Yeah? If nothing's on fire I'm hanging up on you."

Nate shifted, turning his head to the side. "Hi Jamie."

"Yeah, he says Hi, but we spent like…a week on the road today. Yeah. Nope, situation normal, everything okay with you?" She nodded, sighing. "Will. Bye. Love you."

Nate cracked one eye open, looking across the room as Grace dropped her phone on the bedside table. "Did that actually work?"

She flopped back on the bed. "I only threaten to hang up on him when I actually *really* don't want to talk."

"He needs a girlfriend." The instant the words left Nate's mouth he winced. He shouldn't have said that, and he knew he shouldn't have. He didn't comment on Grace's relationship with Jamie. For a whole host of reasons, the largest one being he sort of figured it was amazing he and Grace weren't trying to rip each other's throats out by now and he should try and keep it that way.

"It's been discussed." She sighed, covering her face with her hands when it turned into a yawn. "Crap. I'm too tired to go to sleep."

Nate almost managed to get upright. "Rock, paper, scissors on who secures the room and who gets food?"

She managed to get to her feet, and then pulled him up. She almost over-balanced, and Nate's years of physical training was the only thing that kept them upright.

Grace flushed. "I'm entirely too tired to adequately ward a room, not one you'd want to sleep in. I'll get food."

"'Sure. Might make you double check me anyway, I'm about there."

She nodded. "Towns pretty closed tight, I think. Dinner by vending machine?"

He handed her the ones he had. "Take a weapon with you. Just don't shoot anybody unless you have to."

Grace grabbed a knife and shook her head at his cocked brow. "Sorry officer, he startled me when I was reaching for a nut bar, and I thought he was a vampire."

He chuckled softly. "Well, at least you're with it enough to know you shouldn't be handed fire-arms."

She slipped out the door, and Nate made himself grab their warding supplies. He didn't do this all the time. It was sort of a waste of stuff, for what they normally dealt with. But whatever this thing was—Curt hadn't had a lot of details for them, a couple of missing hikers and a guy who'd eaten himself to death--it had already killed at least one person so he was warding.

If he looked at the clock every minute and reminded himself that Grace was outside, alone, that was just because he was so tired he was in danger of forgetting how long she'd been gone for. He'd done that to Curt once, on a job when Nate was in his late teens. Curt hadn't been in any serious kind of trouble, not anything he could have gotten out of, but it still hadn't been pleasant.

For a guy who was averse to seriously yelling, Curt could guilt a person like nobody's business.

It wasn't an issue. Less than eight minutes, and Grace was back with an armful of food. She stumbled back against the door, shutting it, and dropped her offerings on the water-ringed table.

"So…" She glanced up at him and puffed out a breath. "I'm awake now."

Nate froze, hand already reaching for a weapon.

"There was a goddamn bear hanging out behind the building." She held the knife out to him, hilt first. "And

I'm thinking that probably wouldn't have been very helpful."

He choked, taking the blade from her and stashing it with the others. "Seriously, just hanging out?"

She shrugged. "Minnesota. They've got signs posted all over that it's bear country and you shouldn't leave food in your car and what to do if you accidentally threaten one. Bet you're glad we took some time this afternoon to clean the trash out, huh?"

"What'd you do?"

Grace kicked her shoes off, grabbing a bag of chips. "Waited until a semi drove by and scared it off, and then grabbed the food and got back in here." She smiled wryly. "So clearly we won't be doing a lot of night work."

He shook his head, grabbing a can of something clear and non-caffeinated. "Yeah. I got no desire to shoot some poor animal because I interrupted it's foraging."

Nate didn't remember falling asleep. He remembered finishing the warding on the door, and Grace getting up to check it over. He remembered *I Love Lucy* coming on about when he finished eating, and he remembered Grace reaching up to turn the light off.

He woke up for a moment in the middle of the night, lights all doused and TV off. Grace was crawling back into bed, blinking at him tiredly.

"You good?"

"Fell asleep without brushing my teeth," she muttered, and dropped into bed.

But they hadn't closed the over-curtains all the way, which wasn't a shock given how tired they'd both been by the time they got there, and even this late in the fall apparently the sun in the arctic—Minnesota was in the arctic circle, right?—decided to come up early.

For him anyway. Nate managed to make it to a seated position before he realized why Grace didn't mind the sun coming through the window. Her head was buried under the blankets and a pillow. He had no intention at all of messing with her. He needed a shower, and if he could

77

manage to slip past her bed without waking her up then she could sleep through it.

Nate grabbed his things and edged along the side of his bed. So far, best he could tell, there was about a three-foot bubble around the bed. If he crossed that, Grace woke up. Even if he was completely silent. Somehow, she just *knew*. Nate did some sort of ridiculous, superspy/ninja move that got him to the edge of the bed, next to the bathroom door. He edged through and shut it with a quiet snick.

He dropped his bag on the chipped sink and turned on the shower. He tested the water, biting back a yell when it rained on his hand frigidly cold and spattering. It was only October. Next time, he was going to tell Curt he wasn't taking a job north of Iowa between the first of October and the end of April. He didn't like being cold.

They hadn't had to sleep in the car yet, but he was known to do that more than occasionally, on a string of jobs. If there wasn't a hotel in his price range around. Or one that wouldn't ask too many questions.

One plus to having Grace around, there'd been less of that lately. He didn't know what people were assuming, about their traveling together, but they'd stopped asking outright questions.

Nate stepped into the shower and lathered his hair quickly, because it was warm now but there was no guarantee how long that was going to last.

He stared at the window—it was frosted glass, okay, but it was still a freaking window—taking up one wall of the shower, before he shook his head and shaved quickly. He'd have liked to loiter around in the shower, until the water turned cold and his fingers were all wrinkled, but Grace still needed to take a shower. He didn't need to leave her a lot of water because actually half the time she was faster than he was, but he doubted there was a lot of distance between luke-warm and ice-flow. He turned the water off and grabbed a towel.

"Nate?"

"Yeah?" Figured the sound of the shower would wake her up.

"I braved the cold—b.t.dubs they're supposed to get snow tomorrow—"

"Fucking Minnesota," he muttered, pressing his face into the towel.

"—and got hot coffee and a phonebook," she finished with a soft laugh.

"Phonebook?"

"Didn't figure you wanted to ask the woman in the office where the morgue was," she answered, voice fading away from the door. "Cell reception sucks here."

Nate threw his clothes on, ignoring the pull of denim over wet skin, and opened the bathroom door. He grabbed the coffee cup off his table and dropped the towel he'd used next to his bed. "You with the forethought."

Grace glanced up at him, hands wrapped around a steaming cup of coffee. "It's my superpower." She was sitting cross-legged in the puddle of sunshine across her bed, wearing a thick orange sweater over the sweats and t-shirt she'd slept in the night before. Also, he thought her socks might have had a previous life as a psychedelic green and yellow barber pole.

He tested his and enjoyed the puff of aromatic steam. "All yours, sugar. I like the socks."

She rolled her eyes and grabbed the bundle of things on the bed next to her. "How screwed am I gonna be if the water goes cold?"

He flipped through the phonebook, brow pulling at the tiny print of the county listings. "I think there's a blow-dryer here somewhere, I'll thaw you back out."

The freaking coroner's office was twenty miles away, in the next town over. Along with the sheriff's office, and anything else you wanted that wasn't a tiny library in a converted gas station, or an emergency clinic. He wasn't sure the place even qualified as a one horse town.

But he'd figured out where they were going on the map, and packed up the supplies he wanted for the day by the time Grace came out of the shower, fully dressed and ready to go. She'd dried her hair a little more than the norm, but he suspected that had something to do with the temperature, a balmy thirty-nine degrees.

It was a crisp, uncomfortable morning, and Grace didn't seem inclined to break the silence on their way to the county offices. She sat quietly and stared out the side window of the car, watching the trees go past them in a mad whorl.

It wasn't that Nate minded. Just having her around while he talked his way into the morgue and looked at the body still helped. While he called Curt and figured out what the hell they had that was making people in the back-of-beyond Minnesota literally *eat* themselves to death.

But by the time they'd found it—fucking *fear grass*, seriously—and he'd poured holy water on it, and said the incantations *to make the grass stop killing people* he figured she'd said six words to him in two days.

So maybe it was past time to get back to Curt's.

Now you're messing with a son of a bitch, his phone sang over the deep thrum of the Charger engine.

Grace dropped her head against the car window, breaking into laughter. "I'd say throw it in a puddle—"

Nate frowned, blinking at his phone. "It's not Curt." He hit the speaker button. "Deke, what's going on?"

It wasn't like Deke to call him out of the blue. Deke was pretty much the only person other than Curt who would have called him. Well, Grace probably counted, but still. Usually he just texted.

Deke's voice scratched slightly on the phone. "You say that like I only ever call you when someone's about to die."

"Because you do," Nate answered, throwing his gear in the back of the car.

"Yeah, well." Deke sighed. "I've got a job for you, but Curt said you'd been on the road a while, with some woman I've never heard of. What's with that, by the way?"

He rolled his eyes. "Don't be a dick, you're on speaker and Grace's been on the road just as long as I have, obviously. Say hi."

"Hi Deke."

"Hi Grace," Deke replied at exactly the same time, then snorted. "Listen, if you're too baked for this job, I can...probably find someone else."

He couldn't. Nate could tell by the tone of voice he couldn't, and he looked up at Grace to try and find some way to explain that, completely understanding of the fact she *probably* wouldn't want to take another job.

But she was already digging out the map, handing it to him. "I don't know where he lives," Grace offered quietly.

Nate took the map from her, staring at it for a second, swallowing. "Are you..." He had to physically bite his tongue, not to ask if she was sure. "It's Chicago. I guess we'll be there..." Nate died off, looking at the map. He always forgot when he was in upstate Minnesota exactly how *upstate* he was. "Lunchtime tomorrow. Soon enough?"

"What, could you get here faster if it wasn't?"

"Probably, but I'd have to let Grace drive for a while tonight."

"I don't know what you think I'm going to do to your car. I haven't yet," Grace muttered.

"You let her drive the car?" Deke whistled softly. "Right, well, no point in anything drastic. It'll be fine till then. I'll be at the shop."

"Sure." Nate hung the phone up, dropping it next to him on the seat and dropping his head back against the headrest. "Next time we're going back to Curt's unless the sky's about to catch fire."

Grace buckled her seat-belt, and dug around in the bag at her feet for her editing. "Do you need me to help you stay awake, or are you good?"

"I'm fine." He grumbled. "It was fucking grass."

She shuddered. "Yeah. On the level of weird? Let's try not to repeat the creepy killer grass."

Chapter 5

Deke was one of the few people Nate knew who managed to do this shit and actually get paid for it.

Well, Deke wasn't much of a hunter. Mostly he was supply. Shortly before they'd met, Deke had inherited an old camping and backpacking store in northern Chicago from some uncle, and he'd been trying to keep it open honestly but it just wasn't working. Deke knew other hunters. Actually, he knew lots of other hunters. More than Nate figured Curt and his mother could manage together.

Out of all that, one day Deke had just decided to start offering them weapons. Things they could have made themselves if they had the time. Things they didn't have the tools to make themselves, or the ability to travel with the tools to make themselves.

He didn't charge an arm and leg for them. He even sold them camping and backpacking supplies without a giant markup. He lived in a little hovel over the top of the shop that had better protection and containment wards than just about anyplace Nate had ever been.

But, for the most part, no one wanted to walk into Deke's back room if they didn't have to. It held about three-thousand and twelve things that could kill you without much more than a moment's notice, odd cursed shit he had just laying around until he found a way to un-curse it.

"Don't touch anything," he called, as soon as Nate opened the door.

"Dude, how many times have I been in here?"

Deke appeared from between the shelves, glasses perched on his nose, dark straight hair hanging in his face, and his ridiculous campers vest with god only knew what stuffed in the pockets hanging off his tall lean frame. The weird high lighting in the storage room made his skin look darker than it's normal mixed Native American/African/who knew what else tone.

"That wasn't for you," he said dryly.

Grace stepped in behind him, hands shoved in her pockets. "He told me in the car."

Nate watched Deke give Grace the once over, and felt like someone needed to be making western whistling gunfight noises. "Grace, Deke. Deke, Grace," he mumbled awkwardly.

Deke rolled his eyes at him. "Smooth." He transferred the clipboard in his hand to the other side, holding a hand out for Grace. "Deacon Hughes."

"Grace Cleary." Grace shook easily.

Deke looked at him, brow cocked high. Expectant.

Nate was about to find some way to head him off at the pass because whatever Deke was about to ask was going to be awkward as hell. He looked at the shelves, hoping for anything to derail wherever this was going.

"Right, well." Deke turned and headed toward the back room. "Come on back, so you're out of the line of fire."

Nate stepped aside, waving her past him, and brought up the rear. They tacked back through the piles of junk, and they were within sight of the back office when Nate saw something move out of the corner of his eye. He reached out to grab Grace's shoulder, because it was sort of human nature to catch things with your hands and that would be *bad*.

The ivory totem flew off the shelf, hitting her in the stomach, and Nate and Deke both reached out. Grace let it drop, rolling down her leg before she hooked it up with her foot and caught it in the front of her hoodie.

Deke blinked at her, digging the glove he kept in his left lowermost pocket out. He gingerly grabbed the ivory totem.

"I'm not sure how bad it would have been for that to break, but..." Grace died off, shrugging.

Deke very carefully put it back on the shelf, steady, and gently moved Grace away from it. "I'm not sure it would have broken." He looked her over carefully. "Do strange things usually happen around you, Grace?"

Nate chocked out a startled laugh and Deke turned and looked at him.

"I'll take that as a 'yes' then."

"They have been lately," Grace answered. "So can I ask what it is?"

Deke frowned at the little ivory carving on the shelf. "It's a Tupilaq. It's an Inuit...construct. Or it was, before someone locked it in the ivory totem. I haven't figured out how to get rid of it yet."

"How do you normally get rid of them?" Nate asked.

"Find someone to turn it back on the person who created it, so it will either kill them and then go away or they'll admit what they've done and it leaves on its own." He looked at them, sighing. "This one was trapped in that nearly eighty years ago. Even if I knew who made it, I doubt it would help at this stage."

Deke shot him one last, strange glance before he turned and walked into his back office.

Grace turned around, eyes wide.

"I've got no clue," Nate offered, but waved her on. They made it into the office without any other mishaps, but he was two inches through the door when he nearly tripped over a stack of papers. "Jesus, do you know how to get out if you start a fire?"

Deke glared at him. "I'm sorry, generally people like you need something from me when I'm in the midst of having a clean-up and it never get's finished." He ferreted a file out, from the top of the far desk, and held it out to Nate. "Have fun with that."

"I love it when you say that to me." Nate opened it, angling it slightly so Grace could see it too.

"So how did she get roped into this?"

"She volunteered," Grace answered, frowning. "A Korrigan?" She reached out and ruffled the papers, clearly missing Deke's attempt at silent conversation and Nate's ongoing struggle to ignore him. "Aren't those the water dwellers that lure men to their death at dawn and dusk?"

Nate huffed. "Do I want to know how you know that?"

"I was an English major, much as you like to call me a librarian," Grace teased. "I did more than a few humanities classes."

"I think that's what it is," Deke said. "And I know how much you hate water demons, but a friend of mine has been having trouble with this one. It seems to have moved in up the block from her, and it's scaring her clients away."

"Clients?" Nate rose a brow, waiting for more.

"Not those kind of clients," Deke huffed, unamused. "She's a fortune teller. Tarot and all that sort of thing. But it's been killing people in the neighborhood, and it's not a nice neighborhood so the police presence is a little…um…"

"Not there?" Nate offered.

"Something like that." Deke ruffled his hair. "I'll owe you one, yeah?"

He shrugged, handing the file to Grace. "I'm pretty sure I owe you one as it stands. You might owe Grace." He frowned. "Unless you want…" he died off, not sure how to finish.

"Unless I want?" Grace prompted.

"Curt's only a couple hours away. If you wanted to go back."

She blinked at him. "Is there a nice way to say I'm uncomfortable leaving you with the thing that preys on men after a nearly two-month string of jobs? You're not the only person Curt guilts."

Nate flushed. "Sure. We'll find a place to stay. Deke doesn't really have room for a mouse, let alone us."

Grace flipped through the papers, looking things over. "I'd say we could stay with Jamie, he's only about twenty minutes away." She looked up, handing him the file back. "But that's a bad idea."

Nate snorted. "You're assuming he's not going to somehow psychically know you're within twenty minutes of him and come shoot me for…take your pick, actually."

Deke gave him a strange look, and grabbed his keys. "Let me lock up and I'll introduce you to Rose."

Grace blinked. *Rose?*

Nate held the door open for her. *Hell if I know. Give us a sec.*

"Yeah. I'm going to make a phone-call. Is your statue going to jump at me again?"

Deke glanced up at her, frowning. "Just don't touch it if it does, and try not to let it hit the ground."

"Sure." Grace nodded, and walked out through the store-room.

Nate watched her go, making sure she was through the ridiculous lines of slightly dangerous stuff.

"So who's Jamie?"

He blinked. "Best friend. It's…um…complicated."

"How so?" Deke locked his desk, and set the warding around the door.

"He doesn't know anything and she's not very good at lying to him." He pushed his mind back on target. "Rose?"

Deke looked up, flushing. "Not like that. Much to my mother's everlasting regret, I'm sure."

87

Nate didn't have anything to say for that. Deke's mom had only passed away the year before last, and that wasn't a scab he had any intention of accidentally picking at. Because much as Nate loved his mother, their relationship hadn't been uncomplicated since he was six. "So no."

"No," Deke said dryly. "She's not my type." He looked up from what he was doing. "And normally I'd say she was your type, but..." He glanced through the door, after Grace.

"It's not like that." Nate wrinkled his nose. "Grace is just a friend."

Deke looked at him, hand hovering over the main light-switch. "Just a friend."

"Yes."

"Okay then." He flicked the light off. "Well. Anyway, there's nothing romantic between Rose and I."

~~~~~~

On his list of top ten preferred places to deal with a water anything—spirit, demon, creature, et cetera—in 'a warehouse, down by the water' was somewhere about number eighty-seven. There were worse places, absolutely. In the water. On the surface of the sun. Buffalo.

"OMG, SHE'S COMING THIS WAY!"

Nate winced, covering his ear, and pushed Rose and her broomstick skirt and shawl and flap of quasi-spiritualism through the rickety door before him. If Deke seriously thought Rose was his type, Nate wasn't sure they were speaking anymore.

"She might stop doing that if you stopped yelling," Grace panted, holding a stitch in her side, eyes flicking to Nate for a bare moment of non-verbal *what the crap*.

A door further in the complex opened, and Deke stuck his head out. "Whenever you're ready."

"Whenever we're—"

Grace grabbed him by the shoulder, pushing him toward the door right as their feisty, red-eyed 'I'd very much like to crack your bones and suck out the marrow' friend slammed against it. Rose was already running for Deke, and later Nate was going to give him a ridiculous amount of shit because yeah, there was nothing romantic between them according to Deke. Rose clearly wanted that to be different. In fact, Nate would have bet just about anything he owned—with the exception of his favorite crossbow and his car—that she hadn't actually thought there was a Korrigan in her neighborhood. She'd been trying to get Deke to come around more.

That was probably karma.

Deke had come up with this elaborate plan. They were going to lure the Korrigan through the warehouse district when there weren't a lot of people around. Then they'd trap it and once they had it trapped they could do the Christian rites—which apparently only worked because the Korrigan couldn't handle having the Christian god evoked at them. They literally exploded from anger—and then that would be that.

Rose had insisted on coming along, clearly thinking something about Deke and how nice he was being to Grace.

Some days Nate seriously questioned his life choices.

They were at their last bit of deflection. Deke was all set up and it was time to drag their long-haired nymph from hell into her trap. One last building, and then they'd have her where they wanted her. Nate opened the door, and they all piled through, and this time he left it open a bit to lure their new friend in.

The only notice he had they had a problem was the crash of breaking glass as she decided to forgo the door and jump through the windows overhead.

She landed in the middle of the room, hunched over in a crisp white robe, blood red flowers in her thick hair, fingers sharpened into hard claws, and hissed at them. She knocked Deke back out of the way, sending him sliding across the floor. Nate grabbed his crossbow, aiming a shot, but Rose was in the way and doing some stupid new-age thing she obviously thought was a spell.

The Korrigan laughed at her, fingers reaching—

Right as Grace tackled it from the side, knocking them both over and rolling across the floor. Nate might have managed a shot, but one second the Korrigan was reaching for Grace, and the next the entire room had gone white and Grace was pushed back into a little closet off to the side, the door slamming shut on her.

Nate jumped to his feet, racing after her because if another Korrigan got her in there she wouldn't have room to get away.

Deke threw his last piece of protection into the middle of the room, and the Korrigan screamed in anger. "Nate, I don't know the Latin, so if you'd like to get rid of her—"

"Grace?" Nate yelled through the door. He'd deal with the Korrigan in a minute, rather than leave Grace in trouble.

"It's dark and unpleasant in here, but I'm fine," Grace called, thumping against the door. "Get rid of her."

He stopped at the edge of the trap, watching the long-haired horror twitch around and scream. "*Exorcizamus te, ominus immunde spiritus, omni stanica, omnis encursion infernalis—*"

With one final, horribly high scream she smoked and exploded like an over-filled balloon.

"Wow." Deke swallowed. "I never would have thought they actually *explode* from anger."

Nate threw Deke the crossbow and jogged over to the small door. "Grace." He grabbed the door. He'd expected it to be locked. To somehow have stuck her in that little room and for them to have to pull the door off or something.

The door swung open with a crash, the instant he pulled on the rusty handle, and Grace tumbled out like she'd been leaning on it. Nate didn't think about anything, just caught her and started checking her over. "Are you okay? What the hell."

"I'm fine Nate." Grace brushed his hands off gently, swallowing.

"What in the hell was *that*?" Rose exploded, throwing her hands in the air. "I'm done with you people. That was insane! You're going to get yourselves killed!" She stormed out of the building, throwing a ridiculously stereotypical fit the entire way, cursing them randomly.

"If she ever managed to find the right combination of words that might be dangerous," Deke muttered, watching her go.

"You're welcome!" Grace yelled after her, huffing out a tired breath.

Everything froze, for a long moment, before they all burst out laughing.

~~~~~~

They couldn't just pack up and go. For a start, they had to clean up all the paranormal crap they'd sprinkled all over the lower-Chicago warehouse district. Nate wouldn't have been comfortable leaving all that there. And Deke definitely wasn't, because there was no guarantee they couldn't trace a certain amount of that back to him.

So they'd cleaned up the broken glass, and the salt, and the paint, and the lamb's blood.

Nate was being a little melodramatic. There hadn't been any lamb's blood. He always felt like there should be. Like his life should involve more than salt and holy oil or water. And there were days it did, sure. But he'd only had to go searching for newt entrails once.

Not to mention Deke had taken more than he, strictly speaking, needed and he couldn't have gotten it back to his building on his own.

They used the back door. Nate wasn't sure he could have handled the statue thing jumping at Grace again. The night had been weird enough. He was all for throwing open the alley door Deke almost never used and dragging the supplies back in through there. Grace hefted the second to last box, holding it securely and starting for the door. Deke came back out and grabbed the other half of the giant bag of salt Deke had apparently thought he needed to take with them.

"Why did you need this again?" Nate managed.

Deke didn't answer, just started back for the door. "So how long's *that* been going on?"

"What?" Nate carefully stepped up the curb.

"The white light and *sizzle*." Deke rose a brow, shrugging.

"Second time." Nate sighed. "The first, there was an issue with a Revenant last...um...shit. I don't know. Ask Grace. I don't remember when it was. A week before all this shit. Anyway. It had her and we were trying to banish it."

"That doesn't work on them."

"Did this time," Nate muttered, stomach clenching in worry.

Deke dropped the bag of salt into the pile, wiping his hands on his thighs. "Seriously?"

"Yep."

Deke hit the door control, shutting it down, and putting the padlock on. "You guys leaving town tonight?"

"I don't know." Nate frowned. "Why?"

"I drug you all the way here for that. I can at least feed you."

"Spaghetti Bolognese?"

"The same." Deke nodded, and turned to walk into the office. "Does your girl eat meat?"

"She's not mine," Nate said after him, huffing.

Not that Deke was listening. "Grace, do you eat meat?"

Grace blinked at him, looking between them, and Nate knew she could see the tension there. That something was going on. But like everything else, she let it go.

Grace was a master at letting things go.

"Sure. What kind did you have in mind?"

"I've been told I make a mean meat-sauce. Come on up."

She grabbed her sweater. "Sounds good." She looked at Nate. "Are we calling Curt before we actually leave this time?" Grace asked around a yawn.

"Might actually get there if you don't," Deke offered.

Nate snorted. "Yeah. We're just driving back. Nearly two months on the road in one shot is more than enough for me."

Grace followed them.

Nate looked at the warding Deke had put on the walls going up the stairs. "You've added more."

Deke glanced back over his shoulder. "Comes and goes." He flicked a light on at the top of the stairs. "New neighbor."

"Really."

"Hm." He nodded. "Old Russian woman, and she's definitely an old religion type of person. Means extra protection." He pushed the door open all the way and waved Grace through first. "Make yourself at home. It'll only take me about an hour to make food."

Nate dropped his things inside the door. "Grace, you want anything to drink?" he asked before Deke could offer.

"No." Grace dropped onto the couch, dropping her head back. "I'm good. Thanks."

Nate scrambled into the kitchen and got his drink and got back out of the way before Deke could get around to asking about why he was so twitchy about Deke offering Grace a drink. It was stupid, to feel like he didn't want anyone poking around at Grace. He shouldn't have been responsible for her. It'd been her choice to come along with him, even if he got the feeling sometimes she didn't really *like* it.

But two months in Grace had been not horrible to work with and it made him a little protective. Not that she couldn't take care of himself, or that he understood why she didn't drink—he could guess, it probably had something to do with her crazy instincts for when people were around her, and the fact she moved like a ninja.

He moved back out into the main room and sat down in one of the chairs, letting Grace just relax. He could tell she wasn't asleep, just sitting quietly. He turned the TV on low and settled in himself. Finished his beer. Calmed down a bit.

Eventually he pried himself out of the chair and wondered back into the kitchen, to throw his bottle away.

Deke glanced out in the living room, frowning. "Is she okay? She could go lay down if she needs to."

Nate glanced back, blinking. "Oh, she's still awake."

Deke looked, turning back to Nate. "Does she talk?"

"When she wants to," Nate huffed. And then made himself walk away because if they kept talking he was going to start getting defensive—getting more defensive anyway—and that wouldn't be good for anyone.

He made it through most of a television show before the smell of cooking meat and spices wafting through the house.

"That smells really good," Grace said suddenly, sighing.

"Food's done," Deke called from the kitchen.

Nate kicked her shoe, as he stood up. "Come on." He held a hand out. "Food!"

Grace gave him her hand and let him pull her up from the couch, blinking for a moment. "I'm pretty sure you've eaten multiple times today."

"Diners and fast food don't count."

She scoffed. "You're in the wrong lifestyle if that's true." She stretched. "Thanks for dinner Deke, it looks nice."

Deke frowned, confused, as Grace sat at the table, and he started dishing food up.

The thing was, Nate knew why was Deke's so thrown. When Grace did things it seemed...vague sometimes. Like the words coming out of her mouth were wrong.

Most of the time. She said things that other people said, sure. But there was less emotion behind it. After something like two months of fucking constant contact Nate thought he was starting to figure out how to read that.

Though, in all honesty, he doesn't remember a time when it threw him all that much.

The food's as good as it is any other time Deke's fed him, and once they've eaten and talked for a while Nate's ready to go. It's going to take them the better part of three hours to get back to Curt's, and he'd like that to happen before either of them crashes.

"We should go." Nate sighed. "Otherwise I'll—"

"Have to let me drive," she finished. She tore at the edge of her last bit of garlic bread. "You do realize I have a perfectly clean driving record?"

"I can't believe he's let you drive in any circumstance," Deke said. "Most of us are lucky to be allowed to touch the car."

Nate rolled his eyes. "If you two are done."

"Nope." Grace grinned at him. "This is me getting you back for randomly calling Jamie to translate things you don't need translated."

Deke froze, leaning forward. "So wait. Jamie doesn't know anything about...this, but he's talked to Nate? How does that work?"

"He thinks I'm a bounty-hunter," Nate answered. "And we've already discussed the fact it's probably not going to last long. It's only a matter of time before he turns up at Curt's house."

Grace stood, taking her dishes to the sink, and helping clean up. They moved around each other for a while, the air in the kitchen getting more and more uncomfortable, before it was time for them to go.

"Well." Deke rubbed the back of his neck. "Grace, lovely to meet you. Don't hesitate to stop back in, next time you're in the area."

"Sure," she replied easily, hands sunk deep in her pockets. "I'd say 'you too', but I'm still technically living with Curt."

Nate clapped Deke on the shoulder, giving him a manly half-hug. "Watch out for that Rose, she's special."

Grace stepped into the hall, and Deke glanced at her, before looking back at Nate. "She's not the only one."

He had all sorts of crap to say about that. About it not being Grace's fault. As far as he could tell she wasn't *doing* anything. Things just kept happening around her, and maybe if it was him he'd be a little more worried about it than she seemed to be.

Nate wasn't sure there was a good way to explain to Deke that as easy and with-it as Grace looked, he wasn't sure she was actually dealing.

They stepped outside into the still, Chicago evening, about three seconds before Grace accidentally stumbled into the old woman who lived next door.

"I'm sorry." Grace steadied her easily, swallowing. "I wasn't looking where I was going."

The old woman blinked at her, for a long moment. "I have never seen one before."

"Never seen..." Grace frowned, glancing back at them, clearly wondering what was going on.

She grabbed Grace's hand, patting it easily. "So much pain," she said sadly. "But no amount of darkness will ever hide the light, little one. You mean more to him than he would ever say. Remember that when he tells you." She patted Grace on the cheek. "And don't be afraid to trust people who deserve it."

And then she trundled on in to her door, throwing an arcane protection sign over her shoulder at Deke.

Chapter 6

"So she just…just said it and walked off?" Curt frowned, putting his dishes in the sink.

Grace hadn't really wanted to talk about the creepy Russian woman. It was strange, yeah, and right on the heels of the white whatever it was while they were dealing with the Korrigan she could understand perfectly well why Nate wasn't all that willing to let this slide—he'd asked at least three times in the car on the way back from Deke's if she had any ideas, and been just generally uneasy and uncomfortable.

It was different for them, they were used to a certain amount of this stuff making sense.

"It was freaky," Nate said darkly. "Not as bad as the thing that pushed her in the closet. It was almost like it was trying to keep her from getting hurt, but…"

Grace frowned, looking between them. "But?"

Curt pushed a hand through his hair, scratching anxiously. "But crap with good intentions doesn't usually hide. Even if something was trying to help you, I'd be a little concerned about the why, if they aren't willing to just stand up and say it."

"Why?" Grace asked. "There's nothing special about me."

"Grace, sugar," Curt started, and the paused for a minute. "Even if that were true once—and I'm not saying it was—you've been bitten by a werewolf that wasn't a werewolf, and..." He shrugged. "Doesn't always make sense on the front end what this stuff wants, if it wants anything," he finished. Curt thought for a long minute, fiddling around with his glass, before he looked up at her. "We could find a psychic. There are all sorts of them around, not even counting the probably twelve Deke could have put you in contact with."

"Which would do what?" Grace frowned. She didn't like psychics. It wasn't anything personal, she just didn't. Tarot cards and all that gave her the heebiegeebies.

"It might tell us a little about what's going on," Curt pushed, gently. "I understand you're a little out to sea."

Grace rubbed her forehead. "It's more the creepy extra junk on the back end of however long it's been since we were here last."

"Which is valid," Curt affirmed. "Seriously, I'm a little impressed you're not at each other's throats. In my experience you're both nearly goddamn anti-social and the fact you've been within two feet of each other for two months is almost terrifying." He sighed. "I'm not trying to push. I just...If we don't figure out what this is and it goes bad I'm going to feel responsible."

Why?

She didn't ask it though. Curt was a law unto himself, and she'd stopped questioning why he kept taking her under his wing. Two months on with Nate she was good. Well, she wasn't *good* with where she and Nate were. She didn't understand how they'd managed not to kill each other either. She didn't doubt Nate agreed with Curt, he just wasn't going to push it. She appreciated all of that. Shy of calling Jamie and telling him to put words in her mouth—which he generally wouldn't do anyway—she didn't know how to express any of that.

"Which isn't to say that I'm going to force you," Curt finished. "Go get unpacked and get some rest, you both need it. We'll talk later."

Grace nodded and grabbed her bag. "Yeah. I'm claiming the shower."

"Go ahead, it's your turn," Nate said.

She walked out into the hallway, stopping for a moment to dump their clothes by the wash. "Hey Nate, are we separating our clothes out?"

"I wasn't going to," he said wryly. "If you don't care."

"Nah, it's fine." She dumped everything next to the washer.

"You sure you're good?" Curt asked, voice low and serious, and Grace was about to turn around and answer him, when she realized it wasn't for her.

"I'm fine." Nate huffed, and Grace could see him opening the refrigerator. "It's been…"

"I've never known you to put up with a person in your space for more than a couple of days."

"That's not true." He frowned. "I stayed here for nearly a year."

"And got steadily crazier over that, until you were drinking more than me and your mother put together. And then the instant you had an option to run away, you did."

"What do you want me to say? We did the job, for two months, and it wasn't…" He shrugged, still barely visible from her place in the hallway. "Grace was helpful."

Grace walked away, because she wasn't sure she wanted to hear the rest of that conversation. She thought they'd done pretty well together, and she did sort of like Nate. He was unusual, and willing to let her be herself in a way most people were uncomfortable with.

She made it to the upstairs before her phone rang. She pulled it out, thinking about the psychological dodging they'd started to feel about Nate's phone ringing. But the only person who'd call her now that she was here was Jamie.

"Hey."

She heard a crackle and a pause, and this was clearly going to be one of those times he was walking on eggshells for a bit. "Hey yourself." Jamie sighed. "Where are you today?"

"Back at Curt's." She smiled, relaxing. "We're apparently superstitious. We didn't say anything about coming back, just got in the car and did it."

"Well...that's good then." Jamie settled into the conversation. "So you're back someplace stable and in one piece and I can stop worrying."

Grace dropped her things on the bed, letting out a disbelieving scoff.

"Shut it," Jamie countered. "I said I could, not that I would."

"I know."

It wasn't like there was anything else she could say to that. It was Jamie. It wasn't like he wasn't allowed to worry about her. She just didn't always appreciate it.

"So." He paused. "Plans?"

"Shower?" Grace offered, flopping down on the bed. "Sleep. Finish that paper that's on deadline tomorrow."

"Back to life as usual?"

She rubbed her forehead, wincing. "Something like that."

She stared at the ceiling, old paddle fan spinning lazily over her head. She didn't have anything else to say. *I'm sorry. It's been a really insane couple of months and I can't talk to you about it.* Since they'd been practically babies she'd been running things through Jamie. From the day they met—Grace hiding behind the playground at recess, upset because of *things she didn't think about*—they'd been best friends. Jamie was the only person who'd always believed her.

She wasn't afraid that he wouldn't now. She was afraid he would, and he wasn't the only one who could be protective. He didn't need this shit thumping around in the dark after him.

"I was going to come see you this weekend, if you were back," he said softly.

"But?"

"Last minute faculty thing I can't get out of." He blew a raspberry. "And next weekend is the field study, and—"

"It's fine." Grace picked her head up and dropped it back on the bed, closing her eyes. "You'll make it when you can, or I'll come up and see you when I can." She paused, swallowing. "I'm fine Jamie, really."

"No, you're not." He huffed. "Gracie, you can't lie for shit. Not to me anyway. You aren't fine. I can hear it in your voice."

"Physically I'm fine?" she tried. "And the rest'll keep. I don't think you could fix it anyway."

"Doesn't mean I don't want to try."

"I know." She swallowed. "Hey, what happened with that girl you were taking on a date? Tiffany, or whatever her name was?"

"Ha ha, nice try. No deflecting."

"I'm not trying to deflect, I'm trying to be interested in your life," she answered. "Who's deflecting?"

He grumbled. "Fine, she was marginally insane and she talked about her cat all night. Happy?"

"Thrilled to the bone. Has it occurred to you that your standards are too high?"

"I'm broken. I'm unwilling to saddle myself with someone who can't hold my attention."

"Jameson Williams, not everyone is brilliant all the time," she insisted. "And that's not the thing that turned you off. I'm not the only one who sucks at lying."

Grace waited through the protracted silence. There was something comforting about the amount of dead air they were both willing to leave on a phone call. They didn't talk until they were ready, and Grace wouldn't have had that any other way.

"She was..." He paused. "Close minded? There were a couple of guys on a date and she..." Jamie died off sadly.

Grace closed her eyes. "Bitch."

"It's fine. It's not like I prefaced a conversation with 'sometimes I like guys too' so—"

"You don't have to." Grace frowned. "I mean you probably can if you want to, and it's not like the university is going to give you a hard time about that."

"I know." Jamie puffed out a breath. "Well, I don't. Just because the head of the department is gay doesn't mean he's going to be all that understanding about my being bi. I just don't like to. I feel like I'm defensively over-explaining and..." He stopped, swallowing. "And I'm going to say this even though you're going to get pissed at me. We might not live in each other's pockets anymore, but only talking to you once in a while on the road for two months, and worrying about you—"

"Jamie—"

"Stuff it." He huffed. "Because you're my best friend and practically the sister I wasn't lucky enough to be born with and that doesn't make it unusual for me to want to see more of you."

"Which of our families would you have rather we both been born into?"

Jamie grumbled. "Grace."

"Alright." She rubbed her forehead. "You're right. Just...once I'm caught up on my work I'll see. I missed you too."

"I know." He shuffled around. "Alright, go take your shower or whatever you were going to do."

"Will do. I love you."

"I love you too," Jamie answered warmly. "Light of my life."

Grace stared at the phone, after the call ended, before she managed to get herself out of bed and headed for the shower.

~~~~~~

Whatever she'd expected, after the trip of doom, it wasn't rocketing right back into her and Nate quietly edging around each other.

Nate hadn't been strange about her in ages. They'd gotten over walking around each other on eggshells weeks before. Curt was around so they weren't alone, and they both had things to do. Well, Grace had things to do. She wasn't entirely sure what Nate was doing with himself, other than generally working on cars and things.

But they'd been back for four days and they were still awkwardly tripping over each other.

Things were quiet on the paranormal front. It was a little surreal to suddenly be still in one place, and realize that things didn't pile up the way they had on the road. Curt kept explaining that the last two months had been unusual. That even when you were looking for it, generally there weren't six or eight jobs back to back like that.

Usually Nate cruised around, and watched the papers. Took his time, and found his own jobs as well as taking things that Deke suggested, or things Curt sent him.

There were things out there he could have been doing, but they were things other people could do too. Curt liked to haul Nate in for a while every couple of months.

"I feel responsible for the kid, and I'd like to make sure he isn't about to...take early retirement." he'd explained, when Grace asked the night before.

Grace *hadn't* asked what he meant by early retirement.

She was decently sure Nate wasn't uneasy because he felt like she was too much in his space. He could have avoided her if he wanted to. And it wasn't like she was stalking him outside—so maybe she'd spent a little long staring out the window this morning, while he was working without his shirt—or bothering him. She had enough of her own work to do.

The door opened, and the breeze fluttered her papers. Grace reached out and held them still by wrote, glancing up as Nate came through the door. He froze for a beat, flushing, before he winced and closed it carefully.

"Sorry."

Grace shrugged. "You're fine. Am I in your way?"

"No…?"

She glanced up at him, grinning. "Did you mean that to come out as a question?"

"No." Nate wiped his hands on the rag he was carrying around. "Sorry. I don't want to bother you, since you're the only one in this house that actually makes a living."

"From what Curt said the salvage business was going alright." She rubbed her eyes sighing. "And it's fine. My eyes are starting to cross."

Nate chuckled and moved to wash his hands. "If you say so."

He moved around the kitchen for a while, making himself something to eat, and they didn't *talk*. Grace didn't have anything to say, and she wasn't sure what she'd have said even if she did. It was just strange. Like once they weren't bloody tied together they didn't know how to deal with each other.

Nate finished fixing his plate, and Grace moved a stack of papers, to give him a place to sit, before she finished the last note she needed to make on a page, and folded that away. She hated doing academic articles. She did them, absolutely, but she still hated them. It didn't help any that her brain was a goddamn vacuum and she could never manage to completely forget what she'd read. She could use a break, even if she wasn't hungry.

He cleared his throat, swallowing. "I was thinking, this afternoon if you don't need your car for anything, I

can take a look at the valves for you. I didn't get a chance
to do that, before."

"Yeah. Sure." She forced a smile. "I'm not planning on
going anywhere."

Nate nodded and dug back into his sandwich. And
Grace should have gotten up and gone to find something
else to do. As long as she was here she was going to sit
and stew and wonder about why they were so tense. They
hadn't been when they were sharing a freaking hotel
room, alone in the car for a solid eighteen hours.

Wasn't having more space supposed to make people
get along better?

Nate pushed his plate back and shifted uncomfortably.
Like he wanted to say something, but he didn't know how.

Grace puffed out a breath, leaning forward. "This is
really strange."

He laughed, startled. "It is."

"If I'm making you uncomfortable I can...um..."
Grace frowned. "Talk to Curt? I won't just go, because I
mentioned something about looking for a place the other
day and he got really strange on me."

Nate pushed a hand through his hair. "He's worried.
With the weird stuff."

Grace sighed, nodding. "I guessed. So if you—"

"No." He cleared his throat. "It's not...it's just..."

She waited patiently. Nate tripped like this sometimes.
She was guessing because he was Nate, and he didn't
always do very good at discussing feelings.

But he didn't seem able to spit it out.

"I'd help," she offered. "But I've got honestly no clue
what you're struggling with. Is it about me going with
you if you get another job?"

Nate flushed. "Sort of."

"Well." Grace shrugged. "Just say it. I'm pretty sure
you're not about to insult me."

"No. I just..." He looked away. "That didn't suck. If
you want to... I totally get you wouldn't want to do

another two-month string of them, and I can't always control that, but..."

"If I want to come along next job you get, I'm allowed?"

Nate looked at the table, shaking his head. "You're not tagging along behind me. You're better than that. I wouldn't mind the help." He looked up finally, biting his lip. "Partners? You don't have to come if you don't want to, or if you've got...other stuff, just..."

Grace blinked, shocked. About twelve things went through her head right then. Things Curt had said over the last year about how worried he was that Nate couldn't seem to stand people, about how he never managed to do more than one job with a person, and a few things that basically amounted to 'why am I special' that didn't need to happen out loud. Ever.

"Sure." She nodded, after a stupidly tense moment. "I'd...like that."

~~~~~~

"I'm going to string that boy up from the rafters if he doesn't calm down," Curt muttered, thumping into the kitchen.

People randomly wandering into the kitchen while she was working and starting a conversation was becoming a thing. And actually, given her sleeping schedule and the way she liked to work—and everything else that went on in the house—she wasn't complaining about that.

She was never entirely sure if Curt was complaining *to* her, or in her general direction. He did this more than infrequently, and she got why he was upset. To a point.

Nate had been alright, working on cars and doing shit around the house, for about a week. But with each consecutive day he got twitchier and twitchier having to be in the house. That morning he'd beat the rest of them up and going, and he'd started rearranging shit in the yard. Curt didn't seem to know what to say about that, or if he should say anything.

They were both fun to live with right then.

"My turn to cook tonight," Curt sighed, opening the fridge. "Any preferences?"

"No." She shook her head, finishing her papers and starting to pick up. It wasn't that she couldn't work while Curt was in the kitchen. But he liked to talk, and eventually she'd get short with him having a conversation while she was trying to read.

"You mind checking to see if wonder-boy out there has one?"

"Wonder-boy?" Grace repeated questioningly, standing. "No, I don't mind."

"Well. He's less twitchy with you than he is with me."

Maybe because I'm not grumbling at him, she thought to herself.

Grace moved out into the yard, checking around for wherever Nate happened to be hiding at the moment. The Charger sat, sparkling and perfect, before the garages, and her old knock-around was sitting off to one side. He'd cleaned the engine out, and rotated the tires, and done about every sort of maintenance he could think of on it. She'd started it yesterday and it hadn't even sounded like the same car.

Which wasn't a complaint. If Nate wanted to make himself feel more centered by screwing around with her car, there wasn't anything wrong with that, at least not as far as she was concerned.

"Damn it, Curt," Nate cursed, legs poking out from underneath an old truck. "I told you I was..."

He stopped, sliding out from under it and blinking up at her.

"Not Curt." Grace shoved her hands in her pockets, shrugging. "But he did want to know if you had a preference for food."

"No." He flushed. "Sorry."

Grace waved him off. "Sure. Want me to put him off for a while?"

"No." Nate swallowed. "I'm not too far from done."

She nodded, sucking in a lung-full of warm late-fall air, and blowing it back out carefully. "You could just tell him you don't want to be inside if you don't have to be."

He laughed darkly, sliding back under the car. "That works for you, when he catches you wondering out here. Because you don't have anything else to do."

She cocked a brow, watching him freeze and back-peddle.

"Out here," Nate added suddenly. "You don't have anything to be doing out here. Not—"

"Breathe, Nate." Grace kicked his leg carefully. "I knew what you meant." She turned, heading back for the house. "But when he starts up again you're on your own."

"Thanks."

"You're welcome." Grace opened the door, feeling the pull of the wind as she tried to shut it.

"Tell him it's gonna rain, he might want to come cover his shit," Nate yelled from the yard.

She shut the door behind her, settling her clothes again. "Did you hear that?"

"Yeah." Curt grumbled. "Can you keep an eye on the pasta for a second, and I'll take care of that?"

"Sure," she answered, and threw the last couple of things into her box. It was living in the corner of Curt's kitchen right now—because the tiny upstairs corner bedroom would hold a bed and a dresser and her, sometimes—and she was a little tempted to bring up how she wanted that to not be anymore, but it wasn't that simple.

It wasn't just that she was living at Curt's, and the space issues that came with that. It was him worrying about her—having Jamie worry about her was bad enough, adding more people to that wasn't making her feel better—and her not having anywhere else to be, and a little that she sort of did want to go with Nate next time.

She was draining the pasta when Curt and Nate clomped through the door, Nate shedding his extra layers and heading off to wash-up before they ate.

"Hey, that bag of clothes at the bottom of the stairs is yours," Grace hollered, looking back over her shoulder as he went.

Nate grabbed it, huffing quietly, on his way up the stairs.

She wasn't being difficult. Yeah, his stuff had been sitting in the washer for two days and he hadn't grabbed it. Mostly it was just her trying to put off a journal article she'd been working on, and the washer was right there and tailor made for that. Procrastination was a skill.

Grace helped put a salad together and get the plates on the table. Normally when it was Nate's or her turn to cook they didn't do much of this. Nate pretty much just threw something thawed and already together in the oven. Grace could get a little more adventurous, if she wanted to. Aunt Rhoda had spent more than one summer chaining her to the kitchen stove until she'd managed credible gravy or fried chicken. But simple meant less time, and cooking wasn't her favorite thing.

They might have been leaning on that a little much, lately. Less, when it was Curt making Turkey tetrazzini and not just pasta and sauce, but all the same.

Nate thumped down the stairs, sighing as he sat down at the table. "That smells good."

"Don't look at me." Grace slid a bowl at him. "I just drained the noodles."

Curt stumped back through the door before shutting it solid, shuddering. "Looking nasty out there." He turned, sighing. "Rains coming down sideways."

Down sideways? Nate mouthed at her, eyebrows high.

Grace pulled out her chair, ignoring them both. They'd dished up plates, and Nate and Curt were arguing over whether or not non-Christian techniques would work more frequently if people *used* them more frequently.

"I'm just saying," Curt insisted, pushing his empty plate back. "We don't know everything. It's clear we don't, and I think if people took a chance on the less...standard ways we've been using maybe some of the others would work more frequently."

"Yeah, well," Nate frowned. "This is sort of like the witch thing. Maybe or maybe not, either way I ain't keen to test it while my ass is on the line."

Grace looked between them. "The witch thing?"

Curt blinked. "I told you witches are real."

"Yes." Grace scoffed. "And even if you hadn't, I'd sort of assumed everything was at least a possibility now. So...what about the witches?"

Nate rolled his eyes. "Curt has this idea—and I'm not saying it's wrong," he cut in across Curt who'd furiously opened his mouth. "That since there seem to be...family connections with some of the witches we see doing dark shit that maybe, out there somewhere, there are people doing *not dark* shit we're just not seeing."

Curt huffed. "I just think we only know what we see, and if they're not doing anything we'd notice then maybe we'd never see them."

"Yeah, maybe." Nate shrugged. "But if they're not doing dark shit and they're not going to, then I'm not sure I really care."

"They could *help*," Curt stressed.

Nate scoffed, leaning his chair back and finishing his beer. "Right."

Grace watched them, talking over each other and debating whether or not a people who didn't have to do this would.

And Grace wasn't saying anything. She didn't figure it was the time to point out she pretty much fit in that category, and here she was.

They heard a slam, outside, and Curt jumped, frowning.

"Wind was picking up pretty bad," Nate offered, even if he didn't sound like be believed it.

Curt and Nate were both jumpy sometimes. They heard noises and because they knew all the things that noise *could* be they had a hard time cutting it back to what it was. Grace wouldn't necessarily call it paranoia, but it was a little like that.

Until the door slammed back against the wall, wind gushing through. A female figure with long hair and a dark coat grabbed it and slammed it shut again, dripping wet and stomping its feet.

"Shit it's nasty out there," she looked up at them, dark hair dipping in her pale face, and tried to push it back, shaking her coat off. "Well, don't stand there, one of you could get me a towel."

Curt sat his gun down carefully, shoulders tense. "Sarah. You didn't call."

She laughed, dropping another wet layer. "When the hell do I ever call?" She drew a deep breath. "Wow, Turkey Tet huh?" She laughed, low and manic, looking around the room. "Who're you adopting this time?"

Curt cursed, tensing.

Nate swallowed, blinking for a moment, before moving forward to take the dripping wet coat she held up for him. "Mom…"

"I swear, you two aren't usually this slow."

Grace watched the way she moved, shedding layers. She was just an inch or two shorter than Nate, stick skinny and *mean*. Her features were sharp and her movements were menacing and uncoordinated.

"Sarah, this is Grace," Curt introduced stiffly. "She's been staying with us for a while."

Sarah coughed thickly. "Well, nice to meet you, honey. Why don't you grab me a plate and a drink? There's a girl."

Nate winced, flushing. "Mom…"

"I'll get you a plate," Grace offered, standing. "I don't know what you drink." She spooned up a plate-full, and sat it at an empty seat.

Nate grabbed a bottle of Jack off the counter, shooting her a sympathetic look, before he filled a glass for his mother, and sat down next to her. "You could have told me you were in the area when we talked yesterday."

"Eh." She shrugged, grabbing a mouthful of food. "Didn't know." She downed her entire glass in one shot, and thumped it back on the table.

Nate refilled it slowly, face flushing. And Grace almost told him not to worry about it. It wasn't like she was going to give him a hard time about his mother being an alcoholic.

Curt grabbed a towel, cleaning up the water she'd dripped in the front room, and handing her a dry one. "What's going on?"

She took a giant bite of her food, before taking another swig. "Got a call from Shorty, he's on another gig, so he threw it my way. And here was between where I was and where it is, figured if I needed a hand, I could use my little boy." She scrubbed Nate on the head, smiling. "What'da'ya say, Natty?"

Curt huffed. "You do realize he just got back from an eight-week trip, right?"

"Been back for a few days though." She grinned at him. "I bet you're gettin' twitchy. Come on. Be like old times." She paused, frowning at her phone, clearly not paying attention to them anymore.

Nate looked over at Grace, and mouthed *do you want to?*

He'd let her out of this one if she wanted it.

But she didn't, and she wasn't going to examine why. "I'll go pack," Grace offered, standing.

She was halfway out of her chair when the other woman actually bothered to look at her. Her eyes were just a little darker than Nate's green, and bloodshot.

How much alcohol—and maybe a few other things—did it take to get that look? By the end her mom'd had it even when she wasn't drinking. Her dad probably still had it.

Grace had looked more than one angry, out of control drunk in the eye in her life. She'd learned better than to back down before she was old enough to drive.

"Where you think you're going?"

It was patience and years of practice that kept her from snapping something at that. She was going to walk out of the room without a pause.

"With us," Nate said, jaw tense.

Sarah laughed, harsh. "You don't hunt with people sugar-plum. Remember what happened with Eric?"

Curt glowered, and looked like he was about ready to kick the woman out of the room, which Grace was all about, not that she thought it would help.

"She went with me for eight weeks," Nate said, voice tense. "And—"

"I really don't need to be here for this conversation," Grace interrupted quietly. "I'll go get my ducks in a row."

Grace walked out into the hall, clenching her hands. She needed a minute to cool down anyway.

"I get she's pretty, kiddo," Sarah started around a mouth-full of food as Grace started up the stairs.

Chapter 7

Grace slipped out into the dark, because she knew Nate was out by the garage, and as much as she didn't *want* to have this conversation, she kind of felt like they needed to.

She'd sort of expected Nate's mom to be a piece of work. The way Curt talked about her, with a sort of not-so-subtle undercurrent of tension and disapproval, she'd wondered. It hadn't at all prepared her for the reality. The woman was brash, and harsh, and goddamn *pickled*.

And okay, maybe it wasn't her ideal situation, spending any level of time with that. She was even less interested in sending Nate off with her on a job. She'd give herself an ulcer, wondering if he was going to come back alive.

Nate sighed. "You know normally I'd be looking for a knife right around now." He glanced back at her.

Grace smiled wryly. "Figured it was me?"

He dropped something in the tool-box, closing it with a snap. "Anybody else would have made noise before they got that close." He turned, wiping his hands. "Listen, about—"

"About your Mom—" Grace started at exactly the same time.

They both stopped, tense and uncomfortable. And Grace gave him a chance to say what he wanted to say, but he didn't seem too keen on taking it.

"Um..." Grace swallowed. "That was..." She dropped her face into her hands. "If you don't want me to come this time it's fine."

Nate scoffed, looking down at his hands.

"Really," she insisted. "She's your Mom and if you want..." She died off, because something said mentioning 'old times' would be a mistake. "I won't be upset."

Nate twisted his hands around in the cloth, shifting uncomfortably. He wasn't going to agree with her though. She could tell, was already learning to read him that well. He wasn't negative. Or upset. He was nervous.

"No." He flicked a glance up at her. "I want you to come..." He forced a swallow, pausing. "Just...are you sure you want to?"

Grace blinked at him. "Why wouldn't I?"

Nate shifted, looking back toward the house. "You saw her in there, she's...um...difficult? Even when she's sober."

Where they seriously going to manage some sort of completely non-verbal conversation about her problem with alcoholics? It shouldn't have been a surprise. Whatever else Nate was, he wasn't unobservant, and he'd been pretty careful with certain things around her. He'd obviously keyed into things somehow.

"Yeah." She shrugged. "I got that. You're not leaving me here with six pounds of left-over turkey tetrazzini."

Nate choked out a laugh, shaking his head. "Don't worry, he'll save some for us."

"That's just...disturbing. Really?"

He threw her the pile of rags he'd been gathering, laughing. "You've been warned."

She nodded. "Forewarned is forearmed."

He stopped, wincing. "About that." He looked around, making sure they were alone. "They think it's a werewolf, are you okay with that?"

"I did alright with the last one, I think. Just don't ask me to pet the damn thing."

The door slammed, and Grace had about two seconds to brace for it, before his mom was right there. She threw a collection of stuff into the back of her beat-up old Ram-Charger, and opened the driver's side door.

"You two about ready to go?"

"In a bit." Nate dropped some extra rounds and things in the back of his car, slamming the trunk. "You got your stuff, Grace?"

"It's by the door." Grace shoved her hands in her pockets. "I didn't ask where we were going."

"Ain't you just accommodating," Sarah grumbled.

Nate opened his mouth, clearly thinking he needed to say something.

It's fine, Grace mouthed. "I do my poor best. Need anything else from the house? I should say goodbye to Curt."

"Grab my crossbow?" Nate said, flicking a glance at his mother. Clearly he wanted a minute for he and his mother to have some sort of conversation.

And just because Grace was tired of people staring at her like she was an alien tonight she stuck her tongue out at him. "Only if you let me drive."

"Don't push your luck, woman," Nate said, laughing softly. "Hurry it up."

"I'm going, I'm going." Grace jogged back to the house, glancing over her shoulder.

This was going to be fun.

"Are you sure you want to do this?" Curt asked, the instant she was through the door.

"Yeah." Grace sighed, looking around for the crossbow. Nate had left it half-inside the door apparently, and he wasn't usually, that she'd seen, that lax with it. He must have been in the middle of something else. She turned around, to find Curt watching her carefully. "Seriously."

"Yeah, I know you're serious." He pushed a hand through his hair. "I'm just—"

"Listen, I get it." Grace glanced outside. "We already hammered things out before, and I offered to not. It's his Mom and I thought maybe..." she died off, shrugging.

"That relationship's been a goddamn train wreck since the boy was *six*," Curt complained darkly.

"I guessed." Because her radar for *that* was phenomenal, actually. "Just... If he didn't want me to come, I wouldn't. But he's okay with it, and I'm not okay with sending him on some last minute thing with nobody but her to watch his back, so..." Grace flushed, because if she'd been saying that to Jamie she wouldn't have gotten out of the conversation for the better part of a year.

"Okay." Curt pulled her into a sudden hug, sighing. "He may not be so good at watching yours while he's around her. Take care of yourself."

"We'll be fine." Grace hugged him, kissing him on the cheek on a gas. "And we'll call and let you know if we need anything."

~~~~~~

It was ten hours of hard driving, from Curt's to the little town on the edge of Colorado that's apparently having some sort of werewolf problem. The first night they slept in the car at a rest stop, because that was the way Sarah did things on the road.

Clearly she'd expected this to be some sort of deal breaker for Grace. For her to throw a fit and insist they get a nice hotel room. Because whatever Nate's relationship with other hunters was—and she wasn't sure what was going on there, but she sure as hell wasn't going to ask right now—you didn't take *civilians* on a hunt with you.

Grace wasn't sure if Sarah just didn't like other people in Nate's life, or if it was the fact she was female that was causing trouble, but there was no part of this that was Grace's problem. Nate wanted her along, and he'd said he wanted her along, and as long as that held true then they were fine.

The hours on the road the next day had gone alright. Nate told her about a few different werewolves he'd dealt with over the years. Werewolves were always a pain, and this was going to be another of those times the three of them started doing weird rules about where they went, and when, and with whom.

There'd been a minute there when Sarah had gotten one hotel room, clearly expecting them all to squeeze in, and Nate hadn't been happy. He still wasn't happy, if the stony silence while he unpacked was anything to go by. Sarah had claimed the shower as soon as they got in the room.

Nate's phone started to vibrate on the bed, the ringtone starting up a second later. *Now you're messin with a son of a bitch.* He looked at it, and chocked out a laugh, tossing it at Grace. "That's all you."

She looked down, wincing at the name on the screen. Jamie.

"There's no way I'm explaining why you're on the road again," he said, sitting down with a silver knife and a sharpener. "Have fun with that."

"You're helpful." Grace sighed, and hit the answer button, because the fall-out would be much worse if she didn't. "Hey Jamie."

The pause on the other end of the line went a little longer than it necessarily needed to. "Oh what the fuck is that? He's afraid to answer his phone for me?"

Nate stood, grabbing his keys. "I'll just be a second, I left a bag in the car."

"Alright." Grace frowned, moving so she could see him out the window. She didn't know what was going on yet, but she was understandably uneasy about werewolves. She wasn't leaving him outside alone at dusk.

"Seriously Grace, what the hell."

"Jamie..." She swallowed, pausing.

"What?" he asked, and Grace had this ridiculous premonition Jamie had frozen solid on his way to the car, intent to come track she and Nate down and freak out.

"It's...I completely and utterly can't explain any of this right now because it's not mine to explain." She glanced back to make sure Sarah was still in the shower. "But *I'm* alright. Everything else, not so much."

Jamie sighed. "Grace..."

"It's... I was going to go with him next time he went on a job anyway. My choice," she insisted. "Just... Don't call and bitch at him for a while, alright?"

He deflated, and she could practically feel him relaxing over the phone. "Fuck. I sort of hate you that I'm having to say this—"

"No you don't." Grace smiled sadly, leaning against the window.

"Is Nate alright?"

Grace winced, rubbing her face. "He's...um. Physically, sure. Otherwise it's...complicated. Family stuff."

"Damn it. Fine." He grumbled under his breath. "That doesn't make me any less worried."

"I know."

She heard the shower cut, and Sarah start thumping around in the bathroom.

"I should go." Grace glanced out the window, checking on Nate. "I'll call you in a couple of days, alright? I love you."

"You better." Jamie huffed, hanging up.

Sarah came out of the bathroom, chuckling softly. "I can tell you right now, if you're trying to keep a boyfriend—"

"Not." Grace glanced back at her, leaning against the window.

"What are you doing over there?"

She stopped, taking a second to ground herself. Sarah's grating, brash personality was unpleasant, but Grace was nearly thirty and she could handle it. "Watching Nate. He had to get something out of the car."

Sarah glanced out, rapping on the window and waving for him to hurry up. It was entirely force of will that meant Grace didn't roll her eyes at that. She wanted to, but like Curt had said, she could tell their relationship was complicated, and she didn't figure her non-verbal commentary would be appreciated.

It wasn't as hard to hold in as she'd have thought it would be.

Nate came back in with the bag he'd retrieved, and dumped his kit out on the bed like he did every other time they got to a hotel. He had a rhythm, a way he worked. Sarah grumbled at him, before pouring herself a drink and dropping onto the bed with her headphones on and music blaring in her ears.

Grace helped him sort everything out, because he'd brought a little more than he had on their last trip. She pretended not to notice when he took a minute to pick up the empties his mom had left around the room and dispose of them. They packed things away the way he wanted them after they'd triple checked everything. She didn't think that was something Curt did, and obviously his mother had that personality tic loved by alcoholics everywhere that said planning was over-rated.

No, the fanatical devotion to ensuring all the gear was good was entirely Nate. But he was still breathing, so she certainly wasn't going to say anything about it.

"Are you sure you're alright?" Nate whispered, glancing at the couch.

Grace was going to be sleeping there. Nate clearly kept expecting her to be really upset about that, but it wasn't like it was worse than sleeping in the back of the Charger. Hell, for three months in college she'd slept on Jamie's floor. And Nate wouldn't fit on the damn thing, and Sarah was already passed out on one of the beds so she sort of figured that was the end of the discussion.

"I'm fine."

Grace dropped onto her makeshift bed, and curled into a comfortable position. She could see a little bit of light, coming through the windows, despite how good they'd done at pulling the curtains together. She could see the play of late fall leaves, still stubbornly clinging to the trees here, swaying in the breeze outside.

Tomorrow was the full moon. She hadn't looked it up. She always knew that, probably would for the rest of her life. She just *noticed*. Sometime every month she looked at a calendar, and her brain just seemed to hold it. Like it was something that got slotted into *knowledge required for life* as opposed to *slightly useful on occasion.*

Which sort of made sense, when you figured she'd been attacked by a goddamn werewolf. And sort of didn't, taken with the fact it hadn't been the full moon.

"Grace?"

She looked over, swallowing. "Yeah?"

"If you don't fall asleep before I do I'm telling Jamie," Nate muttered, face half-buried in a pillow.

"He's not my mother, even if he acts like it sometimes. I'm—"

"—a sucky liar," Nate finished for her. "You've already been bitten once. You're allowed to be nervous."

Sarah shifted in her sleep, and they both froze for a minute. Until she'd settled again, letting out a soft snore.

"Fuck," Nate muttered. "I feel like I'm sixteen and I've snuck some girl—"

"Dude," Grace huffed. "I'm not your bit of fluff."

"Bit of fluff?" Nate choked, trying not to die laughing. "Seriously?"

"You know what I meant."

He laughed softly, shifting around in his bed. "Yeah. I did. Hey—"

Grace sighed. "You realize you're trying to make me feel better about something you don't feel grand about, right?"

Nate didn't answer, didn't even shift.

"Yep." She shifted slightly, closing her eyes. "I'm going to sleep."

"It's not..." Nate started, and then died off unsure.

It's not the job, it's my mother, was the sort of unspoken end of that sentence.

"I know." Grace offered, voice low.

~~~~~~

The plus side—probably the only one—to a small community that'd had three murders on the last three full moons was the fact that whatever the locals believed, they all stayed in their houses at night. Sterling, Colorado was probably the most buttoned up it'd ever been.

"I still think I'd have made better bait," Grace said softly, watching Nate pace back and forth at the edge of the high school parking lot. The dark edge of the woods behind the practice field stretched out behind him.

He paused for half a second, before smoothly pacing again. "When have I ever used you as bait?" His voice was a little soft and distant, since he was on speaker and his phone was in his pocket.

"You haven't." Grace shifted, eying down the crossbow. "But you're putting a lot of faith in my ability to shoot this thing."

He snorted. "Nice try. You're nearly a better marksman...markswoman, whatever, than I am."

"I might freeze and miss."

"You won't," Nate said dryly.

"How do you know?"

"Because you wouldn't," he insisted. "Because I'm depending on you, and you won't let me down."

Grace sighed, knocking her head forward. "So no pressure or anything."

"Yeah, well, if you get me killed I'm never speaking to you again." Nate stopped for a minute, leaned against the car. "Can you see Mom?"

Grace looked over, to where Sarah was perched on an opposing building. They weren't high buildings by any stretch of the imagination, but they were decent sniper view-points.

It was almost disturbing that she understood that.

Sarah was sprawled over the side of the building, watching the area around them for their first sight, and then she'd make a signal for Nate. Grace was supposed to keep her eyes on Nate, so if the thing somehow managed to sneak up on the woods he was still covered.

She wasn't sure if she'd have felt better about this plan, if it'd been Nate's.

"She's good." Grace said softly. "No signal yet." *I think she's about at the end of that flask though.*

"Thanks." Nate swallowed. "He probably won't show up for a while yet."

"He? That's a little sexist; you don't think it could be a her?"

"Nothing personal, Sugar." He chuckled. "Most of the ones that attack multiple times are male."

"Seriously?"

"Yep." He paused, looking back at the trees for a second.

"I'm still watching."

Nate turned back toward her, rolling his shoulders to relax. "The sociology of monsters, right?"

Grace laughed softly. "We could ask Jamie, but it's probably something like men are more likely to fight it off and survive the initial bite? More likely to be loaners and therefore have no one notice when they disappear on the full moon for a couple of nights."

"You managed the bite alright."

"He wasn't as big though," Grace said, watching the tree-line for a long moment.

"What?" Nate looked up at her, arms crossing over his chest. "Curt never said that. Because it wasn't the full?"

"Or he wasn't normally a werewolf and it was just the drug thing? No clue. But compared to that one in Georgia he was more like a super large dog."

A breeze blew through the trees, shaking them under the steadily climbing full moon. It was a pretty harvest moon, hanging giant and bright.

"Does your leg bother you on the full?"

She frowned, because she'd have thought all the 'full moon' questions would have happened their first full moon around each other. And she sort of got why they hadn't. They'd been a little busy, and new to being a *them*.

Well, new to hunting together as a them. They weren't in a relationship. Grace didn't do relationships. *Focus, woman*, she chided herself.

"Not any more than it does any other time. I think it's going to rain tomorrow, because it doesn't feel great but it's not hard to move."

"You haven't been limping much, so…"

"I haven't been sitting much, really. Even in the car, I can stretch it out."

"Point."

"Were you worried about it?"

"No." Nate huffed softly. "I figured if it was bad you'd say something. Just—"

Grace looked up, eyes locking on the trees off in the distance. "Shhhh."

He froze, hand instantly going to the weapon he'd hidden under his jacket. "Where?"

"Coming out of the trees." Grace shifted, swallowing, and watched the large, furred head tilt up, scenting the air.

For a solid second Grace couldn't align what was in front of her eyes with anything in her brain. She'd been bitten by a guy with the genes to be a were, and she'd been up close and personal with him. And then the job in Georgia, she'd been back a bit and it'd been over too fast for her to think much about it.

This one was different.

"Nate, I don't think that's a werewolf."

It padded further into the clearing, off at the end by the football field.

"Why?"

She didn't dare look down at Nate. Didn't take her eyes off it. "Because unless I've lost all concept of relative size I'd say it's about as tall as your car. Do werewolves get that tall?"

"On all four feet?"

"Yes."

"Fuck." Nate inched away from the car, she could see him barely out of the corner of her eye. "It's not. Signal Mom."

Grace flicked over to the other roof. "I would, but she's not there."

"What?"

An eerie howl split the night air, loud and deep-chested, and Grace watched the animal lope into the clearing fully, shaking its giant shoulders. It scented the air again, and turned perfectly toward Nate.

"Shit." Grace didn't move, just lined up the crossbow. "You've got a friend. And I doubt this thing'll do anything to him."

Nate cursed darkly. "Piss him off? I'll head for the escape ladder. Try and shoot him in the eye."

The clang of a metal door, off in the distance, was obscenely loud, the hinges screeching, and slamming shut again. The roll of wheels, and the sudden click of lights on the practice field as the old janitor stepped out onto the bleachers, echoed across the parking lot.

The not-werewolf shifted, looking at him, and crouching low, hackles rising.

Grace didn't think about it, just rushed down the fire ladder next to her, ten steps behind Nate who'd already broken for the old man. She hit the pavement running, rushing to catch up with him because if her crossbow wasn't going to be particularly helpful with this thing, his handgun probably wasn't going to be any better.

She was halfway across the parking lot, passing the car, when the tink of metal hitting stonework reverberated, and Sarah started calling. "Over here, you big fur ball. Come get me!"

Its ears twitched, but that wasn't enough. It was scented on prey, and expending energy on it. Noise coming from that far away wasn't going to change that.

Nate ran, until he was less than twenty feet away, and stopped, firing at its shoulders.

It howled in pain, and turned, ready to lunge as Nate emptied the rest of the clip into it. It stopped, pawing at its muzzle for a second, and then pushed its paws in, digging forward and loping toward Nate.

Grace lined up the crossbow, eyes focused. *Breathe, steady, aim...*

The bolt lodged in its eye, and it howled in pain, scrambling off to the side suddenly, trying to paw at the bolt, before it turned and raced back into the forest.

Nate put his hand on the crossbow, stopping her from shooting again. "Don't waste the bolts." He shook his head, swallowing, chest sawing.

Grace snubbed the safety, and held it out for him. "Sorry."

Nate looped her into a tight hug, pulse still thundering. "What the hell are you sorry for? Damn thing had my number," he managed, relaxing. "Told you you wouldn't let me down."

Grace laughed tensely, dropping her head on his shoulder.

Another door slammed, and Sarah—who'd apparently taken the time to come down through the building—came walking toward them. "What are you two waiting for, let's go finish it off!"

Chapter 8

It was by dint of sobriety and superior arguing skills that got his mom back to the hotel. And Nate was epically thankful for the fact Grace let him do it. Because he'd seen the tension in Grace's muscles, and it probably wouldn't have been *easier*—at least in the long run—to just knock his mom unconscious and take her back, but he could tell Grace was thinking it.

The night had been an epic sort of fuck-up. Not all of it was his mom's fault. He wouldn't have gone along with the plan, if it hadn't seemed sound. For a werewolf. The fact it hadn't been a werewolf was another issue entirely.

"Getting soft in your old age," his mom grumbled, stumbling into the room in front of him.

Grace shut the door carefully, and started dropping her gear.

"So it's a little big," she slurred, kicking her shoes off and searching around for something. Probably a bottle. "Still just a wolf."

"Still…" Nate bit his tongue, and pinched the bridge of his nose. "Do you have purified silver rounds? Because I sure don't, not on me." He dug his phone out, turning toward the bed.

"Oh, please. Don't go calling Curt with your tail between your legs. I've got some purified silver."

"What?" he asked, heart stopping. "Why?"

Nate's stomach turned, and his ears started ringing and suddenly he was twenty-one, cleaning his gear in another crappy hotel room in a town he should have completely forgotten the name of.

"Come on Eric, where's your sense of adventure?" Sarah swigged from a bottle of whiskey and wiped her mouth, gun rested on the table. "Thought you were game for the hard stuff?"

"I am game for the hard stuff." Eric glanced at Nate, looking for backup. "This looks like a little too hard for the three of us."

"So what, you gonna run off with your tail between your legs? Nobody's making you stay. Nate and I can handle this fine."

Grace shook his shoulder, fingers digging into the muscle, eyes dark and concerned.

"Never known when you'll need shit, eh?" His mom frowned at him, oblivious. "Whatever Curt's told you, I'm decently prepared."

His jaw twitched, and if he didn't calm down he was going to break a tooth. "Did you know it was a Worg?"

"What?"

"Did you know it was a Worg?" Nate glared at her, mind running through the litany. All the things he convinced himself that meant they could do this.

"Come on Natty, we've—"

"Do you remember what happened the last time we tried to take something this big?" Nate felt his heart beating in his chest, the blood thudding through his veins. He could smell smoke, and the tang of burned flesh. Hear Eric screaming and—

"Nate," Grace said softly, hand reached out toward him.

He looked at her, blinking. She was leaned against the dresser, one hand still wrapped lose and easy around the handle of the crossbow. Ready, just like always.

You were about a million miles away, her eyes said.

He swallowed, looking back at his mother. "You can't do this with just us. Grace damn skippy did better than either of us tonight, but she's not an experienced hunter— no offense Grace."

"None taken," Grace whispered.

"I'm calling Curt." Nate narrowed his eyes. "And you're going to go to sleep and try and sober up enough none of us wind up dead."

Nate grabbed his phone, and was about three steps for the door, when he realized that was a bad idea. Damn thing probably had his scent, at least, so he couldn't step outside. Shit, they'd be lucky if it didn't get over the bolt in the eye and come burst through the wall.

"I can stand here and pretend to be deaf, if you'd like," Grace offered softly.

She was watching him, eyes open and patient. Shitty night like this, one of them should have at least been muddy. Something. Grace had a rust graze on her wrist, from where she'd come down the ladder so quickly, but otherwise she was fine.

"No." Nate forced himself to swallow. "I'm just…"

Grace flicked a glance to his already sleeping mother. "You're allowed."

He rubbed his forehead, taking a deep breath. "For the record, I wouldn't have expected you to manage *that.*"

She nodded, but she was watching him carefully. "I would have."

Fuck they were a mess.

"I should…call Curt. Before it gets later." He looked down at the phone, and swallowed. Dialed the number. Convinced himself not to hang up, or make Grace call.

"Nate?" Curt sounded like he'd been deep asleep. "What's—"

"We're all fine." He glanced up at Grace, before the turned and pushed his fingers against his eyes. "Um...so...job's a little more complicated than we thought."

Curt startled up, Nate could hear his chair bang against something. "Pack?"

"No." He swallowed. "Worg."

Dead air. *One...two...three...four...* "Holy shit, did you have a heart attack?"

Curt let out a low curse. "I'm coming. Do you have purified silver?"

"Mom said she had some, but..." He glanced at the bed. "Might want to bring more. It's big."

"Big." Curt thumped something down. "You've seen it?"

Nate let out a tense laugh. "Emptied a clip of silver bullets into it. Which did about as much good as rocks, I'm sure."

"Fuck. They would." Curt swallowed. "Not that I ain't glad, but how are you not puppy-chow?"

"Grace shot him in the eye with my crossbow." He laughed then, feeling it just bubble out of his chest. "From like ten paces, maybe."

"Go Grace," Curt muttered, awed. "Sit tight. I'll be there in the morning."

~~~~~~

"You realize this should be like a six person job." Curt thumped a large silver crossbow bolt down on the gate of his truck.

He'd apparently come prepared like it was a six person job. Nate wasn't surprised. They needed it, because this wasn't something he'd have touched with a ten-foot pole otherwise. Not if he had any intention of them coming out of it alive.

"Where's Grace?"

Nate grabbed one of the bags. "Inside. She's fine."

"Didn't doubt she was. Just checking."

He shrugged. "She managed last night better than the rest of us did. Saved my bacon. Kept her post."

They unloaded the truck in uncomfortable silence, because they both knew where the rest of that sentence was supposed to go.

"Well. Good training." He handed Nate another bag.

"I don't think I get to take credit for her calm," Nate said, as Curt walked toward the room.

Nate followed him in, as Curt gave Grace a quick hug, and starting to unpack things.

"Where's Sarah?"

"In the shower," Grace answered. "She needed to…" she died off and forced a smile, not sure how to finish.

"Dry out?" Curt offered.

Nate snorted a laugh, and then had to quiet down quickly when they both lost it.

Curt looked between them, cocking a brow.

"We're a little tense," Grace offered, grabbing a bag and starting to empty it onto one of the beds. "Also, I get that this thing is…um…"

"Impossible?" Curt input.

"That. Whatever." She looked at stuff they'd brought in. "Did you bring enough shit with you?"

"Probably not," he said darkly, cocking a shotgun.

His mom stumbled out of the shower, damp and pale with puffy bloodshot eyes. "Curt."

"Wanna tell me why you're the only one packing purified silver?"

Nate winced.

"Not my fault he doesn't," his mom started, digging through her pack.

"Did you tell him he might need it?" Curt asked, striving for patience.

Nate's stomach turned, and his pulse pounded in his ears.

Grace nudged him with her shoulder, still unpacking weapons from Curt's bag. She was laying out the things

131

he normally checked, like it was just another day, just another job.

"DID YOU TELL HIM HE MIGHT NEED IT!"

Nate clutched the half filled clip in his hands, muscles tightening, the cold metal biting into his hands.

"Curt," Grace started.

Everything in the room froze, his mother even stopped digging through her kit and trying to pretend she and Curt weren't about to come to blows over the fact she'd *known* this was going to be a big job, and she hadn't told anyone.

Because he'd never have left without Curt.

"Yes Grace?" Curt asked, breathing loud through his nose.

"You aren't helping." Grace looked up at him, still and easy. "Finish helping us unpack and come up with a plan."

Curt opened his mouth, about to lay out all the reasons that wasn't going to happen. Curt had fundamental problems walking away from the shit with his mother, he always had.

Grace shook her head minutely.

He snapped his mouth closed again, and huffed. "Hand me that clip of purified rounds." He waved at the one next to Grace's elbow. "And tell me where this thing was."

His mom went back to digging through her pack, and Nate woodenly settled their gear and distributed rounds while Curt got all the information he needed from Grace, and worked out a plan with very little help from the rest of them.

When Curt was around, Curt was in charge. That was about half the problem.

"So let's go over this one more time—"

His mom sat on the foot of the bed. "Jesus, how many times we need to go over this?"

"Until I'm relatively sure we're all clear on what's happening," Curt snapped. "Because even if it doesn't work, which it probably won't—"

"So..." Grace cut across them.

Nate wanted to hug her. He had way too many years of Curt and his mother not getting along, and him trying to figure out if he was supposed to be jumping in or not, or where it was safe to jump in at.

Grace had no problems with that. As soon as they started picking at each other she was right there, making them stop. It was subtle, and patient, but it was still there.

"So we're thinking that's his general grounds," Grace prompted after a moment of glared non-verbal arguing with Curt. "And we're setting up there again, only this time we're going to make sure we're the only people there."

Curt nodded. "Grace is going to be bait this time."

Nate winced.

"It's fine," Grace cut him off. "I'm fine being bait. I've got the silver cannon of doom."

"I'm taking her spot on the roof-top, and Nate's going to take the low-point, at the edge of the bleachers." Curt stopped, looking them over. "And you're on the same place, Sarah."

"Fine. Let's go." Sarah stood, taking a couple steps toward the door. "Unless you ladies would like to stop and braid each other's hair?"

Curt rolled his eyes, and shouldered his kit.

Grace grabbed a second clip, pushing it into her pocket. "Alright. One night only, on the Scottish stage..."

Nate laughed, shaking his head. "How badly will this go if I make a Mac—"

"Don't say it!" Grace huffed. "We don't need bad luck."

He chuckled, and held the door open for her.

They weren't talking about how awesome Grace had been, or about how she was putting up with his mother—and what the hell was that about? All the trouble Grace had had with random people drinking, the way she'd been silent and watchful at bars.

Now wasn't the time for that. He could...not ask her about all that later. Nope.

The down-side to a small town was the lack of time it took to get places. He didn't get twenty or thirty minutes to calm down and get his head in the right place on the way there. He was stuck getting out of the car five minutes later, giant gun slung over his shoulder, watching Grace lope over to her spot on the practice field for the night.

The earpiece Curt had insisted on crackled to life in his ear. "Everybody here?"

They all answered with a simple "Yes."

Nate could see them, Grace thirty yards away in the practice field, Curt on the top of the building Grace had watched from the night before, his mom back in her place. They weren't entirely at the other side of the field from him, and it wasn't a regulation size field.

Nate was standing at the edge of the stadium building, with the practice bleachers and an elaborate trap set-up.

"Okay." Curt leaned over the side. "I've got a clear view of everything."

"Wonderful," Grace muttered.

Nate shifted around, glancing behind him. "As long as it comes out the same way it did before." Which he wasn't exactly banking on. He didn't figure something like a Worg was kind enough to hold to any sort of recognizable pattern. A werewolf was dangerous, but a Worg was like a human mind. Capable of a certain amount of reason and thought, crammed into a giant body with razor sharp teeth.

Not that Grace looked like she cared. She hung out in the middle of the field, patient and loose-limbed.

"You really should not look this calm," Nate muttered.

She chuckled softly, glancing around at the tree-line.

"Nate," Curt huffed. "You're not helping."

Grace smiled sadly, glancing his direction, making half a second of eye contact. "Helps that the only person I'm responsible for tonight is me." She shrugged slightly. "The bait messes up, it gets eaten."

"It's still the bait," Nate muttered.

Curt grumbled. "Do you two always lose focus like this?"

"We're focused." Nate turned, watching into the trees for a moment. "This is the way we focus."

"He's not back there," Grace said softly, voice low.

Nate turned, looking at her. "How did you even…"

Grace shifted, one arm going behind her back for the crossbow she was carrying. She'd picked the smaller one again, probably because it was easier for her to manage, and there wasn't much of anything that was going to work *well*. Grace would lure it into the clearing, and crack off a couple of shots at it. Then she'd run back toward Nate in the bleachers, where they'd set up the purified silver netting, with the powdered silver gas canisters. Between the two, that should do for the damn thing. Or at least get it down so Nate could cut its head off.

"It's not back there," Grace said as she took a half-step back, but stopped herself. "Because it's hiding in the bushes in front of me."

Curt cursed under his breath.

Nate took a step forward.

"Nate, stay in your place," Curt ordered, voice low. "Grace knows what she's supposed to do, let her do it."

"Grace does know what she's supposed to do." Grace swallowed audibly, and adjusted the crossbow, still behind her back. "Grace also knows when she's being played with."

"Grace…" Nate hesitated.

"Have you ever looked at something and known what it was thinking?" Grace asked, voice low and easy.

"Don't do anything stupid," Curt whispered, microphone rustling. "Make him come to you."

She laughed softly, taking an aborted step. "He's thinking exactly the same thing. Make her come into the wood. Don't go out there where it's open."

"Grace," Nate warned.

"The part where he's screwed," Grace whispered, muscles tensing. "Is that he's got my scent now, and he can't resist."

Curt cursed again.

"So when I run, you and Sarah should start shooting, and Nate should be at his post, because I won't outrun him for long."

Nate backed up, hand on the button, because he trusted Grace and if she told him she wanted him to be somewhere he'd be there.

"Here puppy, puppy, puppy," Grace breathed out, voice finally sounding as tense as it should. "Who wants the nice rabbit?" She wavered on her feet for a moment.

Suddenly Nate could see it, standing on the edge of the trees.

She'd pricked its hunters instinct, that thing that was telling it the meal it so desperately wanted was right there. Prey behavior, with the half-movements and odd freezes. It was more than a little creepy to realize she'd been doing it on purpose, toying with it.

"Now!" Grace yelled, springing back and around, racing toward him.

The Worg jumped out of the forest after her. Paws the size of side-tables ate up the distance between it and Grace at a terrifying pace, while it dodged around the shots Curt and his mother were firing at it. Someone managed to connect, but it barely slowed the thing down and Nate clutched the button in his hand.

Grace zigged to the side, dropping back suddenly and spinning off just before it connected with a giant paw. She managed to tack across and get it to his mark. He waited until she was over the bleacher, like she was supposed to be, before he released the netting. They only got one shot at this.

The trap sprung, catching it in the netting, cannons going too. It thrashed on the ground, straining. Nate grabbed the giant silver blade, raising it high.

The edges of the netting broke, and the Worg reared up, jaws snapping for Grace. Nate grabbed a handful of the back of her shirt and pulled.

The world around them erupted in light, a giant rush of air that sounded like a goddamn tornado, drowning out Curt's yell as he ran across the field.

Chapter 9

Nate swallowed, hand wrapped tight in Grace's shirt, brain narrowed down to the feel of her along his side, the quiet sound of her breathing. He blinked, trying to clear the spots out of his eyes.

The Worg's head pressed up against his boot, blood oozing from its body a few feet away.

Curt ran up, chest sawing, and looked them both over carefully before he spared a glance for the dead animal at their feet. Nate's mom was just behind him. Later—when Nate wasn't being hypersensitive about his drinking—he was going to have an extra drink just to drown the little voice that was fucking livid his mother couldn't even bother to make sure Grace was okay.

Just because someone was bait didn't mean they were fucking expendable.

"What. The. Shit," Nate said slowly.

Grace laughed softly, pushed a hand through her hair, and gently removed her arm from his grip.

Nate hadn't even realized he'd spoken. Every fucking time this happened, where they were in trouble and Grace's sparkly light stepped in to save the day, it bothered him a little more. Maybe it was being helpful, but he was done with the goddamn element of surprise.

"Let's get this thing picked up before anybody notices," Curt said, watching him carefully. "We can worry about other things later."

His mom dropped a large bag next to the corpse, laughing. "I don't know what you're worried about, that was awesome."

Nate opened his mouth, but Grace nudged him with her foot and handed him a machete. The fact of the matter was, the damn thing was too heavy to just lift. They couldn't leave it where it was and Nate could explode later.

Curt snapped out a heavy tarp, laying it out over the grass at the edge of the practice field, and together they rolled the body onto it with soft grunts. His mom emptied a bag of sand over the blood on the pavement, stirring it with a shovel and then starting to shovel the dirty sand back into the bags.

Nate spent a disconcerting chunk of his life hacking some creature or another into little bits, so he could burn it surreptitiously. The burning never bothered him. There were entire books devoted to the history of the human funeral pyre. What he was doing was just more of that.

He did his best not to actively think about what he was cutting apart. Nothing made him feel more abnormal than staring at a corpse and picking the best joints to sever, the places to cut to render it small, carry-able bits.

They worked in silence, because it was a small town and someone hearing them and coming to investigate would require more talking than any of them felt like, right then.

As he worked at chopping, Grace grabbed their pile of junk muslin and wrapped the pieces, while Curt walked back to the truck and retrieved the wheel-barrows. They filled the first one, and Curt and his mother walked back into the woods. Nate heard the splintering of wood, before the rich smell of wood-smoke started.

139

Burning close to town was a risk too, but it was a chilly kind of night and there were several houses that had smoke pouring out of their chimneys.

He finished cutting and helped Grace wrap the rest of their little friend. He handed her the tools and the tarp, and started pushing the wheelbarrow back into the woods.

Curt knew how to build a fire. Not that Nate didn't, but when Nate built a fire he built one big enough to burn whatever he needed to burn.

Curt built a fire large enough he could pretend he was an aging hippy recreating Burning Man.

His mom swung the last of the bags of sand onto the blaze as they walked up, Grace automatically going to help Curt toss his packages on the flames. Curt always took the bigger ones, got them on the fire first since they'd take longer to burn anyway.

Nate threw pile after pile on the fire, along with a handful of Cedar branches every so often. It crackled and popped, hissing, but the Cedar covered the smell pretty well.

Curt was right. Something that kept doing shit like that but wouldn't just come out and say *anything* probably didn't have pure intentions. Even if it was being helpful, and it wanted to keep being helpful, *why?* They didn't exist in a universe where being special was a good thing. Where Grace could be somebody's new best friend, and someday everything would be clear and happy.

It would have been nice, but he'd stopped believing in fairytales a long time ago.

Grace threw another chunk on the fire, blinking the smoke out of her eyes, and Nate fished the handkerchief out of his jacket, handing it to her. She took it, covering her eyes for a second.

Curt chuckled. "Smoke follows beauty."

"Is that why it keeps chasing you around the circle?" Grace muttered, stuffing it back in Nate's inside jacket pocket.

His mom was watching them. They had a strange lack of physical barriers in their friendship. Nate wasn't sure why. It was just the way Grace was. She didn't touch. She wasn't twitchy with him, the way she was with other people, but she didn't hang on him. But if she borrowed his handkerchief, she was as apt to just stick it back in his pocket as she was to hand it back to him. Maybe that was because every time she used it they were doing this and his hands were full.

She brushed leaves out of his hair, or off his back. Nate grabbed her when they were in danger. Or when she wasn't focusing and she started to walk into something— that'd happened more than once—going down the street.

Somehow it fit in with the weird accommodation. The way Grace didn't ask him questions he didn't want to answer, even when she maybe should, and he did the same with her. The way they actually didn't know a whole lot about each other, but she could tell what he'd have for lunch on any given day, and how he wanted his coffee, and which shirt he'd need clean for working on the car.

Curt threw the last chunk of Worg on the pile, and started piling the rest of the branches on top. He shifted, wiping his hands, checking for sap. "So. Grace."

She blinked at him, cocking a brow. "Yes?"

"About that psychic, just hear me out," Curt insisted. "This is the third time this has happened. I think consulting a psychic is our least worrisome option for getting some answers."

"What do you think a psychic is gonna tell her?" Nate's mom asked, scoffing. "They ain't exactly good for much anyway."

Curt glared at her, and then looked at Nate for help. Because yeah, of course Nate was worried about Grace. But she didn't want to talk about it normally, she sure as hell wasn't going to want to do it in front of his mother.

~~~~~~

Curt had talked off and on for the rest of the night, while they packed up and went back to the hotel and then on the ride back to his house. For the next two days, while things were a little tight because his mother had started an epic bender when they got back.

And Nate totally agreed.

Maybe he didn't like psychics, and he didn't want to start poking things that didn't need poking, but he could use a few more answers. And he'd told Grace that, and then backed off. But right that moment he was having more trouble with everything else.

Grace was uncomfortable about alcohol, had been since the day they met. She'd never said anything, and he hadn't either. He drank less, because he didn't need alcohol to function and it made her more comfortable. Grace made the job easier, for more reasons that just because she watched his back.

He'd expected some sort of fallout about his alcoholic mother.

There was no pretending. Nate might have liked to avoid that, or hide some of the truly spectacular amount of alcohol his mother had managed to go through in the first six hours they'd been back at Curt's. But he couldn't. They were all adults with eyes and functioning brains.

Grace obviously wasn't appreciating his mother. She hadn't said anything out loud, or lost her temper at all, which was a bit of a surprise. He'd always thought there was a line there somewhere, when someone drank enough Grace just couldn't deal with it. There'd have to be, if he was right about *anything* else.

If his mother hadn't found that line yet then he was wrong. If someone did they wouldn't live long enough for it to be an issue.

He hadn't expected violence, or shouting or...he couldn't even *picture* Grace in an emotional confrontation. He'd maybe been prepared for her to suddenly decide to go visit Jamie for a couple of days or something.

Not for her to camp out on the uncomfortable couch downstairs, make a chicken soup run so he didn't have to do it, and put up with the quiet comments.

It might have helped his mother wasn't a violent drunk. She was worse, mopey and irrational.

Nate was hiding outside. Sure, he was working on the Charger, and he'd done a couple other jobs for Curt, and washed Grace's car. He was hiding, and they all knew it. Just because Curt had been through this a few dozen times and Grace wasn't saying anything didn't change the truth.

She'd come out of the house at some point, because Nate could feel her watching him just outside of that distance where he'd have noticed anyone. She'd done this a couple of other times, and he'd started to say he didn't feel like talking, but she'd just left. Apparently she'd figured it out on her own.

"Hey."

Grace smiled, moving forward that last couple of feet and settling against an old junker off to the side. "Hey."

"Everything good?"

"Fine." She nodded. "Curt said it's his turn to cook and he's making chili. I was afraid to ask if that was like making turkey tetrazzini."

Nate chuckled. "Chili's good. There is a lot of it, but it makes good left-overs." He slammed the hood on the Charger and looked around for a rag to wipe his hands with.

Grace held one out, pinched between her fingers. "I feel like you're avoiding me. I don't think you actually are, but...um..."

He looked down at his hands, watching the grease slowly transfer itself onto the old rag. "It's..."

Grace waited for a long beat, watching him. "It's?"

Nate shrugged. Because he was a giant coward, and he liked where they were.

"If this is about the psychic thing—"

"No." He winced, rubbing the back of his neck. They'd both been on her about that a little lately. Curt more than he had, but still. "You know how I feel about that."

"I do." She frowned. "So if it's not that, then what?"

"Hey Natty," his mother called from the house, leaning out a window and slurring slightly. "Where's that book?"

"On the stairs," he yelled back, and then looked back at Grace, about to find something else to say to her that got them out of that conversation.

Grace's shoulders were tense, hands flexing. Every time his mother opened her mouth, Grace had to go searching for her control. Nate got that, he totally did. Half the time he was there himself. What he didn't get was how she kept finding it.

"What?" Grace said darkly, catching him watching her, before she made herself breathe and deflate.

"Yeah, that's what I'm having trouble with," Nate snapped. And later he was going to be thankful he'd managed to do it without actually yelling. "I get why you have trouble with her even if we've never talked about it."

Grace looked away, shoulders tense.

"And I'm not..." Nate swallowed. "You don't have to tell me anything you don't want to." She wasn't asking questions about him, he wasn't going to start asking them about her. "I don't understand why you're still here. Why you came on the job with me."

She looked at him, blinking for a long moment. "You thought I wouldn't because your mom's..." she stopped, swallowing.

And that, right there, told Nate everything he needed to know. The fact Grace couldn't actually say *your mom's a drunk* covered all the bases. "Yes."

Grace frowned at him, shifting uncomfortably. They weren't either of them talkative. Nate was pretty sure they could have managed a conversation about anything but feelings. He wasn't complaining about that, but right that moment he felt like there were things he needed to know that needed one of them to pony up.

Curt called for supper, and Grace waved to say she'd heard, but she still apparently hadn't managed to find something to say.

Nate opened his mouth, to give her some sort of out. Say they'd go into supper and talk about it later, with the full understanding that they never would.

"Just..." she paused, and bit her lip. "If the situation was reversed. If my..." she stopped again.

Nate swallowed, and physically bit down on the question that wanted out. *Grace, where is your family?*

"If that was my mother and...all that." Grace watched him carefully. "Would you have..." Her brow pulled. "I'm stumbling here because 'let me' makes it sound stupid and controlling." She rubbed her forehead. "If I was okay with you coming, but you weren't happy about it, is there a level of uncomfortable that would have kept you here?"

Nate scoffed. "No. You'd wind up dead."

"Pretty much." She looked up, catching eye-contact and actually letting it happen. "I'm not...I get that I'm decently helpful, and I think at this point..." She shook it off. "Anyway. Unenthused about this as I am, she's your mother. I can deal."

He frowned. "Curt deals, but he's not quiet about it."

Grace rubbed her face, smiling. "Curt's older, and feels responsible for you because it's his bloody quest to rescue us from *whatever*. Curt wants to fix people. Even your mother, who I'm pretty sure he doesn't even like." She shrugged. "I wouldn't know where to start trying to fix people, even if I was tempted."

Part of him wanted to push about that. Because Grace didn't say things like that in a touchy feely sort of way. She meant it literally. He was decently convinced Grace didn't lie to him because she just didn't see the point, not because she wasn't capable of it. If he or Curt took things badly that was their own problem. She didn't get invested in their emotional states, any more than she did anyone else's.

Two and a half months, and he was vaguely terrified of what he was going to do if she decided to go back to her own life.

~~~~~~~

Chili was better than Turkey Tetrazzini.

Not that Grace didn't like pretty much anything Curt cooked. Beggars and choosers and all that. He cooked for them, the least she could do was eat it. Even if he always cooked enough for a small army.

It was distinctly possible she just had a problem with turkey. It wasn't like there'd been a lot of turkey dinners in her childhood. Until they'd been in sixth grade and Aunt Rhoda started stealing her and Jamie for Thanksgiving there probably hadn't been any.

Either way, looking down a couple of gallons of leftover chili she could do.

Curt scraped the last of the pot into a reclaimed whipped topping container, and let out a pleased sigh. "That was a good batch."

"It was."

"Thank you for helping clean up."

"It was my turn."

"No it wasn't."

Grace bit back a smile, snapping the last lid on. "I'm pretending it was."

"It is just possible to be too nice to that boy."

Grace glanced behind her, because she did actually kind of want to have this conversation. Nate was outside, she hadn't asked what he was doing because the longer his mother was there the less interested he'd been in talking to anyone.

Sarah was in the living-room, between bottles.

"Well, I don't really know what's going on, so..."

Curt frowned, face dark.

"No, I get that she's trying to drink enough to destabilize wheat futures." She huffed, dumping the pan in the sink. "I don't get why this job was rough."

He winced, and filled the sink with soapy water. He puttered around for a long minute while Grace swept the kitchen floor and generally finished picking up. She didn't push. She'd been around Curt enough at this point she could tell when he was going to answer her question eventually, and he just didn't know how.

He pulled the first dish out of the sink and handed it to her to dry. "It was a few years ago."

She blinked, waiting silently.

"She pulled through here and picked him up on a job. Looked like it was a normal werewolf, possibly an old one which is a bit harder to deal with but nothing..." Curt shrugged.

"Ah."

"No." Curt rubbed his forearm against his face. "There was this boy, another hunter. I never met him, didn't get the chance. From what I heard he was a couple years older than Nate, and they got on like a house on fire." Curt paused, sad and reminiscent. "Nate called me all chuffed he'd made a friend and his mom was gonna let Eric do the job with them."

Grace winced, freezing. "Eric didn't survive the job, did he?"

"He did not," Curt answered, voice cold. "I don't know exactly what happened, I doubt anybody does. Nate showed back up here off the bus, didn't talk to Sarah for six months, didn't hunt for nearly a year."

Her nose wrinkled. "And this job about went really south and she's here and..." Grace blew a raspberry.

"I know you aren't either of you comfortable with actual feelings."

Grace blinked at him, and pushed back on the instinctive desire to run for the fucking hills.

"Don't skip away on me yet," Curt muttered, hands still in the dish water. "I'm not saying anything too touchy feely. Just that boy cares about you. You mean something to him nobody else has, maybe ever." Curt cocked a brow at her. "And I know it's mutual even if you'd rather kill me with a straw than admit it."

"O...kay." Grace cleared her throat. "And that means..."

"That means—"

A shuffle and thump sounded from the hallway, and Sarah worked her way into the kitchen. She grunted at them, and started riffling through the lower cabinets.

Grace dug her fingernails into her palms, clenching her hands tight because she wasn't six anymore. She was long past her days of hiding in the hall closet.

"There's nothing in there," Curt said, making nearly no effort at all to disguise how unimpressed he was with Sarah. "Pretty sure there's nothing left in the house."

Sarah cursed at him, and slammed the door to the cabinet she was going through. "Fine." She stood up unsteadily and looked around her.

Grace snagged her keys off the table, moving over next to the door.

"What the fuck do you think you're doing? Give me my keys," the other woman slurred.

"No." Grace swallowed, focusing on the feel of the cold metal in her palm. Curt was right there. She was fine. "You're drunk."

"Fuck you, Sally do-good." Sarah stumbled against the table. "You can give me my keys or I'll take 'em from you."

Grace squared her shoulders. "You can try. I've been faster than an angry drunk since I was five."

The door shut behind her, but Grace didn't turn around. She didn't want to know if Nate would have let his mother drive off about twelve-sheets to the wind or not.

Sarah grumbled, and shifted around like she going to go back to wrecking the kitchen. Until she turned back and leveled her side-arm directly at Grace's chest. "How are you at bullets?"

"Sarah!" Curt barked, taking an aborted step forward.

He stopped when Sarah turned the safety off.

"Give me my keys."

"No."

"Fine…"

Grace felt a hand on her arm, Nate jerking her aside and stepping between Grace and Sarah.

"What the fuck do you think you're doing?" Nate asked his mother, voice pitched low and *angry*.

Chapter 10

He wanted to close his eyes and walk away.

Except he didn't. What he really wanted, just for a second, was to believe his mother wouldn't have actually shot Grace over the car keys. He wanted to believe he wasn't incredibly lucky he'd come back in the house when he had.

"When'd you get here?"

She slurred, and wavered and Nate reached out and grabbed the gun out of her hand.

"Never mind when I got here, what the hell do you think you're doing?" He poured the ammo out of the pistol, checked the chamber, and tossed it to Curt.

"Don't you worry 'bout a thing, Natty, we was just having a little argument."

Nate clenched his hands, and counted backwards from ten. "You don't pull a gun on someone over a little argument, and if I ask Grace she'll tell me the truth."

"Believe that little slut over your mother?"

"Was that even a serious question?" Nate's pulse thundered in his ears. "And don't insult Grace."

"Don't insult Grace," she mocked. "She's turning you into a right nancy, ain't she?"

"She hasn't…" Nate took a deep breath, because there wasn't any point to engaging with that. "What were you doing?"

"Trying to get my keys," Sarah grumbled, going back to digging through the cabinets. "She took my keys."

"You're drunk."

"I'm fine."

But she nearly overbalanced and fell while she was at it. She would have cracked her head on the counter if Curt hadn't reached out and caught her.

She shoved Curt off, trying to hit him, and cursing wildly.

"You're all fucking worthless."

"Mom…"

"What?" She rounded on Nate, glaring blearily. "What? I wasn't gon shoot her, I just wanted her to give me my fucking keys."

"Can you hear yourself?" Nate clenched his jaw. "Letting you drive a car would be almost as bad as letting you keep the gun."

She rolled her eyes. "Yeah, might as well be his son," she grumbled, pointing at Curt. "Lecture me about driving when I want to drive."

Curt opened his mouth, but Nate shook his head.

"The best thing that's gonna come out of that is you get arrested." He cocked a brow at her. "With a trunk full of guns and ammo."

But she was ignoring him.

"Ain't your problem, I'll take my shit and my self and go."

"You're drunk."

"Points for you," Sarah muttered.

Nate scrubbed a hand through his hair.

"If your Daddy could see you…"

"What?" Nate choked, almost laughing. "If my daddy could see me what?"

She rifled through her bag in the corner, probably looking for her spare keys. Because she was drunk and she'd clearly forgotten he'd taken them the other day while he was working on her rusty death-trap.

"If my daddy could see me what!" Nate stopped, breathing. Yelling wasn't going to help any, and Grace was still standing behind him.

"Letting some *girl* make your decisions for you, running away from a fight, fucking raised you to be a man, not some—"

"You didn't raise me."

Nate hadn't meant to say it, but he wasn't taking it back now.

His mother rounded on him, eyes wide. "What did you just say to me?"

"You heard me. You didn't raise me," Nate countered. "You drug me along behind you while you drank your way into an early grave and looked for monsters to kill."

"These things killed your Daddy! I taught you how to kill them. I trained you because—"

"Because you didn't have anywhere else to leave me and I was all you had of him," Nate spoke over her.

She slapped him across the face, and Nate took it because…well, at that precise moment he was more focused on Grace and the way she'd tensed.

"Don't you speak to me like that, I taught you to respect—"

"You taught me to fear you," Nate said through gritted teeth. "To do what it took to keep you happy because you were the only parent I had and I never mattered more than your revenge. Nobody mattered more than your revenge."

"Your Daddy—"

"He's dead!" Nate shouted, voice sharp. "And I wish he wasn't, I wish I'd ever gotten to know him. I wish…" He stopped, because he wasn't drunk and he didn't need to finish that.

"You wish I was dead?" Sarah asked, eyes narrow and dark. "Cause that ain't much of a surprise. If I'd gotten to pick I'd have—"

"You need to stop," Grace interrupted. Her voice was still, and unexpectedly sharp.

It hit him like a bucket of cold water, the sudden realization that she was right there next to him. She wasn't watching them, wasn't looking at his mother. Her hands were wrapped over the back of the chair in front of her, like she was trying to control herself.

Sarah opened her mouth, glaring at Grace.

"No, I'm done." Nate clenched his jaw again, tried to struggle through all the words that wanted out, to find the right ones.

"You're what?"

"I'm done." He swallowed. "I'm done going on jobs with you so I can watch you take stupid risks. I'm done watching you try and drink yourself into an early grave. I'm done trying to save you from yourself, take your pick."

She blinked at him.

"You're not leaving this house until your sober."

"You can't keep me here." She rushed him, intent on pushing past him.

And normally she had good fighting instincts, she was quick and tough and capable.

She hadn't stopped drinking in days, for more than a couple of hours. A toddler could have taken her. Nate grabbed her arm and drug her toward the basement. Slammed the door open, and marched her down the short flight of stairs.

"Try not to fall down the stairs," he muttered, throwing her into the chair in Curt's little cellar room.

"You piece of shit, get back down here, I'm your mother!"

Nate calmly walked back up the stairs and shut the door, latching it and putting the padlock on too. He handed a silent Curt the key, and turned around and walked upstairs.

~~~~~~~

153

Grace's phone was the first noise she'd heard in more than an hour, and she was going to put a whole lot of effort into pretending that was the reason she jumped on it.

She did glance at the screen long enough to tell it was Jamie calling.

Granted, it was pretty unlikely to be anybody else. Nate was out in the yard, and Curt was in the kitchen pretending the house was quiet.

Grace was hiding in her bedroom, staring at the wall and occasionally wondering if she could come up with a decent excuse to leave for a couple of days.

And the heart to do it.

"Hey."

Jamie paused, and she could practically feel him thinking. "You're breathless and agitated, what's wrong?"

"Um…" Grace bit her lip, blinking.

"Um?" Jamie cursed softly. "Grace, when you answer with 'um' I start to seriously worry. Are you in the middle of a job and I don't know it?"

"No." She swallowed. "No, we're still at Curt's."

"Right." Jamie cleared his throat. "There's so much shit hiding under that sentence I don't even know where to start."

Grace choked out a laugh, dropping back on the bed. "Jam…"

"Does this have something to do with the Nate stuff you won't tell me about?"

She winced. "It's not that I won't tell you, it's just…not mine to tell."

"Make it yours to tell," Jamie countered. "Come on Gracie, it's me here. I'm not gonna do whatever it is that makes you so incredibly nervous about sharing other people's secrets. Whatever it is, it's bothering you and I'd like to help."

"Yeah." Grace swallowed, and closed her eyes. "Nate's mom."

Jamie waited for a beat, and then sighed. "What about Nate's Mom? Is she around?"

"Yes."

Grace swallowed, and mentally pictured the wince on Jamie's face.

"Right. That good, huh?"

She choked out a wet laugh, rubbing her face. "It's a fucking mess. I mean I knew they weren't all happy families but there's all this ridiculous crap rumbling around, and I don't think she's been sober since she showed up. And I didn't try to pick a fight with her, she was freaking pickled and she wanted her keys and—"

"Woah, woah, woah," Jamie interrupted, voice tense. "Slow down a little. Nate's not upset with you about that."

"No?"

"That came out as a question, Grace."

"Well, I mean he's got his own shit going on right now Jamie, I didn't exactly make him talk to me."

"He's not talking to you?"

"He's not talking to anybody, it's not a me thing."

Jamie puffed out a breath. "Alright. Yeah, you're right, it's probably not. So you got in a fight with his Mom."

She winced. "And it went...um...south. And then he came back in the house and they argued."

"The way people do when they're drunk and unreasonable?"

Grace rubbed her eyes. "Yeah."

"And she's still there?"

"We're not sure she's sober yet."

Jamie made a pained noise. "How long ago was this fight?"

"Two days."

"Jesus."

Grace smiled sadly, and sat up. "Yeah. So. I don't expect you to know what to do with all that."

"Yeah," Jamie agreed. "I'm always here if you wanna talk though."

"I know."

They sat there in silence for a long second, and Grace picked at the old quilt on her bed.

"That's not all, is it?"

"You're better at saying the right thing with this crap than I am." Grace swallowed. "It had to hurt, she said *stuff* and I feel like if I was you and he was me you'd say something that made it better."

"Yeah?" Jamie's voice was warm. "I certainly try. I was never sure I managed it."

"What do I do?"

Jamie blew out a breath. "Grace, Nate's not you any more than I am. And since I've never actually met the guy I can't tell you what he needs."

She swallowed. "Alright."

"I can tell you what I always did with you."

"Did?" She snorted.

"Do, did, whatever," he grumbled. "I make sure I'm there, and I accept I might not be able to fix anything. That doesn't mean I shouldn't try. If Nate's not being self-destructive just being there is probably enough."

"Yeah." She swallowed. "Alright."

Jamie cleared his throat softly. "So. How are you?"

"I'm…"

"If you say 'fine' I'm calling bullshit."

"Coping." Grace swallowed. "I'm coping."

She heard a loud bang, and the house shuddered. And they didn't live in a world anymore where Grace could assume that wasn't a problem. She got up and walked over to the door, cracking it open.

There were raised voices, and she listened long enough to decide it was Sarah and Curt.

"Jamie, there's crap happening downstairs. I should go."

"Don't get into trouble, and let me know if you need anything."

"I will. Thanks."

"Anytime, love."

Grace hung the phone up, slipping it in her pocket and carefully tracking downstairs.

She hit the hallway just as Nate came in from outside, the key to the basement in his hand.

Curt shot her a glance, and looked at the door.

"God damn it!" Sarah bashed against the door, voice fraught.

Nate didn't talk to her, just yanked the door open. He stooped down and grabbed the bags he'd thrown Sarah's things in, and dropped them at her feet.

"Listen here—"

"I meant what I said." Nate turned around, heading for the kitchen. "I'm done watching you try to kill yourself, and not caring if you get anybody else killed. You know where the door is."

Sarah looked at Nate's back, squared her shoulders and picked her bags up. "Great job there, Curt."

"Yeah." Curt nodded at her. "You ever decide to sober up for good, you know the number."

She looked at Grace, and opened her mouth on something that was probably unwise.

Grace cocked a brow and folded her arms over her chest. If she was burning her bridges she had another thing coming if she thought Grace was going to help with that.

Sarah snorted, and walked out the door. A second later they heard her engine fire up, and she roared out of the yard.

Grace stood in the hall with Curt and pushed out an uneasy breath.

"Yeah." Curt rubbed the back of his neck. "I don't wanna wish that was the back of her, but I kinda do."

"You're a better person than I am," Grace said softly.

Curt squeezed her on the shoulder, shaking slightly.

Nate walked back in the from the kitchen, face stony. "Deke called, he had a job. You coming?"

"Are you sure that's a good idea?" Curt asked softly. "Nate—"

"Yeah." Grace cleared her throat, watching Nate. "Yeah, all packed. Figured it was just a matter of time."

He nodded. "Leave in twenty." He turned and walked out the door.

Curt muttered darkly, shoulders tense. "Grace—"

"It's that or him just sitting here." Grace glanced at him. "I'll keep an eye on him."

"Who's gonna keep an eye on you?"

"Nate." She shrugged. "He looks pretty focused to me."

"Sure," Curt agreed, voice low. "Yeah. You're right. You and the job is something to focus on that's not...that."

Grace forced a smile and turned to get her bag. She maybe didn't think they'd be *fine* because she wasn't stupid. They'd be better out with something to do, than sitting at Curt's climbing the walls.

~~~~~~

Nate hadn't spoken in three days, when it wasn't absolutely imperative.

Grace hadn't rethought them going on the job. She still felt like it was the best idea. Them being out working a job was better than Nate sitting at Curt's staring at the walls and pretending to work on her car again. It hadn't been a hard choice, really.

They'd rolled into town the day before and Nate had been all about the job.

He'd been all about the job since he showed his mom the door, and she wasn't complaining about that. Being all about the job was better than being a basket-case.

She couldn't actually think of any other response he'd have managed. Nate wasn't any more the crying-in-the-corner type than she was.

The thing they were hunting was new, and Grace had a couple of minutes where she danced around figuring out if Nate was really good enough to pull a job, when she didn't know what they were doing.

Not that she'd wanted to try taking another werewolf or something right then. She'd had a couple of minutes to seriously worry it was going to be some sort of water thing.

A jaculus had been subsiding on hikers and hunters in the local state park for a couple of months before the body-count got high enough Deke heard about it, which wasn't *good*.

But it wasn't anything they couldn't handle. She'd checked the lore—A jaculus was basically a feathered, tree dwelling dragon/bird thing that liked to land on people and eat them—and even without the scary 'I'm not okay' focus going on next to her, she was relatively sure Nate could have handled the job by himself.

She didn't want him to be okay. She didn't want him to be anything other than what he felt like he needed to be. Still, the silently tracking through the woods with a frown on his face and a whole smattering of guns wasn't exactly comfortable.

Nate didn't talk, and since he wasn't talking she didn't talk either. After a while the silence got a little oppressive.

Nate waved her back, looking up into the trees. They'd caught the first one the day before, and taken care of it pretty easily. Grace maybe felt a little bad for it. It was just an animal, trying to do what it did. If there'd been a way for them to get Fish and Game out into the park and not killed by the giant dragon dropping from the trees... She wasn't actually sure Nate would have suggested it right then, but she'd have braved his displeasure and done it herself.

There wasn't, and given the number of people these things had gone through in the last month or so since they showed up, they needed to be stopped.

Grace dropped back where he wanted her, and waited. Now wasn't the time to talk even if she'd wanted to offer being bait. She'd started to offer the day before and the glare he'd given her had made it perfectly, non-verbally clear that was *not* happening.

He looked up into the canopy of trees over them, and then he waved her forward and they started back into the leaves again.

They'd been at it for about another hour when Grace got half a seconds warning before a few hundred pounds of teeth and claws and clawed wings tried to drop on her—they were quiet, but the spring that happened when a large one jumped off a branch was pretty much permanently embedded in her brain now.

Nate hit it in mid-air and slit it's throat, tumbling them both into a messy pile on the ground. He didn't curse, or grumble. He swiftly, efficiently cut its heart out and dumped it in a pile on the forest floor.

It was probably a good thing neither of them needed to be making judgment calls.

Nate grabbed the first branch on the tree it'd dropped out of, and started to climb when it snapped under his weight.

Grace dusted her hands off and walked over. "Why don't I do that? I'm assuming I'm looking for a nest?"

Nate glanced at her, and looked up the tree. He stepped back and seemed to gauge. However much of a mess Nate was right then, he hadn't started taking chances with her. If anything he was being even more careful than he'd been until then. "Do you think you can climb with a knife without hurting yourself?"

Grace pulled a blade out and grabbed it in her teeth. "What am I looking for?" She said, muffled, around it.

"A nest."

"Yes, thank you," she huffed, watching where she put her hands and leaving out half of the words crowding her brain.

Nate sighed softly, and rubbed at his face. "It'll be mostly leaves and sticks. Probably like a giant bird's nest."

"Full of what exactly?"

"Small dragons?"

"Yay."

"Curt said they might be more like largish snakes when they're small. Or we'll get really lucky and they're eggs."

Grace pulled herself up to the nest in the tree. It was pretty close to where the damn thing had dropped on her, so it was clearly the right nest.

"And what are we if it's empty?"

Nate paused for a second, looking up at her when she glanced down. "Define empty."

"Devoid of either dragons or serpents? Lacking in life-forms? Whatever other forms of empty you can picture."

He rolled his eyes. "Are there egg fragments?"

She leaned up further to look in. "No." She frowned. "It sort of looks new."

"New?"

"Well, old bird's nests look dryer. This one looks fresh."

"Okay, come down before you break something."

Grace bit back on her response to that and slowly crawled herself back down the tree, one bit at a time. Until she was on the ground with a dead dragon at her feet.

Nate was already packing up, getting ready to drag the body back to where they wanted to burn it when the tree next to them half bent over and giant wings blotted the sun out of the sky.

Chapter 11

He wiped his hands on the rag in the trunk, meticulously stashing their gear away.

Her phone beeped, and she looked down at the text message screen.

Jamie: How is it?

Grace glanced up at Nate, dumping water over the fire they'd lit to burn their last two friends. There wasn't a special way to kill a jaculus. They didn't need special equipment, they just had to make sure it didn't drop on their heads and kill them with its giant, ridiculous claws.

She wasn't sure the job would have gone as easily if Nate hadn't been in whatever the hell kind of mood he was in. She was also decently certain he was internally beating himself up over the fact neither of them had entertained the possibility the nest was empty because it was new and the ones they'd thought were a nesting pair were the babies.

We're still in one piece, she typed back.

She stowed the rest of her stuff, and wrapped their cleaning rags into a spare bit of burlap, before she shoved them down under the lip for the trunk hide. If someone was dedicated they'd find it, but a cursory examination wouldn't do that.

Jamie: That good?

Nate pulled his phone out, and she didn't need to see it, to know he was calling Curt. "Hey, got anything for us?" He stood before the car, one hand on the handle, and listened intently. "No. Right. Bye."

Nate opened the car door and dropped in, and Grace would have worried, except once he was in the car he stopped and waited, watching her out of the corner of his eye.

"Back to Curt's?"

Nate nodded, and started the car.

How do I get him to talk? she asked Jamie.

Nate didn't turn the radio on. The car was more or less completely silent. It'd been that way for a while, but the job was over now.

Jamie: How do you normally get him to talk?

Grace frowned at her phone, before she started typing. *I've never had to try. He just talks.*

She chanced a sideways look, watching the way his hands snagged over the wheel, knuckles standing out and the tension in his arms, all the way up to his shoulders.

Jamie: Might not be something you can fix.

Grace winced. *Marvelous.*

Jamie: Where to now?

Curt's.

Nate shifted in the seat for a second, still staring doggedly in front of him. He'd driven nearly the entire way in silence before. Stared straight in front of him and pushed mile after mile until he had something else to focus on.

It was looking increasingly like that was going to happen going back as well.

Jamie: Give him something else to think about?

Like what?

Grace glanced up at Nate, because she felt like there had to be a break at some point, and she didn't actually want to miss the beginning of that.

Jamie thought—strongly—that she needed to be careful about that desire to fix things. He hadn't said it in so many words, but she'd heard it in his voice, on the phone the night before.

It wouldn't do any good to remind him she wasn't good at that. Not when she really cared about someone.

She cared about Nate, and it was...novel, absolutely. Jamie wasn't mentioning that because he didn't need to. At some point, when things calmed down he'd probably push the fact she hadn't introduced them yet.

Jamie: I don't know. Whatever might distract him if you think he needs distracting.

Grace stared at her phone for a long minute. *What do I do if he doesn't want to be distracted?*

Jamie: Let Curt try.

Grace was eerily sure he was going to spend a lot of time avoiding Curt when they got back.

Jamie: Or call me and throw the phone at him if you're really desperate.

Grace smiled grudgingly. *Don't throw yourself on a sword.*

"Is Jamie alright?" Nate asked, voice low and tense.

"Yeah, he's good." Grace glanced up at him, nodding. "Curt didn't have anything else?"

Nate shook his head, eyes tight on the road.

~~~~~~

Curt hadn't had another job for them because he'd rushed out and done it before Nate called.

Grace could tell by the set of Curt's shoulders, and the look in his eyes that he'd expected Nate to be on the edge. She understood that, because she wasn't particularly sanguine about where Nate was either.

Nate blew through the kitchen, barely saying 'hello' to either of them, before he was out front working on a clothes dryer for one of the neighbors.

"How was the job?" Curt asked carefully.

Nate had been nearly goddamn scary, but she wasn't going to say that. "Good." She shrugged, grabbing an apple off the counter. "Focused."

"Focused, or *focused*?"

Grace rubbed her forehead, sighing. "Curt—"

"Because it's only going to be so long before Richards or Deke or whoever calls with another job and if you two aren't good—"

"We're fine."

"Are you sure?"

"Yes."

"How sure are you?"

"Curt."

"I'm serious Grace—"

The door opened, hinges loud, and they both froze. Nate walked in and poked around in the fridge for a moment. "Are you bothering Grace about me again?"

"I was just asking how you were. Figured she might get a different answer than I did."

Nate straightened, opening a can. "She didn't ask." He glanced at her, flushing slightly. "Relatively sure she didn't need to."

He walked back outside without another word, and Curt didn't need to say anything either. Just grumbled and started pulling things out of the cabinets to make supper.

She honestly thought that might have been the end of it. Not the real end of it, but they were all prone to walking away from the amount of tension and stress running around them.

Curt finished fixing dinner, and Grace got through most of the paperwork she should have been doing in the few days before they left. Nate worked outside, oblivious to the weather and the hour and Grace was seriously thankful he hauled himself back in before it was time to eat. She hadn't wanted to go get him.

They sat around the table and picked at their food.

"Did you two talk any more about contacting a psychic?" Curt asked suddenly.

"No." Nate shook his head, taking a giant bite of his food.

"I didn't ask..." Curt glanced at her carefully. "Did anything else strange happen on this job?"

"No," Grace answered. "It was pretty normal. Minus the large reptiley things dropping out of the trees at us."

Nate snorted, still just staring at his plate.

Curt glared at her, indicating Nate with his eyes. *See,* he mouthed.

Grace shrugged, helpless.

She took a bit of her food, and her phone buzzed in her pocket. She didn't even get the screen turned on, before Jamie's suggestion flashed across her brain. *Give him something else to think about.* She checked her phone, ensuring it was just an email notification, and then looked at Nate again.

She knew he was worried, and maybe the crap with his mother had over-run everything with her. It was still there, under the surface. Maybe confronting that wouldn't fix everything.

She trusted Jamie to be right, even if he'd never met Nate, even if they'd only spoken a couple of times.

Nate glared at Curt. "If Grace doesn't want to—"

"I'll do it."

They both froze, looking at her shocked.

Grace flushed. "Answers wouldn't be the worst thing ever. Probably. Hopefully."

Curt nearly whooped with joy. But Grace was busy watching the frown on Nate's brow. The calculating look in his eyes, and trying to come up with a reason for her sudden about-face on the whole Psychic thing that wasn't about him.

Nate swallowed. "Are you sure?"

"Yeah, I'm sure."

~~~~~~

"For the record, I think this is a bad idea."

Curt thumped his bag on the table. "Deacon Hughes, I never figured you for—"

"I don't mind psychics," Deke interrupted. He glanced at Grace, standing at the side of the table with Nate, flicked a half glance to him. "And I get how you could be tired of this stuff happening without any explanation."

Nate scoffed.

"But," Deke continued, glaring at him. "Something that hides in the shadows like this, I don't think you want to force it into the light. I mean, in all honesty, I'm not entirely sure you can, but my vote would be for not trying."

"Don't poke the bear," Grace offered quietly.

"Exactly." Deke nodded. "And I've told her we're coming and she's the only person I'd trust with something like this."

Grace swallowed. "Did you explain it to her?"

Deke blinked, thrown. Like they were going to do this and no one was going to make sure the psychic understood things could be dangerous for her. Or because he hadn't expected it to be Grace who asked. "Yeah, absolutely. She understands."

She shrugged. "I'm fine with letting sleeping dogs lie, but other people aren't so much."

Deke frowned at Grace, but let it go. He wasn't any less tense—Nate wasn't entirely sure what was going on with that—and he didn't talk much, while they drove across town to his friendly psychic. That wasn't unusual. Nate pretty frequently got the feeling from Deke that he knew things, or understood things, that he wasn't sharing.

Their psychic lived in a quiet, tree lined suburb. Brownstone houses smushed together down the street, kids at the end in a park that was more cement than grass playing basketball and jumping rope.

Grace waved at a little girl that scrambled across their path.

"Did you grow up in the city, Grace?" Deke asked, leading them down the street.

She looked up at him, blinking at the question. "No." She smiled wryly. "Small town Illinois. Maysville."

"Was it nice?"

She shrugged. "It was probably about like every other small mid-western town."

And Deke was opening his mouth on a question about Grace's parents, he could feel it coming, and Nate was going to interject something. Curt beat him to it. He didn't say anything, just gave Deke a look that said this wasn't a time for that conversation.

Nate was pretty sure there was never a time for that conversation, but that was beside the point.

Deke walked up the small run of steps, to a brownstone with a plaque hanging off the door.

Mother Mary
Neighborhood Psychic and Tarot Mistress.
Yes, you have to ring the bell.

Deke pushed the old bell, and stepped back a pace.

"Deacon Hughes," Mother Mary said grandly, opening the door wide. She wore a cacophony of brassy chains, and crystals, and little vials of things he probably didn't want to know about around her neck. A pile of broomstick skirts, with a denim shirt and three or four shawls. Three pairs of glasses, one on her face, one around her neck, and one on her head. "I knew you'd be to see me today."

Deke laughed softly. "Mother Mary." He cocked a brow. "That wouldn't have anything to do with my calling to tell you we were coming, would it?"

She huffed, and slapped Deke on the shoulder. "Oh, ruin an old woman's fun."

Nate wouldn't have called her old by any stretch, probably in her mid-fifties? She had tawny colored skin, and light eyes. A reddish tinge highlighted her dark hair that Nate was fairly certain was natural. She was an attractive, striking woman now. He couldn't imagine what she'd been like when she was younger.

"Well, get on in here with you," she sing-songed in a deep fake—but surprisingly accurate—Caribbean accent.

"It's disturbing how well you put that on," Deke muttered.

She laughed joyously, showing them into a velvet and lace lined parlor, complete with little round card table covered in spotty material and a crystal ball. "Have to make it good for the coveys, as my Gran used to say." She looked them over, falling on Nate first. "Now this must be sweet little Nathaniel I've heard so much about."

Nate glared at Deke.

"I've mentioned you in conjunction with a couple of jobs, and when she asked if I had any friends," Deke said quickly, flushing. "And I'm sure I never called you sweet."

"But you are." She patted Nate on the shoulder. "And I'm sorry love, but that thing you want isn't going to happen." She smiled sadly. "Some people can't grieve, and some people don't even try. You're momma's gonna pine for that man till the day she dies, just the way she wants to." She squeezed him kindly. "Oh, but he deserved it. One of the best men ever to walk the earth was your Da. You've got a little of that in you."

Curt huffed softly.

"And you..." She narrowed her eyes at Curt. "A woman who loves you loves you no matter what you accidentally drag home with you. You'll find the right one

169

someday. You want to know more than that, I'll have to do a reading for you."

Curt paled, stepping back a half step. "No. I'm—"

Deke chuckled. "Mary, they're more worried about Grace."

Mary tisked. "Yes, introduce me to this poor child who's got something strange thunking along behind her in the ether. There's a first time for anything."

Nate reached back and pulled Grace a step forward, because now that they were in the room he was pretty sure she was having some second thoughts. There was certainly something going on in her head.

"That would be me," Grace said quietly, voice tense.

Mary looked at her, and then froze. She gasped, low and painful, and grabbed a hold of the chair in front of her with both hands, knuckles going ashy-white. "Oh honey..." She blinked, tears springing to her eyes.

Grace tensed even more, arms folding over her chest.

"Oh no... I won't..." Mary composed herself. "I won't say anything." She watched Grace, eyes clear and a single tear slipping free and going down her cheek. "But honey, there are some ghosts you can't walk away from. That boy can't protect you from yourself."

Grace frowned. "I've never asked him to."

Mary scoffed. "You ever asked him to do anything?"

"That'll be Jamie then?" Curt asked softly. "Or Nate? 'cause I don't know that I'd call either of them 'boys' still."

"You call me 'boy' at least once a week," Nate said darkly.

"In his head, he's still ten trying to protect you from things he can't protect you from," Mary said, voice low. "And you're still twelve doing the same thing back."

Curt and Deke were both about to say something, and Mary was about to over-share Grace's life. And as much as he had a few dozen questions about Grace he'd like answers to, he was about eighty percent sure the only reason they were there was him. The other twenty was probably Curt.

"Not to be rude," Grace said softly. "But I don't think any of this has to do with Jamie. Or if it does I don't see how."

"No?" Mary asked.

Grace shook her head. "And I'm not real interested in knowing my future or anything like that."

Mary cocked a brow high, but she didn't offer any more gems about Grace. Just pulled her chair out and sat down. "Right then, sugar, come sit down. You're gonna have to let me touch you for this."

Grace moved over to the chair Deke held out, and sat down uneasily. "Did you think I'd have a problem with that?"

"Honey, you got a bubble that's at least three feet wider than anybody else's." She held a hand out for Grace. "And we ain't discussing it, that doesn't change the fact it's there." She shook herself out. "Bear with me for a bit, this is gonna be damn unpleasant."

Grace frowned. "What are you doing?"

"It's likely whatever it is that's following you around, it's touched you at some point, somehow," Mary answered. "So I'm going to start sifting back through your memories and see if I can find it. Human brain's a miraculous thing. You could meet somebody on a street corner, be absolutely sure they were just another person, but that imprint in your mind will show what they really are. They'll leave a mark, even if they don't want to. Now that might not say what they actually are, especially when I don't know what I'm looking for. But we'll rule out all the regular possibilities. Witchcraft, little people, all that." She blew out a breath. "But it means trolling through your memories."

"Yay," Grace muttered darkly. "How..." She swallowed. "How far back?"

"Far as we need to go." Mary took her hand, braced for it. "And it probably won't go in order, most people don't, so just...let things happen. Close your eyes and relax."

Nate watched as Grace forced herself to calm down, her shoulders loosening, other hand going lax in her lap.

"There ya go," Mary gushed softly. "Now, I want you to start with the first time this happened....that's it. You're at home, and Curt and Nate have come to help, that's it. Let the memory just...flow like it will. Oh my, she's a nasty piece of work, but you're safe. This is just the past, just a memory..." Mary twitched slightly, face leaching for a moment, before she picked back up. "Okay, so it was already there, then...go back slowly, let your mind wander over the past. No destination, we're just taking a nice little stroll down memory lane."

Mary was quiet then, and Nate wouldn't have traded her places for anything in the world. She winced and twitched at odd times, like she was being drug through some sort of horror, but she didn't speak. And over-laid with all that was Grace. Sitting stoic and easy in the chair next to her, letting her mind just...wander.

"No no, don't direct it." Mary frowned. "What was that memory?"

"What memory?" Grace asked softly.

"You started one, on a playground." Mary nodded. "Yes, that. Where did it go?"

Grace shrugged. "It's just Jamie. I can tell you what happened."

Mary's brow furrowed. "There's been lots of Jamie, it wasn't like that. Find something else from back then."

Grace wrinkled her nose, like she was trying to actively find something now.

"Why are they all..." Mary squeezed her hand a bit, leaning forward. "There's some sort of block here. What's... Oh. Your Momma." She swallowed. "But..." She huffed. "I'm going to push at this, if I start to hurt you, you tell me."

Grace swallowed, but stayed calm.

"I can't...quite..." Mary huffed, redoubling her efforts. "I can feel it. Like a big slimy wall at the back of your head, and everything is just stopping," Mary muttered under her breath. "Find a crack, someplace to push against."

Nate could see the tension slowly easing back into Grace. Even when they'd been face to face with a Worg she hadn't been that tense.

"Grace?" Curt stepped forward. "Mary, she's not good."

Grace was pale, almost green, and her muscles were pulled tight, her brow furrowed.

"Almost...just a little..."

Wham!

Nate felt the rush of air, the world tilting under him and heard the crash and splinter of furniture before he bounced off the floor.

Chapter 12

Nate blinked the stars from his eyes, cursing softly and crawling to his feet. He was careful to miss the shards of crystal ball all over the room, but his biggest concern was Grace. The rest of them had been walloped all over, but Grace was still just sitting in her chair, arms wrapped around herself, shoulders tense.

"Grace." Nate reached forward slowly, aware he wasn't entirely sure he wanted to touch her right then, even if he felt like he needed to try.

She swallowed thickly, unbelievably tense, her eyes still closed.

"Grace." He shook her softly, crouching down in front of her. "Come on Grace, look at me." His gut said he needed her to open her eyes. Needed her to stop poking at whatever it was the psychic had dredged up.

It took a moment, but she opened her eyes, blinking at him for a second, still pale and almost green.

"It's alright, just breathe." Nate wrapped his hand around the back of her neck, holding tight to the chair leg because he needed to squeeze something before he fell apart.

"Is Mary okay?" Grace managed lightly.

Nate glanced over, where Deke and Curt were helping a dazed Mary sit up. "She's fine, just thrown for a loop."

"I'm *fine*," Mary huffed, swatting them away, loud and comical and *her*. "Honestly, you'd think I was fragile or something."

Deke stood, helping her to her feet. "I think you just got thrown halfway across the room."

Mary settled her skirts, huffing.

Nate leaned his head down, trying to catch Grace's eye. "What about you?"

"Working on a major headache, I think," she muttered. "But I'm fine."

Curt looked around the room. "What the hell?"

Mary tisked, standing one of her chairs up and looking at what was left of her crystal ball. "Whatever that is, it's big. You wanna go poking at it, I think you're going to need a better plan."

Grace stood slowly, using his arm to steady herself for just a second. "Mary, do you mind if I use your bathroom?"

"No." Mary frowned at her. "It's right down that hallway, Honey."

She nodded and walked off, quiet and tense.

"I vote for not poking at it," Deke muttered.

"What the hell kind of solution is that?" Curt grumbled. "It's protecting Grace, sure. That ain't the first time it's not been precisely careful with the rest of us while it was at it."

"Well, arguing with each other isn't gonna help anything," Mary said darkly. "Curt, you can come help me make some coffee for everybody while these boys sweep up what her mysterious guardian did to my house." She handed Deke the broom, and practically drug Curt into the kitchen.

Nate hadn't missed Deke's momentary freeze when Mary said guardian. "Something you want to share?"

Deke cleared his throat. "No."

"Just because I don't say anything about the fact you're keeping secrets doesn't mean anything, really." He shifted, grabbing one of the tablecloths off the floor. "I'm looking for a handle here, and if you could help—"

"I can't."

Which was true, but he was guessing not the whole story.

"Just..." Deke stopped and rubbed his forehead, pushing his glasses off the bridge of his nose for a second. "I get that you like Grace, or whatever you want to call what you two having going on."

Nate flushed, opening his mouth.

"Even if I had answers for you, I don't think they'd be the ones you want."

He scoffed, going back to picking up. "I don't know what you think I want."

"Her, safe, without any caveats or addendums," Deke answered. "I think you and Curt need to accept, something that hides like this, it has its reasons. If it's protecting Grace I think you might have to wait until Grace starts looking under rocks."

Which would be about a quarter to never.

Finding out he had a wall of repressed memories in the back of his head would have driven him crazy in about two seconds flat. Grace came out of the bathroom five minutes after she went in, refreshed and normal.

There wasn't anything that had happened today, that shocked him. Even before Mary literally freaked out at the sight of her, he'd had a fairly good indication Grace had more than the normal amount of shit stacked in her past.

Still, her calm wasn't doing much for the rest of them.

They sat around the old blond kitchen table at Mary's, drinking coffee and talking about old jobs and strange creatures. Well, Curt and Deke did. Nate didn't feel like he had a lot to say right then, and it wasn't the sort of conversation Grace would have jumped in the middle of even on a normal day.

"I don't know." Mary frowned, leaning back in her chair. "You hunters usually seem like a blood-thirsty lot to me. Shoot first and let God sort them out. Like you've all watched too many westerns."

"Oh come on," Nate grinned. "Everybody loves a good western."

Grace scoffed. "Not all of us can watch Bonanza for eight hours straight."

He pushed at her shoulder. "Uh huh. Which of us can sing the entirety of Ghost Riders in the Sky from memory?"

Grace finished her coffee, chuckling. "That only counts if you're going to call Blues Brothers a western."

Deke's phone chirped in his pocket, and he excused himself to answer it.

Curt was three-quarters of the way through an explanation as to why he disliked Chicago so much, when Deke came back in.

"Nate?" Deke looked up from his phone, watching him. "How willing are you to do a job right now?"

He shrugged. "I'm good, and if Grace wasn't she'd have said something by now."

Grace rolled her eyes. "It's not like I do much. I'm occasionally bait, and research help."

Mary laughed darkly. "Nice try, Sugar. Don't underestimate how much easier you make his life."

Nate ignored them, and kept his eyes on Deke. "What's the job?"

Deke handed him a scrap of paper. "Sounds unusual. And those are usually the ones I call you for. Less chance of someone who doesn't deserve a bullet to the head getting one."

He took the paper, frowning at Deke's crazy sideways handwriting. "I don't know, Grace is pretty scary with that crossbow."

~~~~~~

Two Harbors, Minnesota was *unreal*.

"Whole goddamn place looks like a postcard," Nate muttered, watching as Grace jogged out of the office at a cabin rental, jangling a key at him. They were just outside of town, which worked for him in a place this small. One of those reasons having Grace along made his life easier.

She was a built in cover story. They were just a couple from the city, down for a random mini-vacation. It was a cute little place, one room log cabin with a giant fireplace, a tiny kitchen, and pretty much everything else was bed.

"Sorry." Grace thumped one of the bags on the end of the giant king-size bed. "I sort of figured it'd require a lot of explaining if I asked for a double." Her nose wrinkled. "I also might have said something about celebrating our anniversary."

He laughed, and dropped the things he was carrying. "And that was without the explaining?"

"She's…sweet." Grace wrinkled her nose. "I have trouble with 'Minnesota nice' sometimes."

He cocked a brow.

"They don't *stop* and I don't know how to make them without hurting their feelings." She flushed. "Anyway."

Nate unpacked, dropping his long succession of guns and things on the bed.

"Do you ever wonder if the assumption that strange things are going to be violent is part of the reason they always tend that way?"

He frowned, blinking at her. "What?"

"I mean we don't know anything yet. Deke got a call about a weird death, and we're here with a medium sized arsenal. I don't know. It seems harsh. Are they actually always super scary monsters?"

Nate blinked at her. "That depends on your definition of scary."

"Werewolves and revenants and stuff, yeah. Most of the ones we've run up against in the last couple of months, sure. I don't think anybody could have reasoned with that Korrigan." She shrugged. "That can't be all of them."

"It can't?"

"No." Grace scoffed. "The only way this crap stays secret from the rest of the world is if the body count's low enough not to get noticed. Given all the books Curt has, I don't think they can't all be using us for snacks."

Nate finished unpacking, moving on autopilot. Was he too harsh? That was absolutely his mom's way of hunting. That assumption that if she heard about something then it was automatically evil and needed to die. He knew some of the creatures out there lived in their own societies, with rules about hiding their existence from humans.

Did they punish people who broke that? Could he have used that? Not the Korrigan, sure. He'd dealt with a Selkie once, and he hadn't wanted to shoot him, but he hadn't felt like he had a choice. Was there some sort of person in charge he could have handed that one to?

"Sorry," Grace said softly.

"No." Nate looked up at her, blinking. "No, you're fine. I don't know if you're right. I deal with them the way it feels like I have to deal with them. But I suppose just because I'm less trigger happy than most hunters doesn't mean I couldn't do better."

He thought about it, while they finished unpacking, and found a nice little diner for food. He didn't stop thinking about it, even as they were working their way into town.

One plus side to this job, the person who'd called Deke because there was a strange death was Jon Anderson, the county coroner. They weren't trying to talk their way in to see the body, they were invited.

The Coroner was just like half of them he'd met. Everyone always thought they'd be squirly and small. Strange.

Sometimes they were. Most of them were like Anderson, capable and robust. Medical Doctors who didn't want to be medical doctors for whatever reason. Anderson was tall and blond, with a wide Norwegian face.

"Thank you for coming so quick." He shook Nate's hand seriously, before turning to Grace. "I hope the drive up wasn't too bad."

People in Minnesota seemed to assume they were 'up' from bloody everywhere except Canada.

"Traffic in Chicago," Grace shrugged.

He nodded, commiserating.

"So, this body," Nate prompted.

Anderson waved them both over to a sheet-covered table. "His name was Hank Jansen, been living in the area since he was in his twenties." He pulled the cover back. "So about ten years. Didn't know him well, but he seemed like a nice guy." He sighed. "I called Deacon because I've got no real cause of death."

Nate leaned over the table, looking the poor dead bastard over. He was about their age, fit and healthy. Well muscled, like he was active, and attractive. "Nothing?"

"Nada." Anderson shook his head. "Far as we can tell he just...stopped breathing. I convinced his wife to see you." He twitched the sheet back into place. "Said you were a friend of a friend, a private investigator. Because it looks better if all the lines are filled out on the county death report." He smiled sadly. "Even if that's not possible."

Nate straightened, stepping back from the table. "Any chance she just smothered him with a pillow?"

Anderson shook his head. "Not unless it was a pillow of air, and if it was I'd rather not know."

Nate laughed at the attempted joke, and thanked Anderson for his time. Said they'd be back in touch, and then drove them across town to a quaint little fisherman's house right on the edge of the water. It was all sweet flowers and herbs, and pale yellow siding sitting against the ridiculous black water of Lake Superior.

He didn't want to know what was in that water. Shit like Kraken grew dependent on how large the body of water they inhabited was. He'd stay well back from that.

"What do you think?" Grace asked softly, stepping up next to him.

A little boy played in the yard, sitting on a slab of patio, drawing in the cool fall air with sidewalk chalk. Clouds were rolling in over the lake, gathering overhead.

"That we're going to get rained on," he muttered. "I don't know. There are a few dozen options. Most likely is some sort of witchcraft, which means she's not going to like us much when I start asking questions."

Grace nodded. "Alright."

"Can I help you?" A young woman stood at the edge of the house, hand shielding her eyes from the lowering sun.

Nate took one look at the sweet curve of her face, the wide pretty brown eyes and silky light brown hair blowing in the breeze, and felt his blood run cold. "Shit."

Grace turned to look at him. "That's a new one for hello."

He tensed, rubbing the back of his neck. "She's an Ondine."

The woman tensed, instantly looking at her little boy, taking a half step toward him. "What... Who are you?"

Grace frowned between them. "Alright, so whatever an Ondine is, you're obviously right. Can we calm things down a bit?"

Nate's jaw twitched. "That depends on whether or not her husband knew what she was before she killed him."

"Hi, my name's Willy," the little boy said brightly. He'd moved, apparently, while they weren't paying attention to him. "I like numbers."

Nate could see the cold terror in his mother's eyes and all he could hear was Grace, hemming around the fact that he kept expecting these things to be violent and possibly making them violent.

"Hi, Willy." Nate forced himself to swallow. "That's cool. We need to talk to your Mom for a minute—"

"I like to calculate birthdays," Willy rambled off.

Nate looked down at the boy. He was fidgety, and plucking at the sleeve of his sweater, talking to Nate but looking at the ground or at his chalk or off at the lake. Nate looked at Grace, wondering if she knew what was going on with him.

She shrugged, equally confused.

"If you tell me what your birthday is and how old you are I can figure out what day you were born on."

"February twenty-third, I'm thirty-one," Nate answered, watching the kid scamper off to his chalk-area again.

"Please." His mother bit her lip. "We've had enough trouble, can't we just..." She died off, blinking back tears.

Grace grabbed his wrist softly, tugging. "Let me? At least try."

He looked between them, and took a step back. He'd stay there, and stay watchful, but if Grace was right he figured he owed her the chance to prove it. "Sure."

She tossed him a half smile. "Hi. Sorry. My name's Grace." She held a hand out to the woman, easy and uncomplicated, but not unknowing.

"Hi." The other woman swallowed. "Erin."

"Erin." Grace shook her hand. "Is your son alright out here alone if we go inside and talk?"

"What..." She looked between them, confused.

"We're interested in what happened with your husband," Grace said softly. "I'd just like to talk."

~~~~~~

Erin hadn't spoken, once they'd gone in the house. She'd made her son come in—she thought it looked like rain too—and he was enthroned in the corner of the room with a dry erase board bigger than he was, trying to figure out what day of the week Nate had been born on.

Erin had silently made coffee, and put some cookies on a plate—what the shit was *wrong* with people in Minnesota?—and sat things on the table. She'd sat down, and doctored her cup after they'd helped themselves, and never said a word.

"He didn't cheat on me."

As opening gambits went, he'd heard worse.

"I'm sorry?" Grace frowned. "I don't actually know what an Ondine is."

"Type of water nymph," Nate offered softly. "They can marry a human man, and have his baby, and then they can stay human if they like." He cleared his throat. "But they carry a curse, because the one the legend comes from... He promised to be faithful all his waking hours or something ridiculous like that, and then she caught him sleeping with a maid or whoever and she cursed him that he'd die when he fell asleep."

Erin nodded. "He didn't cheat on me." She huffed. "And even if he had, it's not..." She stopped, struggling to speak, face canted toward the table, tears gathering in her eyes.

"It's a curse you can use, not one you have?" Grace offered softly, handing the woman a Kleenex.

"What are we going to do?" Erin sniffled, looking at the table, hands in her lap. "Hank was so good, and with Willy and how...special he is." She swallowed. "My parents aren't..." She wiped her face. "They didn't approve of Hank, and even if they had, I can't take Willy to live with them. He's human." She blew her nose. "Sort of missing some required equipment for living at the bottom of the lake."

Grace winced. "Oh. Well, there are all sorts of programs, to help single mothers." She grinned. "You don't live in the socialist republic of the north for nothing."

Erin almost laughed, looking up at her.

"And it sounded like people in town liked Hank. I'm sure they'll help."

Erin wiped her face again. "Why are you being so nice to me?"

"Do I need a reason?" Grace frowned. "From where I'm sitting you've had a pretty crappy week."

"You're hunters." Erin bit her lip, like she didn't want to insult them.

"If you haven't done anything wrong, you became human when you married Hank," Nate offered. He wasn't entirely sure that was true, but he'd give her the benefit of the doubt. "But if someone's done this to him, we need to know who."

Erin looked away, watching her son in the corner.

Nate opened his mouth, intent on pressing her. He got that these were her people, and she was going to have to sell someone upstream, but clearly they were dangerous.

Grace shook her head no, motioning him to silence.

Erin looked back at them after a moment. "I can take care of it myself."

"Take care of it?" Nate swallowed.

"Erin." Grace winced. "I'm not saying that I doubt you could. If something happens to you, Willy—"

"Nothing will happen to me." Erin balled the Kleenex in her hand. "Thank you for your concern, but—"

"Mommy?" Willy came over suddenly, tugging at her shirt. "That woman's standing out in the yard again."

They all jumped up, Nate instinctively going for the knife he kept in the hidden sheath on the back of his belt. Grace—just as instinctively, apparently—grabbed his wrist before he got there.

An older woman stood on the sloped, rocky shore between the house and the lake. Tall and willowy, with gray skin and clumpy hair, watching them through eerily wide eyes.

"I want to go see her," Willy stated.

Nate watched in horror as the kid tore out the door before any of them could get a hand on him.

Grace wasn't as slow as he and Erin were. She was out the door two steps behind Willy, reaching out to grab him, before he stopped a few feet from the older Ondine. They could hear his voice, through the open screen.

"I like birthdays, they tell a lot about people." Willy paused, looking up at Grace like he didn't understand why she was there. "People born on a Tuesday are always nice. People born on Thursdays are selfish."

The Ondine standing on the shore watched him coldly. "And what do you say about people born on Saturday?" Her voice floated, light and beckoning.

The problem with water nymphs was even if they were nice, they were perfectly capable of luring you into the water and letting you drown. He'd dealt with more than one who would have, just for fun.

"My Daddy was born on a Saturday, and he used to be kind of slow out of bed on Sundays, and he never wanted to go to church even when Momma thought they should take me because that's what people do, but he worked hard and he loved her very much. She misses him."

The Ondine frowned, cocking her head to the side. "Don't you miss him?"

Willy shrugged, looking down. "Yeah."

Nate swallowed, watching through the kitchen door. "Erin, who is that?"

Erin's hands were white over the back of her chair, shoulders tense. "My mother."

The Ondine looked at Grace then, face leaching of anything that looked remotely kind. "I'd like to speak with my daughter. Eri-en, come out here."

Erin pushed the chair away, and took three steps toward the door before Nate caught the edge of her shirtsleeve. "I'm not sure that's a good idea."

"What?"

"If she hurt your husband…"

Erin blinked at him. "It wasn't my mother."

He swallowed. "Okay. Still, I'd be careful around her like that." He motioned to Erin, who looked human and soft.

Erin glared at him, shrugging him off and going out the door. "I'm here, Mother."

Nate slipped out behind her, wondering how badly this was going to go.

The Ondine glared at him. "Keeping company with hunters now?"

Erin wrapped her arms around Willy, holding him tight. "They're only here because they had questions about what happened to my husband!"

Erin's mother didn't have anything to say to that, apparently. They watched each other in silence for a long while, before she cleared her throat. "What is wrong with the boy?"

"Nothing." Erin spat, glaring at her. "There's nothing wrong with him. He's brilliant and perfect and—"

"Mommy." Willy huffed. "The doctor said it was okay to tell people I have Asperger's." He looked at his grandmother. "My brain doesn't work like everybody else's. There's nothing wrong with me, I'm just different."

Nate winced, feeling like an intruder. Talk about a family matter.

"Tell her if I see her again I'll rip her apart with my bare hands," Erin said, voice low and hard. "And I don't want—"

"You won't," her mother interrupted. "She was given to the sea."

Grace swallowed, paling. "What does that mean?"

The Ondine looked at Grace, but decided not to do anything about her having the audacity to talk, which he was good with. The knife behind his back would have worked, and he'd have used it to protect Grace, but it'd be grand if they didn't need that.

"She was judged, because she killed a human unprovoked and brought hunters to our midst." She looked at her daughter then, gray-brown eyes sad. "But I have already lost one daughter."

Erin narrowed her eyes. "You told me I was dead to you the day I got married."

"I simply—"

"Right." Grace cut across them. "Um...I think you probably don't want to air your family business in front of complete strangers?" she offered, smiling tensely. "So I'll leave you a phone number Erin, if you need anything." She turned to look at Erin's mother. "If you can promise nobody else is going to wind up dead over this we'll get out of your way. Sound good Nate?"

"Works for me," he managed, biting back on his instinctual laughter.

"You do not stipulate only humans will be unharmed?" The older Ondine asked, cold and haughty.

"No?" Grace looked between them all. "I apparently missed the memo that put stipulations on what sort of life was precious."

"There will be no more violence," Erin's mother said easily, like she was doing them a favor.

And Nate maybe wanted to call her on that, but Grace was looking like she was about ready to drag him for the car.

"Unless you really *wanted* to watch them have a mother-daughter moment. I get the feeling Erin can take care of herself, and Willy," Grace said, opening the car door.

Nate looked back, as he crawled in the car, watching the two women have a conversation over the head of a little boy.

This whole touchy-feely, mending families thing was going to take a little getting used to.

~~~~~~

Grace slid onto the hood of the Charger with him, passing him a bottle of some local berry drink before she twisted the lid off her own. "Please tell me you're not sorry you didn't have to shoot anyone."

Nate rolled his eyes, shoving her with his elbow while he opened his own. "I'm not."

"Good." She took a sip, settling in. "Because then I'd have to call Curt, and he'd make noises at us for the next twenty or thirty years."

He coughed, shaking his head. He was maybe a little weirded out by how the job had ended. They'd stuck around long enough to make sure things were actually alright. For the coroner to have a somewhat believable prognosis no-one was going to argue with, and for Erin to say she and her parents were working things out and the Ondine in the area were back to hiding like they should be.

They'd leave in the morning, barring incident, which meant sitting at the edge of Lake Superior on the hood of his car, sharing a drink and watching the sunset.

Well, watching the sky change colors. They were pointed the wrong direction to watch the sun sink down. He was fine what that. The sun went down fast that time of year in Minnesota anyway. Seemed like when they sat down it was bright and evening, and now the first stirrings of stars were popping into the blue over his head, crescent moon hanging off to their side.

"Okay, I'm going to say this out loud, because I'm sure we're both thinking it, and you're just being nice to me." Nate nudged her with his shoulder. "It's a little throwing, like I'm missing some closure, but you were right and I'm glad we played this your way."

Grace smiled, leaning against his shoulder. "We could find some random thing to burn in the woods, if it'd make you feel better?"

"Don't joke, it might," Nate muttered, taking a sip.

He could see why people looked for this. Someplace quiet to just put down roots. It maybe wouldn't be so bad, if you had someone to share it with. Not that he was angling for anything.

Grace made a noise, next to him. "Shooting star."

Nate instantly looked up, even if he knew he wouldn't see it, and missed Grace leaning in and pressing her lips against his cheek. "What?" He had to clear his throat, heart pounding in his chest. "What was that?"

"Star magic," she answered perfectly seriously. "Haven't you ever done that?"

"Um...no?"

She shrugged. "Sharing star magic. Figured you could use some."

Nate swallowed. With anybody else on the planet, he'd have called that a pick-up line. The problem was, he was never entirely sure if Grace realized she'd crossed a boundary with him. Or if it was just him, crossing stupid lines in his head because they'd been sleeping in the same bed for the last three days.

And he knew her, well enough to know he could have reached forward and kissed her, and if he got something wrong she wouldn't hold it against him. They'd still be friends and still work together and everything would be fine.

Only he was probably already a little more invested than that, whether he wanted to admit it or not.

Grace leaned back on her hands, humming along with the radio and watching the clouds and the stars.

"So what do you do if you see a satellite?"

She laughed, glancing at him. "Wave to Mother Russia?"

He laughed, shaking his head. "I'm not sure they'd like my wave."

Grace grinned. "I think we're in the wrong state to have issues with socialists."

"Minnesota is really known as the socialist republic?" he asked, shaking his head.

"It is." Her head fell against his shoulder. "But it seems like it'd be a nice place to live. Well, not so much if you don't like water, but still."

Nate opened his mouth, because he was fine about water. It was the shit that lived *in* the water he had a problem with.

Now you're messin' with a son of a bitch, his phone sounded.

He groaned, dropping his head back.

Grace blew a raspberry. "If it's a job we've...I don't know. One of us broke a long bone or something. Just until tomorrow."

He chuckled, fishing the phone out. "We've been temporarily decapitated." He glanced at the screen, wincing before he answered. "Hey Curt."

"Good." Curt sounded rushed. "I thought you'd still be in the middle of that thing in Minnesota."

"Nope. All wrapped up." He scuffed the side of his shoe. "We were leaving in the morning. Theoretically back to you, unless you're changing that."

"How difficult is it to leave tonight?"

"Not." Nate frowned, shooting Grace a look. She sighed, and hopped off the car. "We've paid for the room, and there's a night drop for the keys. What's up?"

"I found a spell."

"You found a spell." Nate rubbed the back of his neck. "I'm not *fond* of those. What's this one do?"

"It makes whatever's following Grace around come say 'hello' properly," Curt answered, the sound of a cardoor slamming in the background. "I'll meet you at Deke's."

Chapter 13

Grace watched the now familiar sight of the edges of Chicago start to roll by the window. It wasn't as if it'd been particularly unfamiliar before. She'd driven by the outer bit frequently enough, between her and Jamie.

Deke was on the other side of town and considerably further south. She was starting to learn that bit now, to recognize the landmarks between the main circle and the turn-off for Deke's neighborhood.

It'd been a quiet, long night. They'd spent a couple of hours of it pretending to sleep at a rest stop —she was pretty sure that'd been mutual—before throwing themselves back onto the road again. Curt had called once to check in and see where they were.

Deke had called while they were stopped, and whatever that conversation had been about Nate had felt compelled to walk away from the car for a bit to have it.

Nate and Deke's conversation hadn't fixed everything. Hadn't fixed much of anything actually, that she could tell. Deke and Curt had opinions. And even if she wasn't all that interested in their opinions, Nate had so much stuff hanging over his head—his willingness to walk away from any relationship he'd had with his mother cast a long shadow—Grace thought maybe getting one more thing out in the open might help.

Mostly she was grasping at straws.

Nate pulled up to the curb outside of Deke's shop, and cut the engine. His hands wrapped tight around the wheel and he twisted them, knuckles turning white.

Grace cleared her throat.

"Are you okay with this?" Nate asked softly, voice low.

"Am I..."

Nate looked up at her, eyes clear and sad. "Because last I remembered your vote was for leaving this...whatever it is, alone."

Grace shifted, settling her sleeves. "I'm not..." She stopped, and swallowed. Actually *saying* that she didn't want to but she'd play along to make him feel better was going to go badly.

"Yeah." Grace forced a smile. "I'm good."

She stepped out of the car, and watched Nate crawl out on the other side. He pulled on his jacket and reached into the back to retrieve his bag. Curt's truck was just a bit up the street, and the lights in the downstairs of the shop were turned off, the sign turned to closed.

Nate walked up and tried the door, hauling it open. The jingle of the bell on the door echoed through the dark space.

"Lock it behind you," Curt shouted down from the back stairs.

Nate rolled his eyes, and snubbed the lock after she stepped through.

Curt was standing at the top of the stairs, waiting for them. "You look undamaged."

"Grace took care of it. It was quiet," Nate said.

"Grace did?"

Nate waved it off, looking around him.

"Deke's in the kitchen," Curt muttered, and turned back to the pile of books spread out over the small coffee table.

Grace followed Nate into the small kitchen, listening to the somewhat ominous sound of cabinets opening and closing rapidly.

Deke slammed the one in front of him, muttering as he dug through a small pile of bottles.

She didn't know how Deke managed not to poison himself. Most of the nondescript things he had lying around in his kitchen nobody wanted to eat.

He turned, and stared at them both. Grace watched something quiet and tense pass between he and Nate, before Deke nodded to her and went back to what he was doing.

"I think Curt needs to chalk out of the bottom cabinet still," Deke grumbled.

Grace grabbed the chalk, because she'd met Deke twice and if he was going to talk to anyone it was probably Nate. It was better for her to just get out of the way of that.

She helped Curt for a minute, while he chalked something on the floor in the living room. When he finished he went downstairs to find something he'd left in the office, and Grace wandered back toward the kitchen.

Grace stopped at the door into the kitchen, the tight sound of Deke's voice floating through the doorway.

"No, this isn't going to go badly," Deke muttered.

A loud clang echoed, and Grace jumped, one hand pushing at the door.

"Sorry," Nate muttered.

There was a long pause, and a scoff she pegged on Deke.

"Dude, if you've got a complaint, then *tell me.*"

"It's a bad idea," Deke said at the same time.

Grace winced, and stayed on the other side of the door. She could have walked into the room, and they'd have stopped arguing and gone back to pretending.

Deke was about to burst something.

"Damn it Deke," Nate started.

She heard a bang—probably another cabinet, Deke hadn't exactly been nice to those so far. That was most of how she understood how tense he was.

"I've said until I'm blue in the face this is a bad idea. I'm still letting you do it in my *house*. I'm still letting you use supplies." Deke paused, shuffling around unseen on the other side of the door. "I don't know what level of cooperation you think you're entitled to that you're not getting."

"Right," Nate snapped, low and dark. "You've told me twelve times you don't think this is a good idea. You won't tell me *why*. Or what about this has you so spooked," he growled. "Because I can tell you, from where I'm standing, you being scared of this thing when I don't even know what it is isn't convincing me not to try and find out."

Grace swallowed, feeling the silence stretch, and started trying to decide when she should walk in. If she should walk in.

"And you've got your secrets man, and I'm fine with that." Nate paused. "Usually."

"You're doing this because of Grace and she's doing it to keep you happy, or Curt happy. I'm not sure anyone or anything knows what's going on in that girl's head. Including her."

"Grace said she was okay with it," Nate reminded.

"Yeah," Deke scoffed. "Because you're attached to her. I got that. I'm sorry if I'm not doing real good on where that leaves you."

"It doesn't leave me anywhere," Nate said, voice dark. "And fuck you very much, I'm an adult and I can take care of myself."

Grace smiled, shaking her head.

Deke huffed out a chuckle, and suddenly they were both laughing, letting out some of the tension. "That was nice."

"Sorry." He huffed. "Just, much as Curt can forget it, I'm an adult."

"Yeah." Deke paused. "Trust me on this? This isn't one of those things you want me to make easier for you."

Curt's footsteps sounded, coming up the stairs, and Grace walked in the kitchen then, rather than being caught hanging around outside the door. Deke went back to what he was doing, letting an uneasy silence settle over them.

They'd been at it for a while when Grace blew out a breath, flopping into a chair with a mortar and pestle. "Double double, toil and trouble, fire burn and cauldron bubble..."

Nate laughed. "Which witch am I again?"

Grace's lips twitched. "Well, if Curt's running things, I figure he's witch number one. And I'd say Deke was witch number two, but he's pretty unwilling, so I guess that makes you number two."

"And what's that make you?" Deke asked wryly.

"The newt," Grace answered. "I'm pretty sure that's preferable to Lady Macbeth."

Nate picked up his pile of supplies to add to the main one, and walked them out to the cleared space in the living room. Grace watched him leave, and almost started counting in her head. She figured there were maybe ten seconds until Deke exploded.

"Are you seriously just going along with this?"

He'd made it about ten seconds longer than she thought he would. "I understand that you're worried."

"Yeah, I am," Deke agreed. "Because not that I don't like you..."

She scoffed, watching him, because she and Deke were civil, but they weren't comfortable with each other.

Deke cleared his throat. "Well, I don't know you, but I can't imagine they do either, it's only been a couple of months."

"I've known Curt for two years," Grace said. "If you've missed that story I'm impressed."

195

"I did." Deke frowned.

Grace twisted the pestle again. She didn't understand why Nate wouldn't have shared that, but it didn't matter. If it'd been imperative she keep it secret he'd have said. "He saved my bacon when one of the local guys turned into a not-werewolf."

"That makes a little more sense. Nate?"

"Nearly three months," Grace answered easily. "That we've been within twenty feet of each other probably ninety percent of the time? So I'm sure that's something ridiculous in normal people years."

"Normal people years?" Deke asked, smiling.

Grace shrugged.

"He's...fond of you." Deke managed, careful and strange.

"Curt?" Grace questioned. "Yeah, I think he's got a saving people thing. Well, I mean I'm pretty sure everyone in this business has some sort of saving people thing, or revenge thing, or whatever. But I do like Curt, I know that's a bit of a concern."

Deke blinked at her, vacant. "I didn't mean... um...yeah, I suppose they do."

Nate stumbled back through the door, empty bowl in hand, and headed back for the counter. Deke flushed, turning back to what he'd been doing, back straight.

Which was weird, but Nate smiled at Grace, and shrugged like he didn't understand it either. "I think we're about done with all this." Nate grabbed another pile of supplies from Grace.

"Yay," Deke muttered, grabbing one as well.

They all moved out into the main living area. Nate glanced over the chalk circle on the floor, checking the rune work and symbols around the edges.

Grace wasn't sure about spell-work. It wasn't the first time she'd seen something that looked more at home in medieval times than modern day, but it still felt strange, gearing up for that.

"Right." Curt stood from the center, looking around him. "That's all of it." He nodded. "I do this stuff in order, and say the words, and it should make whatever this is come—"

"Whoop your ass for bothering it?" Deke muttered softly, voice tense.

Curt glared at him. "Yes, you've given us your opinion."

"It's a fundamental issue you don't seem to be grasping though," Deke said angrily. "You're insisting you have to do this because you aren't sure this thing is friendly, and therefore you're going to *poke it with a stick.*"

"I'm doing something, before things get so bad we're stuck wondering where we lost the thread at, when it starts—"

"Randomly saving someone else's life?" Deke countered. "Perfect. Grand plan. Did you check to make sure Grace wasn't going along with this just for you? Do you even know what this spell is? Did you tell them where you found it?"

Curt looked at him, eyes narrowed. "What would you know about spells? Been keeping more secrets then normal there, Deacon."

"Curt," Nate warned softly.

"Because you seem to know a lot about this," Curt continued.

Deke crossed his arms over his chest. "I'm not the issue here. There's serious possible blow-back from this, never mind how I know, and I'd like to know if you mentioned that to Grace. Or Nate, for that matter." He cocked a brow. "Didn't want to make him choose? Or were you just that sure he'd tell you to go ahead anyway?"

Grace sighed, rubbing her temple. Aside from how little help them all standing around yelling at each other was, they were already there. "Am I allowed to express an opinion here?"

"No, because if you wind up dead I'll never forgive myself," Curt said.

Deke huffed, and crossed his arms over his chest mulishly.

Nate winced, pushing a hand through his hair.

A white flash lit the room next to them, and Grace felt all the blood whoosh out of her head.

"I think she is," a strange, male voice snapped, echoing in the small space.

Chapter 14

Nate pulled his knife out, hand hard around the hilt. His heart smashed against his chest. Deke had some pretty serious security set up. Whoever their new friend was he'd just popped right into the middle of all of that like it was nothing.

The new guy was tall and broad, with blond hair and a sort of strange stillness to him. He looked like a Greek god out of a classic painting. Eerie light blue eyes watched them, dusting a speck off his shoulder. He looked around the room, letting the silence stretch. "Well." He looked at Curt, then Nate. "You were so keen to meeting me."

Deke swallowed, and twitched like he'd finally decided to reach for a weapon.

Curt had a pistol out, leveled at their guest and Nate didn't need him to try to pull the trigger to know it wasn't going to work.

"Who the hell are you?" Curt asked.

Grace stumbled, fetching up against his side, hand pressing to her temple.

"Grace?" Deke turned, his face darkening.

Nate grabbed her elbow, feeling her knees go weak, her weight dragging him forward. "Grace?"

"I'm...fine. There's this...buzzing...and..." She shook her head. "It's like I remember something but..."

"No!" The new guy, whoever he was, took a giant step toward Grace, reaching out for her. "Do not push at it, you cannot—"

She gasped, and Nate felt her start to collapse. She shook her head, and blinked at him.

Deke cursed darkly, suddenly there, grabbing the back of Grace's head in his hand. "Grace, listen to my voice, you have to calm down." He shook her slightly. "*Pes ahanet nea matal nea fea*," he muttered.

Grace twitched, sucking in a breath and turning ghostly pale.

"Shit. Shit shit shit..." Deke pulled a strange stick out of his pocket and pressed it against Grace's temple, voice low and commanding. "*Tahalamat eset duoath.*"

Her eyes rolled back in her head and she went limp, falling into Nate's arms. Nate locked his knees, keeping them both up, and watched the steady rise and fall of her chest.

Deke turned back to the new guy, cursing darkly. "For future reference, telling a human being not to poke at the...guard you've put in their head is probably the worst thing you could do!"

Nate shook her softly, pushing her hair back with his free hand. "Grace—"

"No." Deke grabbed his shoulder, fingers digging in tight. "Don't wake her up."

Nate swallowed, heart beating like crazy. "Okay, what do I do?"

"Get her on the couch," Deke said, already patting the cushions. "She's got this giant poisonous sore in her head, I didn't push at it so I don't actually know what caused it. But she needs to heal past it."

"And the spell?" Curt asked darkly.

The new guy glared at Curt, huffing. "The spell was less problematic than all that." He looked pointedly at the floor. He turned toward Grace then, movements tense and jerky. "Will she heal?"

"If she sleeps all the way through it she'll probably be fine," Deke answered. "If she was weak she wouldn't have survived whatever that was in the first place."

Their new friend frowned.

Deke looked at Nate expectantly, and normally he'd be all over jumping in with questions. If he had any. If he could really focus on anything beyond Grace, lax and unnaturally still on the couch.

Deke looked expectantly at the new guy. "Would you like to give us a name?"

"Samriel."

"Samriel," Deke repeated. "You weren't showing yourself because?" he prompted.

He looked at Deke, then right back to Grace. "Grace created the block herself, as a child. She was..." He frowned. "She would not want me to explain that. Excuse me." He looked between them. "I did not appear to her because I was afraid that my presence would..." he died off, unsure how to continue.

"Make that happen?" Deke muttered, making sure she was settled.

He nodded. "We are not adept with human mental injuries."

~~~~~~

Nate stood in the open kitchen door and stared at them.

At the moment Samriel was sitting in an uncomfortable folding chair, watching Grace like the universe depended on her continued health. They'd all left him to it. Because however much Nate might have wanted to just plant himself next to Grace, he did have a question or two he'd like the answer to.

"So." Curt huffed, arms folded over his chest, zeroed in on Deke. "You wanna bring the rest of us up to speed?"

Deke shifted, back straight and defensive. "My personal history is mine." He flicked a glance at Nate. "I'm not...I was struggling for a way to make you understand why this was a bad idea without telling you any of this about me." He pinched the bridge of his nose around his glasses. "What you think you know about witches doesn't even scratch the surface."

"Tell us something we don't know," Curt grouched.

Deke rolled his eyes. "You talked about thinking there were family connections in dark witches, so maybe..." He shrugged. "Surprise."

"So what are you?" Nate managed, glancing away from Grace for a second.

"Nothing," Deke answered, maybe a little too fast. "I'm not the issue here. My family is...we lost our Warder generations ago."

"Warder?"

Deke winced. "I'm not supposed to explain this to normal people, so you'll have to bear with me if I'm not sure where to start," he grumbled. "That thing in my living room, watching Grace sleep, is a Warder. Technically he's a Maeleket? They're like *everything*. The genesis for the human concept of angels and demons and fae and whatever else." He swallowed. "There's a group of them that works with *not-dark* witches and wizards. They assign somehow, I couldn't tell you how, to a family and stick with the first born child of every generation in that line." He puffed out a breath. "Which I'm guessing would be Grace."

"Would he ever hurt her?" Nate asked, the words just popping out.

"Never," Deke shook his head. "She's presumably clean and she's the First, he's been going to a lot of trouble to keep her healthy, I'm sure." He frowned. "Which probably means her line isn't in good shape."

Nate swallowed, shifting. "So you're a wizard?"

"No," Deke answered. "I can do...it's not really magic the way you think of magic. It's mostly family magic though, and my family's not in much better shape than Grace's likely is."

"Is that your coven?" Curt asked.

"It's what they use covens to replace," Deke explained. "Listen, I am sorry. You're all pretty decently anti witchcraft and I don't practice."

Nate cocked a brow at him.

"With the exception of when your not-girlfriend is about to accidentally break her brain," Deke huffed. "It's complicated. We lost our Warder because my grandfather was leaning a little dark."

"And then?" Curt prompted.

"And then everyone ostracized them, as they do, and that was that," Deke answered. " The society is a little strange and insular. Lose your Watcher and you might as well be dark, whether you are or not."

"So these Watchers..." Curt glanced into the living room, curious.

Deke watched them, shaking his head. "He's probably been showing a ridiculous amount of restraint."

Samriel made a noise, not even shifting.

"But I don't understand why she managed to get into trouble in the first place," Deke continued. "If he's supposed to be watching her."

Samriel sighed. "I will explain to Grace, and if she does not mind that you hear I will not hide anything. You have all protected her when I was unable."

None of them had a response for that. Eventually Curt pulled a face and went to start cleaning up. Nate moved around with him, scrubbing the chalk lines off the floor with a damp rag, and rolling the rug back into the center of the room. He settled the coffee table back into its normal place, and tried not to stare at the man watching Grace.

It wasn't just because of Grace. Sure, he was a little freaked because she was goddamn unconscious and there was something *wrong with her brain*. But Deke had said at least three times she'd get better, as long as she slept through it. They just needed to keep her asleep and give her time to heal.

He chanced going close to the guy, picking up the last of their aborted supplies. The bowl in his arms was full of five or six different herbs, a couple of twigs, and something that looked suspiciously like a dried chicken liver.

Samriel didn't move. Just sat there, staring at Grace. Nate wasn't even sure he was blinking. He made his way back into the kitchen, swallowing. "Are they all like that?"

Deke looked up, blinking. "Like?"

"Creepy?" Nate asked.

Deke laughed. "You're asking me like I've ever seen one before. I told you my family lost ours long before I came along."

"Then how do you know what he is?" Curt asked, voice dark.

"My Grandmother was full of stories," Deke answered. "And there are very few things that could just slide right on through my warding. And the way the Tupelaq downstairs jumped at her."

Nate blinked, swallowing. "It recognized that she was whatever you said?"

"A First, yeah." Deke shifted, wrinkling his nose. "And there are all these signals kids in the society are taught, to see our own. Things that won't mean anything to normal people."

"Like a mason's handshake or something," Curt said, impressed.

"Something like that," Deke agreed. "Anyway. She didn't do any of that."

"Probably doesn't know," Curt offered. "Or it's suppressed with whatever else all that was about."

"Yeah, I guessed." Deke leaned back against the counter. "But usually if she's a First—and she'd have to be for the Tupelaq to just jump at her." He shrugged. "Even if the line's broken and the First is an orphan or whatever, usually one of us tracks them down and tells them something."

Curt puffed out a breath. "If his presence is what triggered that he might have kept that from happening."

Deke dumped a pile of herbage into a bag, throwing it in the trash. "Okay, so you were wrong to force this stuff out, because it's not good." He wrinkled his nose. "But I wouldn't have depended on a memory block like that staying solid. That sort of blocking is a dangerous business, and it doesn't actually fix anything. I can see it being instinctual, because I don't know anyone who practices healing who would do that to her."

Nate poured himself a cup of coffee. "Does Samriel eat or drink? Should we offer him something?"

"Might as well try." He scoffed. "I wouldn't even talk to him. You're probably okay. You're normal, and Grace is attached to you."

Nate grabbed an extra cup, filling it. He took a breath and walked into the living room. He felt Samriel's attention shift, right away, but Nate hadn't ever been a chicken. "I didn't know if you wanted a cup of coffee."

Samriel stared at it, confused, and took the cup. "No, but I'll take it from you."

"Sure." Nate swallowed. "Listen…"

"Grace is resilient. She will heal well."

Nate frowned, and just gave up and pulled up a chair. "I'm sorry, I'm just…I have questions."

Samriel looked at him, watching him sit down.

"Deke thinks you'll put up with me. Because I'm a normal human."

"No." Samriel looked back at Grace. "But Grace is fond of you."

"And you're fond of Grace?"

Samriel sat utterly still, watching Grace and didn't answer.

"Okay. Are you only watching her because it's a job?"

Nate was taking a chance, asking questions about Samriel because he'd said he wouldn't share answers about Grace unless she said it was okay.

Samriel glanced at him for a moment, jaw tense. "I no longer have a regular job as a Warder. I requested that I be allowed to continue watching Grace, even though they consider the line broken."

"But she's still alive."

"She has no child, and she is untrained." Samriel looked down at the cup of coffee. "What is this?"

Nate coughed, and choked on his drink. "Coffee?"

"Ah."

"You've never had coffee?"

He shrugged. "Grace didn't drink coffee before college." He wrinkled his nose. "I stopped watching her daily then. She was an adult." He sniffed it carefully. "It contains caffeine?"

"Yeah."

Samriel sat it down carefully. "I do not believe this would be a good time to find out if it causes any reaction with my strange physiology."

Nate snorted, finishing his. "Probably not."

He watched Grace, the way she settled into the couch. The way she slept peacefully. Well. Sort of peacefully. He could see the slow build-up of pressure between her brows. The way she started to shift uncomfortably.

Deke showed up suddenly. "She's having a nightmare. You need to calm her down."

Nate watched carefully, waiting for Samriel to do something. Eventually he realized Samriel and Deke were both looking at him. "Me?"

Deke rolled his eyes at him. "Whatever he is to her, she doesn't know his voice, brainiac. You've been what, three feet away for two months? Calm her down."

Nate swallowed, and leaned close, pulling the blanket up near her shoulders. "Shhh...Grace." Nate brushed her hair back carefully. "You're okay."

She shifted for a moment longer, before curling in slightly and settling again.

He sank back into his seat carefully, head spinning.

The steady ring of Grace's phone echoed through the room, and Nate looked around, wondering if he should find where she'd put it.

"Someone should answer that," Samriel intoned darkly. "Jameson will worry if she does not answer."

Curt dug the phone out, from a pile of papers, and swallowed. "Right. Here ya go Nate."

"Why me?"

"He talks to you on the phone, and you and Grace are usually together."

Nate swallowed, taking the phone. "I hate you all." He paused for a second, before connecting the call. "Hey Jamie."

Chapter 15

Nate had been lying to Jamie basically since the first time he talked to the guy. Maybe not outright. He'd never said Grace was alright when she wasn't, or that he could keep her safe when he didn't think he could. He'd never *said* he was a bounty hunter.

He'd never said he wasn't, either. He'd said they had a job, and let the other guy think they were just hunting down tax evaders or something. Whatever bounty hunters actually did. He'd said everything was fine, and left out the part about them tracking a werewolf, or a Korrigan or…whatever.

He didn't precisely feel guilty about that. It was Grace's choice whether or not she wanted to share everything with Jamie. He'd never thought she wasn't telling him because he wouldn't believe it. She had her own reasons, and he respected her enough to leave them to her.

So when Nate answered Grace's phone and the first words out of Jamie's mouth were "Where's Grace?" Nate hadn't had an answer prepared. In his defense, it'd been a long day, and things were still strange.

"I feel like a broken record," Deke said, voice dark. "But this is a bad idea."

Nate sighed, leaning against the doorway, waiting. "It's the way they are. There's no amount of 'It's under control' that was going to work." He swallowed. "And I've talked to him enough he can tell I'm uneasy."

Deke sighed. "I know. And I'm not saying you should have managed some sort of lie, or not told him where we were, I guess." He rubbed his brow. "If they're that close it might help Grace to have him around while she's dealing with whatever poisonous thing is locked in the back of her head."

Nate snorted. That probably hadn't helped him not fail at lying. It was stupid, given he'd never met Jamie, but if Grace was in trouble something in his gut said Jamie should be around.

"Talk about dropping someone in the deep-end."

"I suppose there's no chance he knows," Nate muttered.

"If he did, he's never said anything *their entire lives.* Does that seem likely?"

Nate thought over all the conversations he'd overhead, and the few he'd had with Jamie. "No. He doesn't know." Nate looked out the shop window at movement. A car pulled to the curb, the engine cutting almost immediately and a door popping open.

Nate blinked. He'd talked to Jamie on the phone a lot, and he knew he was harder than you'd expect, given the fact he was a social worker and a sociology professor. But he'd still slotted him somewhere in the 'professor' mind-frame. The guy jogging up to the door was taller than he was, and broad shouldered. He wore rough ratty jeans and an old t-shirt, and his face was all business.

"Is that him?"

"I think so." He nodded. "Grace didn't keep a lot of pictures around." The ones he'd seen, he could see the kid in them growing into the man in front of him. He had the shame careless shaggy hair and sharp jaw line.

Jamie hauled the door open, and stepped through just as it started to rain, and looked right at Nate. "Where is she?"

Nate swallowed. He'd maybe sort of expected to be greeted with a fist to the face. "Upstairs. Listen..."

Jamie slapped him on the shoulder. "It's...whatever. Nice to meet you Nate, you can explain later," he said easily, and then pushed past them and took the stairs two at a time.

Nate followed him up, not quite as quickly, but he wasn't sure Curt was going to naturally assume that the guy running up the stairs was okay.

Jamie didn't pause, brushed right past Curt with a mumbled hello, and headed straight for Grace. Nate had expected some kind of introduction. Samriel obviously knew who Jamie was. He'd have to, if he'd been watching Grace for any length of time. So he'd thought maybe there'd be a 'Nice to meet you' or *something*.

Instead as soon as Jamie got near Grace, Samriel took two steps back, standing next to the wall. Like if Jamie was there then he wasn't allowed to be.

"Christ," Curt muttered.

Nate seconded that, he wasn't sure how much more complicated things could get, but he just about expected them to find a way.

Jamie grabbed Nate's chair, and pulled it close. He tucked Grace in just so and pushed her hair off to the side, making sure she was comfortable. "How long's she been asleep for?"

"About four hours," Deke offered, moving forward.

"And she's not hurt?"

"No." Deke shook his head. "Well...she's hurt but it's not recent. It's...complicated, and there's a lot I'd have to explain before that would make sense." He pushed a hand through his hair. "She's in a sort of healing sleep, and we need her to stay that way for as long as she can? And then she'll wake up naturally. How she is then is contingent on exactly what she's healing from. And I don't know that. I

210

could find out, but I'd rather not go poking around at her brain without her consent."

Jamie looked them over. "So I've got Deke," he said and nodded to Deke. "And Curt," he said, before looking over at Samriel. "Who are you?"

Samriel watched him, tense and quiet, like he didn't know how to answer.

"We're all sort of waiting to find that out," Curt offered eventually. "Samriel said he'd explain to Grace when she was awake."

"I would not want to share her secrets." Samriel twitched slightly. "To them."

Deke huffed out a laugh. "Long story short and vastly over-simplified, his name is Samriel and he's… Whatever else he is, he's an immortal being that's called a Watcher. They're supposed to help certain, special humans."

Samriel frowned. "The families are not human."

Deke blinked. "What?"

"You are not human," Samriel reiterated. "Though I suppose at this point there is little difference. You are Nephete because you are a different race, once a blending of Maeleket and human. If you were simply human we would leave you to your own devices."

Deke huffed, and glanced at Jamie. "Right, so clearly you're not the only one who needs explanations still."

Jamie swallowed, looking annoyed, and Nate was waiting for the blow-up because he'd heard bits of Jamie's temper over the months.

"Right." Jamie turned, looking back at Grace.

~~~~~~

Deke moved around the kitchen, trying to make food. Nate felt for him. The space was starting to feel a little over-taken for him and it wasn't his house. What with Curt, and Samriel, and Nate in the kitchen with him, and Jamie still in with Grace.

"Feel enough like Sardines yet?" Nate offered, taking a bowl from him.

Deke grumbled. "Something like that."

Nate sat the bowl on the table, and shifted things around. It was going to be tight at the tiny little table, but they'd manage. "Sam, have a seat and grab some chow."

Samriel blinked at him. "My name is—"

"I know what your name is," Nate interrupted, holding a plate out to him. "But you're probably gonna be around a while, and m's and r's shouldn't touch. So..." He cocked a brow. "Sam. Sit and eat. We're human, even if Deke's a little further away from it than the rest of us, and we're going to have a meal. You can sit and talk with us."

Maybe ordering Sam around wasn't his brightest move, but whatever else the guy was capable of, he'd put a lot of effort into keeping Grace in one piece and he obviously cared about her. Nate didn't have it in him to walk around on eggshells.

Sam swallowed, and edged down onto a chair around the table, taking the food that Curt shoved on his plate.

"There ya go." Curt smiled at him, slightly forced.

Sam nodded, picked up a fork, and started mechanically eating.

Deke shook his head. "Does that even taste like anything to you?"

"It does." Sam took another bite. "Though probably not what it tastes like to you."

"So the coffee?" Nate asked.

"I have not had close dealings with humans or Nephete in many years."

"Wouldn't following Grace around for however long have been close dealings?" Curt asked, around a mouthful.

Sam shook his head. "I followed only Grace. I did not interact."

Curt frowned. "So that Revenant, that said Grace was so special, how did it know?"

Sam blinked at him, blank and confused for a moment. "I was not there for the entire issue. What did it say?"

Nate swallowed. "It said they'd been looking for an unprotected one like her. I thought it was just general smack talk."

"I do not know what that is," Sam said with a frown.

"Insults," Deke offered.

Sam wrinkled his nose. "I do not know what it thought it knew about her. There are ways I could check." He glanced at the living room. "But I am loathe to leave before Grace awakes."

Curt scoffed, standing up to grab something out of the fridge. "Yeah, none of us are explaining this for you."

Nate glanced into the living room, Jamie leaned forward and settling the blankets around Grace again.

"So is there a type of spell you're better at than others, Deke?" Curt asked, sitting back down. "Like protection spells."

"I don't practice," Deke nearly sing-songed. Like he'd already said it six or seven times.

He might have, actually.

"Right, and all that warding?" Curt asked.

"Is me taking in the crap you people kick up and expect me to keep in the storeroom, and not letting it take out random passers-by?" Deke stabbed at his food. "It's not the same thing."

"That sounds like splitting hairs," Curt groused.

"Sure, call it that." Deke leaned back. "It's mine to split, and my distinction to make."

Nate tried to follow their conversation. It wasn't that Jamie intimidated him. Not really. So in all honesty, professor or not, he looked like they'd be at least an even match in a physical fight. He was relatively sure at least Curt would make sure Jamie didn't beat him up too badly.

And the beating up would be because there was pretty much no way imaginable Nate was going to take a swing at Grace's best friend.

It was just the *lying*, and he'd talked to Jamie on the phone a lot. He'd maybe sort of grown to like the guy, and obviously the weird in Grace's life didn't have anything to do with him. Maybe the poking at it did, or had to do with Curt, whatever.

They finished eating, and Nate put his plate in the sink—he'd finished it, not that he'd been paying much attention to what he was eating.

"Here." Curt handed him a plate piled with food, and a fork. "I doubt seriously we're going to get that boy away from the couch any time soon."

Nate looked at him, and sighed. He wasn't enough of a coward to try and throw Deke under the bus, or Curt. And there had been some sort of weird tension with Sam and Jamie. He didn't think he wanted to have to deal with that before Grace was awake.

~~~~~~

Nate stared at the ceiling in Deke's office for probably three hours.

It wasn't that he didn't like being downstairs—he didn't, as far as he was concerned he was way the crap too close to the storeroom—or that he was uncomfortable sleeping on the floor. He'd slept worse places. Probably close to more dangerous things, though that was debatable.

He just *couldn't*.

He tried for three hours, listening to Curt's soft snores on the couch in the office, and then he called it. Got up and carefully put his clothes back on, rolled his sleeping bag up and crept back up the stairs. Deke had turned most of the lights off, except the one in the kitchen where Sam was sitting—probably to give Jamie space— and a single light in the living-room.

Jamie wasn't asleep either. Just sitting on the chair with his elbows on his knees, watching the steady rise and fall of Grace's chest.

He heard Nate pause at the door, and looked up at him, sitting up and pushing a hand through his hair. It was sticking up in all directions now, and he awkwardly patted it down.

"Hey."

214

"Hey." Nate dropped his things, and glanced at Grace, then in to see Sam watching them from a distance. Which was just weird all its own. Had they even spoken?

"Come to join the night watch?" Jamie offered, leaning back.

"Sure." Nate pulled up a chair, dropping into it. "I couldn't sleep anyway. How's she been?"

Jamie shrugged. "She started to have a nightmare, I think. Calmed down pretty easy, thankfully. I'm not as good with those as I used to be."

"I don't think she's been having problems normally." Nate flushed. "We've been sleeping in the same room most of the last three months, I feel like I'd have noticed."

Jamie glanced at him, then looked back a Grace. "I think we were twelve the last time she slept hard enough to actually have a nightmare in the normal run. Not that she was pretty much ever a hard sleeper."

"I can see that. I've developed some impressive moves, trying not to accidentally wake her up on my way to the bathroom."

Jamie cracked a small smile. "You've managed it though, that's pretty impressive." He glanced at Nate, before looking back at Grace. "She likes you, you know?" He grinned. "Well, no, you probably don't, given its Grace."

Nate blinked. "I..." He cleared his throat, swallowing. "We get along pretty well."

Jamie looked at him, interested. "Do you normally spend three straight months with people?"

He scoffed. "No."

Jamie nodded. "And when do you think the last time was Grace spent more than a couple of days with anybody but me?"

"I never asked."

"Well..." Jamie looked back at Grace. "She lived with her Dad until we graduated, but you can ask the guy in the kitchen why that doesn't count." His jaw twitched. "That's pretty much it."

215

"So I'm...special." Nate tripped over it, trying to roll it around in his head.

"I'd say yes." Jamie sighed darkly. "But I haven't pushed much."

Nate laughed. "Dude, it's weird for *us*. I sort of expected you to say 'hello' with your fist tonight."

Jamie laughed, rubbing the back of his neck. "I hit someone over Grace once, when I was like twelve." He smiled, looking at Nate. "And I've talked to you on the phone enough to know she's still making her own decisions."

"Who'd you hit?"

Jamie waved it off. "It's a long story and we were stupid kids. She liked this boy and he was being kind of an ass and I..." he paused, rubbing his forehead. "Acted like twelve-year-old boys do, even though I should have known better." He pulled a wry face. "I've never repeated the mistake."

Nate grinned. "I could always ask her."

Jamie looked at him, really looked. "Would you?"

"Yeah," Nate answered. "We do talk. I don't know why everyone's always so surprised about that."

"Because most people feel like she's not interested in what they're saying so they get uncomfortable and stop talking, or they talk more, but either way it's not really a conversation."

Nate blinked, thrown. "Is that what the problem is?"

Jamie just looked at him. "You didn't do that?"

"No." Nate huffed. "I never doubted she'd tell me to shut up if she didn't want to talk. Or...whatever. I didn't analyze it. She offered to help, and then we sort of got sucked into a whirlwind of jobs, and by the time it was done we were just...here."

Jamie chuckled. "I think there's something to be said for what nineteen hours in a car together in one day has to do to your shields."

Nate cracked up, shaking his head. "You know she went to get food out of the vending machine that night and almost ran into a bear? Freaking Minnesota."

"A...seriously. Just stumbled on a bear."

"Yeah." Nate shook his head. "Woke her up good. Which was probably for the best, because we weren't either of us one-hundred percent after that."

Jamie shifted, rolling his shoulders. "Alright. So ignoring all the immediate supernatural shit that I haven't heard about. What have you two actually been doing while I thought you were chasing criminals?"

Nate winced. "You're seriously okay with this?"

"No," Jamie scoffed. "But it's not like I've got much hope of making her stop. Nobody makes Grace do anything. I'd like to know."

Nate scrubbed a hand through his hair. "Okay. Um...in order? The leg injury when she met Curt was a...not-werewolf. The short answer is the guy had the genes to be a were in there somewhere, and a butt-load of recreational drug use released them."

"But it didn't—"

"Didn't make her a werewolf." Nate shook his head. "Guy wasn't actually a werewolf, and it wasn't the full moon. Major bite injury and all that, but no curse, or disease or whatever you'd call that."

Jamie swallowed. "Okay."

"Then there was some spirit action that Curt gave her the incantation for because he was on a rough job right then." He wrinkled his nose. "And then a couple of months ago there was a Revenant—which is like a cross between a poltergeist and a ghost on steroids—and she called Curt for help, and he decided it was strange enough he wanted an extra hand and drug me along. Grace had to shoot the police commissioner in the head." He winced. "He'd have been dead anyway, and he was about to kill someone else. We tried to get rid of it again and that the first time we met Sam...sort of. He fried the Revenant, he didn't introduce himself."

Jamie cocked a brow.

"And then there was..." He frowned. "Shit, I don't even remember it all. I think, over the course of the two-month stint we did a werewolf—a real, on the full moon one—a couple of vengeful spirits, a patch of fucking hunger grass you can ask Deke for an explanation about because I still don't get it, a Korrigan—that's a sort of Gaelic water vampire? Sam hauled her out of the fire on that one too."

Jamie blinked at him. "In like two months?"

"Yeah." Nate shook his head. "It was a little much for *me* and I kept waiting for Grace to crack because right out the gate, that's boss."

Jamie smiled softly, almost proud. "I'm not sure Grace knows how to crack."

Nate nodded. "There was a moment there where I think she was a little worried our psychic friend Mary was going to share some things."

Jamie winced.

"It's fine, she didn't."

"Was it just Grace?"

"No, she was over-sharing all of us." Nate pushed a hand through his hair. "I can tell there are things in her past she doesn't want to share."

"How?"

Nate blinked. "What, you don't—"

"Oh no, I know." Jamie huffed. "I was there for it. How can you tell? She doesn't talk about *anything*."

Nate swallowed. "She's watchful in a bar, pretty much always. She moves like a goddamn ninja *all the time*. My mother was a pushy, drunk, pain in the ass and she never said a word." He shifted, shaking his head. "But mostly, even before me, Curt said if you mentioned her family she changed the subject like a pro. But she'll talk about you.

About your Aunt Rhoda. I always sort of felt like that was her talking about her family."

Jamie smiled crookedly. "Rhoda'd certainly say it was. I'm only marginally better in the family department than Grace is. I think we're probably closer to treating each other like siblings than anything else, though I've yet to have a significant other who was capable of understanding that."

Nate opened his mouth, but stopped suddenly when Grace shifted, groaning softly and blinking her eyes open.

Jamie grinned, leaning forward. "Hey, look who's back with us?"

Chapter 16

Grace blinked, trying to find her mental feet. "Jamie?"

He grinned at her, ridiculously wide and bright.

Grace jumped up, never mind how her head felt and everything else, she hadn't seen him in freaking ages. She wrapped her arms around his neck, squeezing tight.

Jamie laughed softly, pulling her tight against him, pressing his face against her shoulder. "I missed you too."

Grace just soaked him in. "Did you threaten to hurt Nate?"

"No." Jamie laughed, pulling back finally and brushing her hair back, kissing her on the forehead noisily. "He's entirely too nice a guy for his own good, and I called and he couldn't lie to me."

Grace reached out and grabbed Nate in a tight hug, kissing him on the cheek. "You look really worried, but I'm fine."

Nate had to clear his throat, flushing slightly. "If you're sure."

Grace nodded, shifting so she was sitting on the couch. "Shut up Jamie."

He laughed. "You get a freebie for that one."

Grace punched him in the shoulder lightly. She looked up at the figure standing in the doorway of the kitchen. She'd seen him pop in, and that had triggered the whole buzz in her head. But it was fine now. Well, she generally agreed to Jamie's aversion to the word fine. There'd been a fairly terrifying level of shit locked underneath there. She wasn't poking at it, but she knew it was there now.

Except none of that was about the tall strangely classic looking man in Deke's kitchen. "I don't know your name."

He coughed softly, clearing his throat. "Samriel." He winced. "I will explain, but if you could have Mr. Hughes make sure you are well."

"I heard my name," Deke said, strolling out of the bedroom fiddling with his sleeve.

Grace sort of wanted to hug him, too. Whether he'd been easy about her or not, he'd jumped right in there when she was in trouble.

He stopped, looking at her, and sighed dramatically. "Of course you wouldn't need the full time."

Grace smiled wryly. "Maybe you're just good."

"Oh, I am." Deke insisted, coming over and shooing Nate out of his chair. "And if you're feeling up to it, I'm going to poke around at your brain for a minute, make sure we're not going to do that again."

Grace nodded.

"Good. And then Samriel and I will explain the whole...three quarters of everything."

"I'm telling you. Sam," Nate insisted. "M's and r's shouldn't touch."

Grace shook her head at him. "You're trying to nickname him already? And people think I'm strange."

Nate huffed. "You say that like there's something wrong with you."

Grace wasn't touching that with a ten-foot pole right then. Never mind the ever increasing headache in the back of her brain, or everything else that'd happened in the last couple of days. Jamie was *right there* and maybe with most people the things she said got lost in context. Not with Jamie, and he was already staring at her like they were going to talk.

Grace blinked, looking around the room. "Where's Curt?"

Nate cursed and jumped up. "Asleep downstairs in the office. I'll go get him, don't blow anything up until I get back."

"Was that for me, or the room at large?" Grace asked.

Nate pulled a face, but loped off down the stairs without answering.

"So." Deke pulled out a strange little stick, knotted wood smooth and bleached. "It's exactly what think it is. It's a wand." He smiled wryly. "Fiction has to get some things right."

Grace nodded again.

"I'm going to see if I can figure out what's back there, and if it's contained in such a way you're all good." He swallowed, perfectly serious. "Which means I'm sifting around in the back of your head. But I won't see anything. This isn't like a psychic, you don't have to take a trip down memory lane or anything like that. The best way I can describe it is that there's a sort of poisonous thorn hidden away, and you've grown scar tissue around it, but it's still trying to poison you."

Curt came up the stairs then, smiling happily, Nate right behind him.

"So I'm going to search around and find where it is, and—"

"August 13th, 1993," Samriel said quietly.

Grace froze, muscles locking, feeling Jamie's hand fasten around her wrist instantly.

Deke swallowed. "That was...exact."

Samriel glanced between them, then swallowed. "I felt the...spontaneous block on that date."

Deke rubbed his forehead. "Did something happen that day?"

Grace sighed, forcing her muscles to relax. "My mother died."

Jamie had to take a deep calming breath, and Grace looked at him, because he was working really hard to stay in control.

"Just..." He forced a smile and shrugged. "First time I've ever actually heard you say that."

Grace blew out a breath, bearing down. She was safe here. Nate, and Curt, and Jamie. There was no reason for her to start upping her shields just because she was going to have to stop pretending her past was blank.

Jamie tugged softly.

"Sorry." She swallowed, and smiled at him. "That's because you're entirely too easy on me."

"Ha," Jamie scoffed. "Nate's too easy on you. I know better than to push things it wouldn't help to push."

Deke winced. "Right. Um... Can I ask how she died?"

"Alcohol poisoning," Grace said wryly. "Presumably it was the alcohol, there might have been other things in her system."

The discomfort in the room ramped up and she looked at Jamie, focusing on the fact that he knew all this.

"Burned her bridges before that, huh?" Deke offered, voice rough.

Grace blinked at him. The general response to her lack of emotion about her mother was at least confusion, if not actual negativity. Not understanding. That was part of why she never talked about it.

Jamie sighed, rubbing his forehead. "Now's probably not the time for self-discovery." He watched her carefully. "And maybe I'm too easy on you, whatever. I can cover the basics and you can work on how to say this shit out loud later."

Because Jamie knew perfectly well she'd said all of this out-loud once, to the therapist, so they'd stop making her go to appointments.

Grace smiled softly at him. "One breakthrough at a time?"

223

"Something like that." Jamie kissed her on the cheek.

"You're supposed to be freaking out about all this," Grace reminded.

"Gracie, the first thing you ever said to me was about the voices in your wall at night. I'm not sure I ever expected normal."

Grace frowned, blinking at him. "What?"

Jamie leaned back, confused. "The day we met?"

"I remember. It was the fear assignment and Mrs. Holiday said I could write about anything I wanted so I wrote about Dad trying to hit me and she thought I was lying."

The room went stone quiet, and Jamie cursed softly. "Um…I'm pretty sure they knew about that too, but I saw your paper Grace. You wrote that you were most afraid of the voices in your walls that talked to you at night."

Grace bore down, past the instinctual push to not think about it, and tried to remember.

"Woah, don't push at that blockage." Deke grabbed her elbow. "Let's not do that yet."

Grace looked at him, blinking.

"I've got a date, I'll start there." Deke swallowed. "Just slow down a little."

She nodded, settling her shoulders. "Alright."

Deke canted her head down gently. "Close your eyes and stay relaxed and loose. You should feel strange, but there shouldn't be any pain, or anxiety." Deke pressed his wand to her temple. "If you feel like you can't handle it, or you're overwhelmed squeeze my hand and I'll stop." He left his other hand right there next to hers. "Nate, watch her, and if she starts to get like she did with Mary—"

"I'll stop you," Nate offered softly.

Deke paused, looking back at Samriel. "Are we good?"

He nodded stoically, watching Grace carefully.

"Right then." Deke smiled at her. "Close your eyes and relax."

224

Grace could feel it, moving around in her brain. Almost like a caffeine high. Like something was lighting everything up in there but it wasn't...doing anything. She breathed deep and easy, intent on staying calm. Deke wouldn't hurt her, and Nate was right there and he'd notice anything strange going on. She trusted him, completely.

She felt Deke jump suddenly, swallowing. "Sorry, caught me by surprise." He cleared his throat. "Still good, Grace?"

"Yes."

"Okay." He shifted around a little. "I'm just finding the edges. Relax, nothing's wrong..." Deke pulled off suddenly.

Grace opened her eyes, looking up at him. So that he could just stare at her, horrified. "Yes?"

Deke swallowed. "Sorry, just..."

Nate nudged him softly. "All fixed?"

"I..." Deke rubbed a hand through his hair, almost shaking, and looked back at Samriel. "Did you know?"

"No," Samriel answered, jaw tense. "Whatever caused it had moved on."

Deke stood started to walk off. He stopped halfway to the kitchen. "Will you be super uncomfortable if I need a drink to explain this?"

Grace cocked her head at him. "No."

Jamie huffed. "You get like a six drink threshold before Grace really get's uncomfortable, just so you can stop asking all the time."

Six? Nate mouthed.

Grace pulled a face at him. "It's complicated."

Curt flopped into a chair he'd pulled from the kitchen. "I've never met an alcoholic that the drinking was really their problem."

Deke came back with a bottle of beer, and sat a few on the table, like he thought somebody else might need one. He sat down heavily, sighing. "Alcohol is no excuse for being an asshole, and anybody who says differently deserves to have their ass beat."

Grace shifted, wrapping her arms around her middle. "Someone drill that in you?"

Deke smiled dryly. "My grandmother. In our family alcoholism was more a religion than a way of life." He sighed. "Right. First, sorry if that made you nervous but I'm going to break myself trying to find a way to say I'm surprised you're functional."

She watched him, waiting.

Deke swallowed. "You've got massive mental scarring. Not even... The date that Sam back there gave me was the day it should have killed you." He watched her carefully. "You weren't blocking the memory. That was a side-effect. There was a thing—there are a couple of options and I don't know which one is more likely—that was slowly poisoning you. The fact you held on until nine is epic, actually."

Nate frowned. "Options?"

"On the best option I'd say it was a strong Lupara," Deke said as an aside. "On the worst a Coco."

Curt cursed darkly, grabbing a beer.

"And that is?" Grace asked, looking between them.

Nate winced. "A Lupara is a kind of house spirit, it mostly just generally wreaks havoc. Sometimes if there's enough...unhappiness in a house they can do more." He shifted uncomfortably. "A Coco is less of a ghost, more a non-corporeal critter? They torture children. Well, technically they feed off negative energy and emotion, but the like to play and adults don't have the right temperament to notice them, generally."

Grace blinked. "Wow. That's lovely."

"Yeah." Nate made a face. "They're a bitch to get rid of too."

Deke swung around, shocked. "I didn't think you could."

Nate flushed, shrugging. "I'm inventive."

Grace laughed softly. "Is that like 'here, have a crossbow, you can just shoot it in the eye again.'"

He snorted. "Don't knock what works."

Deke rubbed his forehead. "You two are just..." He blew out a breath. "Anyway." He smiled at Grace. "I can't do anything more about that. It's just scarring now. I wouldn't go poking at those memories, it won't be pleasant."

Grace laughed darkly.

"You don't anyway?" Deke offered quietly.

"Something like that."

Grace didn't really have a better description for it than that. She'd never been all that adept at self reflection. She'd spent so much of the years people learned that intentionally avoiding it.

"Okay." Deke swallowed. "If you can give me some kind of assurance you'll let me know if you start to feel strange or unusually panicky we can leave it at that."

"Sure," Grace agreed. "I can't exactly walk into the ER."

Deke shifted back slightly. "Now, for the white elephant in the room. No offense Sam."

Sam frowned. "In what way am I a large pachyderm?"

Deke dropped his head forward. "It's a figure of speech. How long has it been since you were around humans?"

"Routinely? Five-hundred and seventy six years."

"Wow." Grace swallowed. "So immortal *is* a thing."

Deke scoffed. "Sam back there is a Maeleket, and presumably he'll jump in at some point and explain this to you, but I think he's been following you silently for so long he's forgotten how," Deke muttered. "Maeleket are the genesis for all those things we see, Angels and Demons and Fae and..." He waved a hand. "That's all them, in one way or another."

Grace looked at Sam, still standing uncomfortably near the door to the kitchen. "So the random white light that kept saving my bacon was you?"

"Yes, although, in all fairness, I empathize with Curt's desire to 'put a bell on you' as you kept getting into trouble at odd times when I was otherwise occupied."

"Alright." Grace drew the word out, confused. "Thanks. Why?"

Sam didn't answer though, and Grace was going to come up with a secondary question, maybe one he'd be more comfortable with, but Deke shifted, and shook his head.

"And now for the grand explanation about witchcraft," Deke muttered. "Unless I can just skate past it."

Grace blinked at him. "I'm pretty sure I could manage with the short explanation."

Deke relaxed suddenly. "Good. Have you heard Curt's theories about witches?"

"There are connections in families, and there may be not-assholey ones too, only you never see them."

"Exactly." Deke nodded. "They call themselves the Nephete, and they run in family dynasties basically? They consolidate a lot of power in a distinct family lineage, passed straight down a line to the first born in every generation of these special lines." He smiled. "My grandmother was the first born of a line of Ojibwe Nephete, though they didn't separate themselves from the rest of their population, they were just...medicine people."

"Okay," Grace said. "And?"

"And one of your parents was the same thing," Deke continued. "Which makes you the new First once they've died. These families that stay on the light side of witchcraft are given a Watcher, someone of the Maeleket that helps them and guides them as needed. If you go dark enough you lose that, but general speaking they do their best to keep that from happening." He huffed out a breath. "Now, given the strange situation we find ourselves in I'm guessing your family doesn't have a Watcher any longer, for whatever reason, but clearly the Warders—which as best I can tell are the ones who oversee the Watchers—are still interested in you, because you've got a Sam sitting on your shoulder."

Grace wrinkled her nose. "So either side of my family. Probably Mom, since—"

"Both," Sam interrupted softly, shifting suddenly. "Your father was a Nephete also, though his family had gone more like Deacon's. His grandmother chose not to deal with the Warder's Council any longer—she was not dark, she just left her family and..." he died off. "I am...*was* the Watcher for your mother's family."

"So what happened?" Grace asked.

Sam crossed his arms over his chest, shoulders tight and defensive. "I will claim no fault for this, but I am not...making excuses as you say." He watched Grace. "I was rotated away from your family because someone had locked another Watcher into a special contract. The council decided as he was stuck, that they would have him be the family Watcher and I would fulfill other functions until the end of his contract with a member of your family. A term of five-hundred years."

Grace swallowed. That was one hell of a contract.

"He did not do his job well though. I kept track as well as I could, despite the fact you were no longer my concern."

Deke frowned. "How long had you been Warder for...whatever line it is? I'm assuming one of the larger ones."

"The oldest stretching Rom/Rus line."

Deke blinked. "Wow. Sure."

Grace cocked a brow.

"The Rom/Rus line is...um. To borrow a modern euphemism, they're the red-headed stepchildren of the magical community. Or they used to be, I'm not sure there's much of that left." Deke rubbed the back of his neck. "They're sort of assumed to be dark. Anyway."

"I was Warder for the line for one thousand, six-hundred and thirty-eight years before that."

Deke choked. "Seriously? You just...crap." He winced. "How ticked are you that they broke it?"

Samriel huffed darkly. "I was not pleased." He glanced at Grace. "During the 1930's things were, understandably, hectic. Hitler, and Stalin, and all of that," he grumbled. "We were all trying to put out fires for nearly two decades. By the time anybody was in a position to look at the lines in the new world it was more than a decade later." He frowned darkly. "And your line was...broken."

"How, if Grace is here and it's supposed to go to the first born?" Nate asked, frowning.

"I was wondering that," Grace muttered.

"Your Grandmother, Mary. Her father was in line to be the next First and he was..." He wrinkled his nose. "I have followed you long enough to know you value honesty. He would have lost the line its Watcher had he become the title-holder." He huffed. "He was also cruel and abusive, and therefore should have been weeded from the line as quickly as possible. The temporary Watcher in charge did not fulfill his duty well, and he was not. His wife was addicted to human medicines, the ones that come in bottles?"

"Opium?" Grace guessed, swallowing.

Samriel nodded. "I did not know what actually happened until much later, but she was killing herself. Rather than leave her husband with the child she took your grandmother to a catholic orphanage in the city, and then committed suicide in the river." He shook his head sadly. "She convinced everyone who saw her that she had jumped in with the baby. And the council believed the report. They termed the line broken, and ensured he would have no more children." He stopped and cleared his throat. "After his wife and child were gone he crossed lines."

Deke winced. "Which is Warder speak for very bad things."

"I guessed," Grace muttered.

"I was displeased," Sam continued. "It is a point of professional pride that your family do well, and I had managed to keep a line everyone assumed was going dark on the right path for a very long time."

"And he screwed it all up in less than five-hundred years?" Deke asked.

Samriel gave him a dark look. "In less than a century." He shook it off. "In any case, I went on to other things." He waved his hand. "Suddenly it's 1993 and I was between jobs and there is this jolt in the ether that feels like your family magic. But there should have been nothing left of that."

"Surprise!" Grace said, complete with jazz hands.

He almost smiled, face softening. "It took me a considerable amount of effort to find you, and then once I did I—"

"Followed her through all those years and didn't—" Jamie started, agitated, but Grace reached out and grabbed his wrist, stopping him.

"He couldn't," Grace said softly, turning back to Sam. "Because if you had, what happened now would have happened and—"

"I couldn't save you from that." Samriel looked terrified, actually, compared to how relatively emotionless he'd been until that point. "We have learned long ago not to interfere with the human psyche. Had I known there was some sort of human healing magic that could help that, I would have found someone." He swallowed. "Different lines have different focuses and I am not familiar with the minutia of them all."

Deke grumbled. "Curt's spell would have caused that to happen anyway, so the risk associated with showing up the way he did was the much better option."

Jamie glared at him. "He's how old and he couldn't just ask someone how to do what you did?"

231

Deke scoffed. "He could ask. And, I mean if he'd asked *me* I would have. If he'd asked my grandmother she'd have told him to go away because he wasn't connected with our family."

Grace shook Jamie slightly, and glanced at him. She understood how he felt, but whatever the reasons, it was in the past. She turned back to Sam. "Alright. So now? I'm not a witch, I mean maybe I have the genes…"

"You have no training," Sam agreed. "You were too old for that to be a consideration once I found you anyhow, and the Council urged caution because of your family situation."

"So why are you still here?" Deke asked frankly. "If they've lost their watcher. That's supposed to be the end."

Samriel looked at him, shifting slightly. "According to the council the line is broken. It may stay that way." He looked at Grace. "But I felt responsible for it, so I insisted I be allowed to watch you until you were an adult. Once you were they felt that perhaps the line didn't need to be *broken.* Any children you had could be trained, with enough care, and…" He frowned. "Not that I'm implying you should have children you are not sure you want."

Nate blinked. "You're not following orders. You're just here for Grace."

Grace looked at Nate, frowning. "What?"

Jamie sighed. "Grace. He's been following you around for…ages. Whether he was supposed to get attached or not, he did."

Grace blinked at Samriel, watching the tense set of his shoulders and the way he shifted uncomfortably. Crap. "Oh." She winced. "Um…okay. Thank you."

Samriel stood suddenly. "I discussed with Curt that the Revenant seemed to know something about you. I will go check and see if there is a connection we should be concerned with."

And he was just…gone.

"What the hell?" Curt muttered, shocked.

Jamie broke, laughing and dropping his face in his hands.

Grace frowned, and looked at Nate. "Was that something I did?"

Nate laughed, shaking his head. "No, I think he got embarrassed." He nudged her shoulder. "Are you good? I'm going to go steal Deke's shower."

"I'm…" Grace wrinkled her nose. Fine might have been overstating the case. "Does 'in one piece' work?"

Nate nodded. "Don't slip off alone for a while?"

"Yeah." Grace shook her head. "No, I'll sit here and answer Jamie's eight million questions. I'm good."

Nate laughed softly, and walked from the room. And about two seconds later Curt and Deke were gone too.

Grace looked around them and Deke's suddenly empty living room. "Did they plan that, or did you?"

Jamie laughed darkly, hugging her suddenly. "Don't care."

Grace leaned her head on his shoulder, laughing. "I am the most high-maintenance person in the universe, aren't I?"

"No comment today."

Grace sighed. "I said I missed you, right?"

"You did." Jamie leaned back, shifting so he was sitting on the couch next to her.

Grace leaned into his side. "I don't think we're supposed to go three months without seeing each other."

He smiled. "I think I could get used to this, if it makes me stop being the only clingy one." He ruffled her hair softly. "Are you really okay?"

She pushed a hand through her hair. Her life was a mess. "When I find the bottom of the crazy I'll let you know."

He shook his head. "Yeah. The stalker bit is new."

She frowned, shifting to see his face. "You don't like him."

Grace loved Jamie with pretty much everything she had. They weren't friends, they were siblings and they

233

had been for so long some days she thought they were too close for that. And because of that there were no walls left. There hadn't been since they were children.

It didn't just mean she was honest with Jamie, even when she didn't want to be. It meant he was honest with her.

"No." He leaned his head back, thumping it on the couch cushion. "I don't."

"Why?"

He rubbed at his eyes, obviously starting to get a bit tired. He probably hadn't slept while he was watching her. "Because the rest of them can let go of the fact he just left you to deal with all that. Maybe he couldn't have or he didn't know how." Jamie looked at her, eyes sad. "They didn't have to live through all the background shit with you. It's just background now."

Grace leaned her head on his shoulder. "True. You seemed okay with Nate though."

He snorted. "I like Nate, and we're gonna talk about that later."

"Ooookay?" Grace frowned. What were they going to talk about, with Nate? If Jamie liked him wasn't that the end? Or did he mean the traveling? She didn't think so.

"And Curt, and Deke even though you two haven't figured each-other out yet. And I'm not being crappy. It's absolutely a little strange that there are suddenly all these new people you're close to. I'm not jealous of that. Well..." He winced. "Maybe that they get to spend time with you that I don't get anymore, but just that." He thumped his head back.

"Alright." Grace nodded. "Just... Sam's kinda saved my butt a lot the last couple of months."

"Are you sure you'd have been here without him?"

"Decently." Grace looked at him, both of them sprawled out across the couch, sighing. "Did Nate tell you about the not-werewolf that took a chunk out of my leg?"

Jamie patted her leg sadly, nodding.

"I didn't get in its way; it was trying to have some kid who lived up the block for a snack," she said dryly. "And that's how I met Curt. So...yeah. Fairly sure all that would have happened even if Samriel wasn't following me around." Grace settled in. "Just...give him a chance? Because I might need you to help when I say or do something that massively alienates him."

Jamie huffed. "I don't know, you've done alright with Nate."

"That's because, as you said, Nate is entirely too nice for his own good."

Chapter 17

Grace shifted through the books Curt kept leaving on the desk—massive piles of them about witchcraft—trying to search through all the random dross of information for the things that were actually true. Samriel hadn't come back yet. At least not as far as they could tell. If he was just hanging out with her that would be awkward.

Grace was not thinking about that. Seriously. The concept that he'd been following her around for years was just creepy beyond all reason. She sincerely hoped there had been some boundaries there.

Her phone rang, and she looked down at the ID, huffing out a laugh, before she answered it. "Hey."

"Hey." Jamie swallowed. "Still at Curt's?"

"Yeah." Grace looked at the spine of a book, deciding which pile to set it in. "Nate felt like a week off and a little quality time with his car."

"Really."

"Well, he'll probably start messing around with mine while he's out there. It's what he does."

"Other than hunting monsters."

"That too," Grace agreed. "So. How's your life? I've got nothing new to report."

"That's news all its own," Jamie deadpanned.

"Yes yes, I already admitted I'm high maintenance. Moving on?"

He laughed softly. "I'm not any different than I ever am. Teaching. Students are..." He sighed. "We can't have been like this, can we?"

She let out a startled scoff. "That depends on what sort of 'like this' you're talking about. Because I could come tell them some stories about what Professor Williams was like in college."

"You aren't funny," Jamie said dryly. "And it's Dr Williams to them. I'm too young to go by Prof."

"I don't know. I think if they give you the job you should make all the hay you can out of the title."

Curt walked into the room, frowning at her.

"It's Jamie," Grace said, before he could ask. "Who else would I be talking to on the phone?"

"Deke called you yesterday," Curt offered, shifting through books.

"Hm."

"Why are you no-commenting that?" Jamie asked, intrigued.

Grace quietly waited until Curt was out of the room, she didn't want to hurt his feelings. "Because he wanted to see if I could do anything about Curt calling him every ten minutes to ask if another piece of lore he'd found was true," she answered. "Apparently the witch in your pocket isn't worth much when she doesn't know anything."

"There is no way Curt said something like that," Jamie huffed. "And even if he did, Nate would have corrected him."

"It's implied, even if it's only implied in my head," she insisted.

Grace sorted through the last few books. "So. I don't have anything worthwhile to say. I'm doing good, and I can hear you tapping your pen around, trying to avoid going to do your grading or whatever it is you're putting off right now."

"I hate you."

"No you don't." Grace grinned. "So…"

"Fine. I'm going. Say 'hi' for me."

"Will do." Grace sat the book in her hand down, and switch which hand was holding the phone. "Oh, hey, before I forget, you said you wanted to talk about something about Nate."

Dead silence hung on the line. That was ominous.

"Jamie?"

"I'm…" He blew out a breath. "It's a relationship thing."

"Okay." She swallowed. "Um…"

"Are you sure you want me to tell you?"

Grace glanced out the window, watching Nate move around out in the yard, stopping to shield himself from the sun and guzzle half a bottle of water. "Did I miss something?" She snorted. "Stupid question. What did I miss?"

Jamie shifted, the phone crackling. "I'm still on the fence about this. I think you could figure it out on your own eventually, and he probably won't thank me for telling you."

"Right, well, I can't say anything about that until you tell me. Did I say something to hurt his feelings and not notice? I don't think I did, I sort of think he'd *look* hurt, unless I've just been missing it for ages."

"You noticed hurt." Jamie sounded sort of impressed.

"He looked like someone kicked his puppy pretty much the entire time we were around his Mom. It was quiet, but it was there."

"Ah." Jamie gulped. "Right. Well."

"Just say it, you're killing me here."

"He's in love with you."

Grace froze, nearly dropping the phone.

"Or nearly there anyway," Jamie finished. "And I'm pretty sure he knows it, but he thinks you either don't feel the same or you aren't there yet."

She heard a book fall over behind her, and turned around.

To find Samriel, standing uncomfortably behind her.

"Grace?" Jamie asked, concerned.

"Sorry." Grace swallowed, shaking it off. "Right. Um…Sam's back and…yeah."

Jamie laughed. "Call me when your brain restarts."

"I hate you."

"Liar." Jamie chuckled, hanging up.

Grace looked at her phone, swallowing. He… What?

Samriel frowned at her. "It is concerning that you look close to panicking. You do not panic."

Grace hauled in a giant breath, looking up at him, and shoved all of that into the back of her head. She'd just call Jamie back later and freak out at him. Because—

"Did Jamie tell you that Nate harbors feelings for you?"

"You know?" Grace burst out, startled. And nearly kicked herself for that. There were better ways to have this conversation.

Sam almost smiled at her. "I've been watching you together a great deal." He cocked his head to the side. "Is that a problem? Don't you feel the same way?"

"I don't know!" Grace swallowed, feeling her chest start to constrict again. Nate was awesome, absolutely, and attractive sure. He had really nice eyes, and he was so nice to her about everything and she was just a mess. Every time she had a relationship things went badly because she wouldn't share things or she wouldn't and—

Samriel grabbed her shoulder suddenly, shaking slightly. He looked at her with eerie blue eyes, hand still holding her steady.

Grace looked at his hand, confused. Jamie did that. He had since they were kids. "How long have you been watching—"

Samriel winced, and answered before she finished. "You were thirteen when I found you again."

"Please tell me you didn't follow me in the bathroom or anything?"

He winced. "I gave you what privacy I could. I understand that crosses a boundary."

She swallowed. "Sorry, I'm just struggling with that."

Sam cocked his head to the side, watching her expectantly, because apparently he'd taken a page out of Jamie's book and he was going to push certain things.

"And bloody everything else." She pushed a hand through her hair.

"I understand," Sam offered softly.

"Should I go get the others? Did you have news?"

"I do not. I did ask about, and look where I could. If someone has nefarious designs on you they are being quiet." His brow pulled. "Which means diddly-squat, as you say."

"Alright." She watched him for a minute. If he'd been watching her that long then presumably he knew what to expect from her. "So the random terrified popping away. Are we done with that?"

Sam flushed, looking away. "I…apologize. I did not mean to give offense."

"Sam." Grace pinched the bridge of her nose. "How long have you been watching me? Am I offended by that?"

He blinked at her. "No." He frowned, cocking his head to the side. "You are…concerned?"

"A little." Grace shifted. "I just… I'm not always good at telling what normal people are thinking, generally, so…"

Sam hemmed around for a moment.

"Come on Sam, you followed me into the bathroom. Nothing can be more embarrassing than that."

He laughed suddenly, like she'd surprised him out of it. "I did not follow you into the bathroom. But you may have a point." He shrugged. "I spent so long following you and from nearly the beginning I liked you very much. I have never personally bonded with a human."

"But you did with me," Grace offered, when he paused.

Sam nodded. "And it did not occur to me, until you were...there..." He waved demonstrably. "That you might not...feel the same way about me." He flushed. "Not right away, obviously. You know nothing of me, but—"

"You did go to a lot of trouble to keep me breathing."

Sam shifted, uncomfortable.

"And Nate thinks you're alright."

"Jamie does not."

Grace winced. "Jamie has...history," she said. "You were there."

He nodded, eyes sad. "It was not just hard for you." He swallowed. "If I could..." He cleared his throat. "I know it was not good, but if you'd been struggling inconsolably at any time when I was there I most likely would have risked it." He huffed. "Which would have ended rather badly, obviously."

"Just a little." Grace smiled wryly. "It is what it is. I'm good if you are, and we'll give Jamie some time."

Sam relaxed slightly. "I would like that." He cocked his head. "You keep calling me Sam, and I know you do not have Nate's issue with m's and r's."

She laughed and squeezed his shoulder. "I like 'Sam.' Do you not?"

"No. I..." Sam cleared his throat. "It is acceptable."

"Good." She smiled. "Sticking around? If Curt see's you he's going to insist you stay for supper."

"As long as it is not Turkey tetrazzini."

~~~~~~

It was Curt's turn to cook, but somehow she still wound up in the kitchen with Nate.

She'd gotten suckered into cleaning the peas for dinner—at some point she'd made the mistake of mentioning that Aunt Rhoda made them shell peas and snap beans and anything else she could manage, to fix their woefully inadequate big-city upbringing when she had them over the summers.

Jamie used to joke that it was sweet, how Rhoda thought it was the city that was inadequate about their upbringing.

Grace grabbed another handful of pea pods, cracking them in half one at a time, and using her thumb to scoop the peas into a bowl in the sink.

There'd been a bit, in the ridiculous long run of jobs they'd gone on that first time, where they'd been awkward. For a solid five minutes anyway. And then while Sarah was around.

Grace was good at awkward. If she was going to have a skill, it was awkward. Mostly—according to Jamie in any case—as a sort of long run attempt at not freaking other people out. Because she realized how abnormal she was and when she started trying to act normal it just didn't work.

So they'd been awkward, until somewhere around the werewolf it suddenly occurred to Grace she had literally zero need to be normal for Nate. Nate wasn't all that much better acquainted with normal than she was.

Nate shifted past her, grabbing something out of the fridge, before he went back to the bowl of...she wasn't sure what he was trying to make, and given the fact he'd started with things that weren't edible and ended with eggs she wasn't going to ask.

There had never been all that many people Grace could just be herself with. She liked Curt alright, and after he'd followed her around forever she was sure she'd be alright with Samriel. Deke was nice.

Nate was... She didn't want to hurt him. Jamie was right, she wasn't good at romantic relationships and she never had been and if he was in love with her and she fucked it up it would make things awkward and not just stuck in a hotel room together awkward. Properly awkward.

"You alright?" Nate asked, frowning at her.

Grace blinked at him, heart pounding. "Fine."

She didn't need him to refute the lie, they both knew it was one. He opened his mouth, and whatever he was going to say Grace had to come up with an excuse right then, because she'd never manage it if he said something stupid and helpful like he was worried about her.

"Just...everything." She turned back to the sink, ignore the weight in her chest. She didn't like lying to him.

"It has been a crazy week," Nate offered wryly. "Still. Sam looks like he's willing to stick around." He smiled at her, trying.

"Yeah." Grace smiled back. "Yeah, he is." She could spend a few minutes pretending that was going to fix anything.

~~~~~~

Grace glanced into the kitchen, making sure Sam was still trapped in Curt's never ending run of questions about witchcraft, Nate with them, before she zipped her hoodie on and slipped out into the yard. She looked down at the screen of her phone, and pressed the call button, it automatically going to the last number.

She determinedly didn't think about the fact three months ago she wouldn't have had to make sure that was Jamie's.

"Hey." Jamie answered right away, breathless from his dash to the phone.

"What... How..." Grace managed, completely incoherent.

"Breathe," he ordered softly.

"How do you…"

"Keep breathing." Jamie snorted, laughing. "Do you need to arm-flail for a while until you remember how to talk?"

"No, just Sam said that too and what am I supposed to—"

"Grace," Jamie cut across her. "If you have a full on panic attack here I'm going to have to call Nate and tell him how to calm you down and I don't think you want that."

"No, Sam's still in the house and he knows."

Dead silence. "I suppose he would."

"Jamie." She pinched the bridge of her nose.

"I'm working on it," he defended. "Really. What's rule number two?"

"Jamie's allowed to remind me I'm not the only one with issues," Grace recited, sighing and rubbing the back of her neck. "Sorry."

"It's fine." He huffed. "You're allowed once in a while."

"What do I do?"

He paused for a long moment, Grace glaring at a cricket somewhere in the car she was sitting on that chose then to be really loud.

"What do you want to do?"

"I don't know." Grace thumped back, covering her face.

Jamie sighed. "Would you like me to tell you why I told you?"

"Yes." Grace bit her lip, shifting. "I don't understand how you even know that."

Another dead pause, and she could nearly hear him head-desking. "It's not the first time."

"What!"

"There have been a couple."

"And you didn't share because?"

"You either didn't even like them as people—there are a disturbing number of those—or I could tell from the get-go they weren't going to—completely honest here—handle you well in a relationship."

She frowned. "And Nate doesn't fit that?"

He scoffed. "Dude's been with you basically around the clock for the better part of three months. You and I both know you're not capable of that level of acting," Jamie answered. "There's no way he doesn't realize you've got issues. From what I saw, he's compensating. Maybe a little more than he should, but nobody's perfect."

Grace whimpered. "Which means I at least need to tell him to stop doing that."

"No you don't." Jamie huffed. "Grace, people are allowed to help you. Life doesn't have to be fucking hard every second."

"It's not--"

"It is," Jamie cut across her again. "You absolutely need to tell him the Grace rules, you're allowed to do that without them being The Grace Rules, but..." He sighed. "Just don't make him stop. Because you're a lot more comfortable than you've been pretty much ever and I think at least part of that is him."

"Why would that be him?"

"Because, sunshine, level of emotion aside, he's not me but he still likes you."

Chapter 18

The problem, more or less from the start, with sitting around at Curt's waiting for Sam to sound out the quasi-backseat over-arching magical organization he still sort of worked for, is that they aren't any of them good at sitting still.

It wasn't quite the level of itch to get on the road they'd had to deal with when they were stuck waiting for Sarah to detox. Nate and Curt were both jittery, but they didn't either of them seem to want away. Grace didn't want away. She wanted something to break, and breaking in such a way they actually got some answers would be nice, but she didn't want away.

The bigger problem with that seemed to be quasi-backseat over-arching magical organization Sam *still sort of worked for.*

Grace is relatively sure even if they knew exactly what that meant for Sam, or for them, they still wouldn't know how to peg what that meant for the moment.

So they're...settled. In as much as they can be, squished into Curt's tiny house without climbing the walls. They took turns cooking, and doing the dishes, and Nate spent most of his time out in the yard keeping busy in whatever way he could. Curt muttered about them and worked on the same projects he'd been tinkering with since she'd "moved in" with them.

Grace organized Curt's books.

Organized might have been slightly overstating the case. She felt a bit like she was rearranging deck chairs on the Titanic. Curt had books everywhere. Whole shelves of them squirreled away in the downstairs bathroom, and going up the side of the stairs. Bookshelves lined the upstairs hallway—all fourteen inches of it—and nearly every available inch of both the bedrooms she'd seen.

She hadn't ever opened the door to Curt's room and she fully intended never bearding that particular Lovecraftian horror.

She liked organizing the books, even if she wasn't necessarily accomplishing much. Books had been her safe place for so long, it was calming. Almost like being back in college working the library stacks, humming to herself and stroking the spines before the put them back in their places.

They'd had a couple of calls, people throwing jobs Curt's way. So far Curt had managed to throw them back off on someone else. She'd told him, and Sam had told him too, that Sam could find her wherever and there was no reason for them to stay right there.

She wasn't surprised neither Curt or Nate seemed particularly comfortable dealing with normal life—normal according to them in any case—without more answers.

Curt stopped in the doorway, wiping his greasy hands on a rag, looking around at the neat little piles she'd managed on literally every available surface. "Enjoying yourself in here?"

Grace scoffed. "It's a party."

Curt chuckled softly. "Who's turn is it for dinner tonight?"

"I'm taking it."

He tilted his head to the side. "Was yours last night."

She nodded. "It was. And it should be Nate's tonight."

"Saving him from that, are you?"

She'd caught Nate hanging out of the freezer that morning, blinking in confusion because he was exactly the sort of person who could have run an armory but didn't know what to do with a pound of ground turkey.

"I'm helpful," Grace said vaguely, grabbing a giant Hollywood book on werewolves. She blinked at the cover for a second, before she held it up for Curt. "Joke?"

"Blind," he answered wryly. "It's actually scarily useful at confusing people."

"Alright then." She put it in the pile with the others. "Are we planning a movie? Or maybe—"

The wall phone rang, and Curt held a hand up, stopping her, before he answered it. Even if they weren't going to take whatever job somebody offered, he still got it just as quickly. Grace wondered if he didn't have his own feelers out, about what was going on. But he hadn't said, and she didn't ask.

She didn't lie to Curt, and he didn't lie to her. That didn't mean they told each other the whole truth.

Grace went back to organizing, and gave him space for his phone call. They might have been living ten inches away from each other, but it wasn't like it was with Nate. Her and Nate could spend months on the road, in each other's pockets, and deal.

"Yeah, it changes I'll let you know." Curt hung the phone up, frowning at it.

"'Nother job?" Grace asked, glancing at him.

"Yeah." Curt scratched the back of his head. "Strange."

"What was it?"

Curt blinked at her. "Oh. Nothin'. Poltergeist. Nothing serious."

There was no part of that sentence Grace was going to touch. "Ah."

"Richards was being strange. Usually only asks for help when he's either outnumbered or it's something real strange. I mean he's been having problems lately anyway..." Curt died off, and shrugged.

"He's the one Nate said kept getting arrested and stuff, isn't he?"

"He's certainly been having problems," Curt said, shaking his head. "What're you making for supper?"

"White turkey chili." Grace glanced at the mantle clock. "Eat at six?"

"Sounds good." Curt turned, and headed for the door. "Holler if Sam shows up."

Grace rolled her eyes, and went back to the books. "Yeah, sure."

Pretty much every conversation she'd had in the last three days had ended with that. She wasn't in danger of forgetting.

~~~~~~

Grace had to remind herself to stop watching for Sam every possible second. She could have chanted 'a watched pot doesn't boil' in her head over and over again, and it probably wouldn't have helped.

She'd known he'd get there in his own time, and he had.

Suddenly appeared in the hallway six feet away without any warning at all, shoulders tense and eyes watchful. "Grace."

"Sam." She cocked a brow at him. "Should I grab the others?"

Sam nodded slightly.

"Alright." Grace forced a smile. "Go on into the kitchen." She opened the door to the cellar, and yelled down. "Curt!"

"Yeah?"

"Sam's here." The door opened behind her, and Grace looked back over her shoulder. Nate stepped in, wiping his hands, and looking around him.

"Hey, Sam."

"Nate." Sam stood still and careful.

"Have a seat man," Nate ordered, slapping him on the shoulder on his way past.

Sam looked down at his shoulder, confused, and subsided into one of the kitchen chairs. Grace wondered over to the sink and poured herself a glass of water because she felt like she was going to need it, all the more when she could hear Curt thudding up the stairs two at a time in his haste.

He burst into the kitchen, face red, looking hopeful. "You have news for us then, Sam?"

Grace gently pushed him into one of the chairs. "Don't stand there and tower over him." She slid into a chair herself, watching as Nate took the seat next to Sam. "Go ahead, Sam."

"I do not have news," Sam said stoically, "because there is no news to be had."

Nate frowned. "No..."

"I asked in all the ways it was possible to ask without garnering a bit more attention that I think any of us would like. But the fact remains, we have very little to do with any of the Nephete when they transgress to the point they lose their Watcher."

Curt cursed softly.

"So the point when you really should be watching them," Nate started.

"Indeed." Sam made a displeased face. "I agree, it is not a... Clearly that is something that should be addressed, and I will do so as soon as I possibly can without making it about Grace."

"Is there a reason we don't want to make things about Grace?" Curt asked, frowning.

"A few dozen, I would imagine," Grace offered. "Given we're here at all. Whether they're officially watching the wicked witches or not, the bad guys are getting information from somewhere."

"Indeed," Sam agreed. "Them being interested in a First could be a very bad thing."

"If we can find them, or prove anything," Curt muttered. "Which, right now, we can't."

"Is that all?" Nate asked, eyes narrowing. "Because you don't look like that's all, Sam."

Sam blinked at him, before he flushed. And at some point in time Grace was maybe going to have to ask about that. As far as she could tell Sam didn't really have blood, so the flushing was a little strange.

Which was strangely second to the fact Nate had pegged that small curl of avoidance Sam was apparently trying to hide.

"That is all that pertains to the present issue."

Grace blinked at him, picking through that. Sure, the language could have been Sam stumbling through English sideways from who-knew-where. But it sounded more to Grace like one hell of an evasive non-answer. Like there were reasons he didn't intend to share.

Sam looked at her, strangely imploring, and Grace swallowed her questions. From what Deke had said Sam was sharing a lot more than he really should have. She could respect where he wanted to put those lines. Particularly right then when she didn't have any legitimate reason not to.

"Okay." Nate sighed, shrugging it off. "So we're back at square one, and we wait and see if Deke's contacts, or the questions Curt keeps pretending he's not asking, bear anything."

Curt grabbed a bottle of water off the counter. "If they're planning something I'm sure they'll get around to it sooner rather than later."

"Yay," Grace dead-panned.

Curt smiled sadly, and patted her on the shoulder. "Don't wander anywhere, sugar."

"Hadn't planned on it," she answered.

~~~~~~

"You avoiding that boy for a reason?" Curt asked, sitting next to her at the rickety old picnic table, out on the edge of his land.

"Curt." Grace blinked at him. They'd all sort have been at sixes and sevens since Sam left the day before. They were in a holding pattern, and she'd needed to get out of the house for a bit.

"Relax," he assured. "He's got his head shoved up his own ass at the moment. I don't think he's noticed yet. So."

Grace swallowed. She could do this. She didn't want to tell Curt about any of this. Not because she did trust him, but the whole thing was supposed to be private. And she'd never managed to put Jamie in that category, and Sam was equally a no-go, but Nate obviously liked to keep certain things private.

"I'm just…" Grace swallowed.

Curt huffed. "Sugar, I've known you for more than two years, and you've been here for a couple of weeks over the last few months. Something's on your mind."

She shifted, leaning back on the edge of the bench. "I'm working on it." She frowned suddenly. "Are you sure you don't mind me staying?"

"Hell no." He burst out laughing. "You think I wanna deal with the moping that happens if you leave?"

She chuckled, reminding herself of Grace Rule #2. She wasn't the only one with issues.

The problem was she knew all Jamie's. She could navigate them perfectly well, even when they weren't about her—sometimes, shocker, the world didn't revolve around her. And she'd figured out a few of Nate's, obviously.

"I'm just being strange." She forced a smile for Curt.

He nodded. "I thought maybe there was a problem with Sam. I know Jamie wasn't fond of him."

"It's a protectiveness thing. He'll…grow past it eventually. He knows he will. He just needs time. I told Sam that, even if I'm not entirely sure it sunk in."

Curt looked up at the sky. "Well, there's that then. Certainly has been—"

He stopped suddenly, and they both heard crashing through the path, a bare second before Nate and Sam appeared, both running full tilt.

Curt leapt to his feet. "What's—"

He didn't get a chance to finish, before Sam was there and he'd pulled Grace to her feet, crushing her into a tight hug.

"Sam?" Grace swallowed, awkwardly patting his back.

"I don't know." Nate swallowed, leaning forward and putting his hands on his knees. "He showed up at the house, white as a sheet..." He paused, panting. "And wanted to know where you were."

Grace cleared her throat. "Sam...air... You're crushing me."

Sam shook his head no, not releasing her. If anything he clung tighter.

"What happened?"

"Blinding spell," Sam muttered, face practically buried in her hair. "If I hadn't known where you were, I would never have been able to find you."

"Alright." Grace pushed him off a step gently, swallowing. "That's absolutely creepy, but I'm right here. See, all good."

Curt cursed darkly. "But somebody must be planning something."

Nate sighed. "I better call Deke."

Sam frowned, and waved his hand in some kind of symbol Grace wasn't fast enough to catch.

Deke popped up in the clearing with them, looking around him, hand going for his pocket before he saw them. "Son of a... Can we do that without the bloody element of surprise?"

Nate blinked at him, then looked back at Sam. "That was interesting."

Deke huffed, and rubbed a hand to his forehead. "There's obviously something wrong."

"Someone performed a blinding spell," Sam said, still looking like he'd like to be physically holding onto Grace.

"That's lovely. So?" Deke asked darkly.

"I spoke to Grace yesterday morning," Sam answered, voice tense. "She agreed to tell me if they were leaving—"

"And I didn't, so here I am," Grace finished for him.

She didn't have to ask why Sam was so freaked out. If someone could normally just snap people around and follow her anywhere with no advanced warning, the concept of someone taking that away was probably terrifying.

Deke pushed his sleeve up. "Well, there are only so many people who can do that." He looked at Nate. "What have you brushed up against lately? Obviously something has Grace's number."

Grace felt her phone buzz, starting to ring. "Speaking of having Grace's number..." She pulled it out of her pocket. "It's just Jamie."

Grace didn't think about it, just pressed the talk button because even when she couldn't talk, she didn't let Jamie go to voicemail. "Hey Jam, now's not great. Can I call you back in a bit?"

"Jamie thinks now's probably the best time," a voice she didn't recognize oozed across the line, laughing harshly at the end.

Chapter 19

Sam took the phone away from Grace, passing it at Nate, before he physically sat Grace down on the bench behind her.

Which Nate understood, because he'd seen notebook paper with more color than she had right then.

He frowned at the phone, heart stopping in his chest, and hit the speaker icon. "Who is this?"

"Listen carefully, Mr. Carter," the voice answered. It crackled and pitched, because there was some kind of masking going on there. "Tell your little wizard friend that he won't be able to find Doctor Williams, we've taken care of that." He laughed darkly. "If Darling Grace would like her friend back, she has to meet with me. The Warehouse on Seventh and Sycamore, St Louis. Eight PM tomorrow."

Nate winced as the call disconnected with a loud crackle.

Curt cursed darkly. "That's just *wonderful.*"

Deke sighed. "They probably don't know about Sam. I'd guess the blinder was meant to block me from using Grace to track Jamie down. They're pretty...connected."

Nate swallowed, watching Sam with Grace.

But clearly Sam didn't really know what he was doing with this. Because he was trying to make her feel better and Nate sort of figured better wasn't an option right then. Nate cursed under his breath and kicked the side of her shoe. "Come on. Come help me pack."

Grace blinked at him, swallowing. "What am I grabbing?"

"We'll, you'll need the crossbow obviously," Nate said dryly. "We'll take a smattering."

She stood, slipping away from Sam carefully. "Alright. I'll—"

"This is a trap Grace. You can't..." Sam stood, face dark. "You can't go."

Grace frowned at him, eyes hurt. "Of course I'm going."

"I know you care about Jamie, and you want him to be safe, but I will not let you endanger yourself!"

Deke huffed. "Can you do that?"

Sam glared at him, actually looking faintly terrifying. "I do not care, I will—"

Curt cleared his throat. "Why don't you kids go pack? Sam and I'll talk for a second."

Nate winced, and started to grab Grace by the arm, because that wasn't a conversation he felt like being around for. Especially when people's emotions were running high.

"I will not let her—"

"You can't...order," Curt said softly. "They're adults, even if they don't always act like it," he offered. "If you order her she can't go she's going to slip off when you're not looking."

"I swear the way he talks you'd think I was a difficult teen," Nate joked, trying to loosen the tension. Not that he thought it was going to work.

Someone had Jamie and he was pretty sure that was the sort of thing that was going to make them figure out exactly how Grace cracked.

Curt smiled sadly. "This is one of those times you just have to help. Trust me, it's better than getting left behind."

Sam looked at Grace then, uneasy, but eventually despite how tight his jaw was, he nodded.

Nate didn't wait for more, just drug Grace off with him to pack their things. He was ten steps down the path when he realized Deke was coming with them.

"I'm not staying back there." He pulled a face. "Holy hell."

Nate glanced at him, cocking a brow.

"Not that I don't get that things are bad." Deke swallowed, glancing at Grace carefully. "Guy's forgetting all his lines. That doesn't end well."

Nate huffed. "For those of us in the cheap seats?" Nate handed Grace the nylon bag he kept out by the workbench, and pointed her toward the locked chest with the crossbow and everything. "Don't accidentally shoot yourself."

Grace almost smiled, grabbing the bag from him. "Sam said before, Maeleket aren't supposed to order, they're supposed to help. Sort of defeats the purpose if he started making decisions for me."

"Also," Deke continued. "The…randomly shifting people is a little sketchy. I get obviously something was wrong, but he should have found a way to check with me first."

"I should have," Sam said suddenly, standing next to the car. "I apologize. I should not have moved you without your consent."

Deke shrugged, letting it go.

Sam looked at Grace, swallowing. "Would you like me to help," he managed stiltedly. "Or go away?"

"Why would I want you to go away?" Grace frowned. "I thought you were coming with us?"

"I am. I meant until you've packed."

"Oh." Grace rubbed the back of her neck. "I'm just...
It's Jamie."

Sam looked away. "Jamie would say the same thing if
he were here."

"Probably." Grace huffed at him. "I wouldn't listen to
him, either."

Sam blinked at her, and relaxed slightly. "I want you
to be safe. They've gone to a great deal of effort to lure
you into a trap. One that I cannot predict at this point."

Nate couldn't imagine how uncomfortable that had to
be, when you factored in Sam's age. If he had one.

"But I do want Jamie to be safe as well." Sam
continued. "You are attached. I would never cause you
pain."

Grace swallowed. "Okay."

If he thought it would have done any good, Nate
would have suggested he and Deke go do *anything* else.
Give them a little privacy.

"I have to do this," Grace said simply.

Sam straightened his shoulders. "Then tell me how I
can help. With the packing, I can ascertain the rest on my
own."

Deke cleared his throat. "You can help me get some
ingredients together, since I'd have to explain what I
wanted to anyone else."

"Of course." Sam nodded, and glanced at Grace. "You
will stay with Nate or myself, until we go?" He flushed.
"So I know you are safe."

"I'll stay with Nate." Grace forced a smile.

Sam turned, and walked off with Deke, toward the
house.

They both watched them for a long moment, and then
turned and started working almost simultaneously. Nate
focused on the job. He'd been doing this stuff with Grace
long enough to know she wasn't going to let herself think
about anything other than what she was supposed to be
doing. Grace was good at focus.

So he shoved the ridiculous intense desire to crush her into a hug and promise everything would be alright, and packed every weapon they could conceivably need.

Which turned out to be a lot, when you considered they didn't have the first clue what they were up against.

Grace pulled out the bag of C4 he'd stashed in a safe box, and an old Claymore mine. "Do you ever wonder if you've gone so far beyond over-kill you're becoming comedic?" She choked out a slightly manic laugh. "C4 and a Claymore?"

Nate snorted. "They'd have come in handy with the Worg."

"Point." Grace held them up. "In the box or not?"

"Not, I think," he said dryly. "If we need the C4 or the Claymore with humans, or whatever this is, they probably wouldn't be that helpful."

She blew out a breath, and went back to her packing. Nate kept at it, until he'd finished his last bag. Until he'd packed literally everything he could possibly need for any possibility he could think of. He zipped it closed with a flourish, and dropped it next to the car.

He looked up, and watched Grace for a long moment. She was mechanically shoving rounds into a clip, just staring into space. Nate carefully put his hand on her shoulder. "Hey."

Grace blinked at him, eyes large and luminous. She sat the clip down carefully, flexing her fingers. "It's... I just..." She swallowed, and shook her head.

Nate swallowed. "Would it make things worse or better if I gave you a hug?"

Grace blinked at him, and suddenly her forehead was pressed against his neck, her arms wrapped around his middle, clinging tightly. Like if she could burrow into him and be safe, she would. Nate carefully wrapped his arms around her, smoothing her hair down gently.

"Jamie's tough. And just because Deke can't find him doesn't mean he can't tell if they've done something to him. He'll be...fine."

Grace swallowed.

"No, I don't know that." Nate squeezed her. "I believe it. We'll get him back and he'll be fine." He kissed her on the forehead. "If I have to believe it enough for both of us, I will."

He pulled her back into a hug, listening to the evening sounds descend around him, trying not to think too much about what tomorrow would bring. Grace needed one of them to be coherent and capable, and it was his turn anyway.

~~~~~~~

Nate ranked St Louis right up there with water-demons.

Not the city so much. It wasn't *great*. Dark and a little gray and somehow just as depressing as Chicago without the angst. The Arch was neat, but that was about all he had to say for it.

St Louis drivers were...

It was like someone had dropped stupid into the water, and it only acted up when they got in a car. Freaking two inch following distance, with no clue where their indicator lights were, and some freaky sexual thing for their car horns.

St Louis wasn't his favorite town, and he didn't like being in a tense car for *hours*. Grace wasn't normally talkative when they drove. She didn't speak when she didn't have something to say and he was fine with that. Always had been. Even appreciated it.

This was not 'Grace doesn't feel like talking.' This was 'Grace is falling apart in next seat.'

And he just...drove because it wasn't like there was anything he could do about it.

Sam had elected to ride in the back of the Charger, Nate suspected just so he could keep an eye on Grace. He didn't have the guts to ask if Sam could un-manifest—or whatever the term was Deke had used for when Sam made himself look like a person—and still be able to find her.

Because Sam wasn't doing much better. Nate got that the blinder had freaked him out a little. The rest of them hadn't seen how bloody terrified Sam had looked when he'd popped into Curt's yard. Nate was more than a little concerned if this somehow went badly and Grace got hurt...

He didn't hold out much hope of any of the rest of them getting Sam under control. From what Deke said there was some question as to whether other Watchers could get Sam under control.

Just one more thing to add to the steaming pile of fun the day was turning out to be.

Remember that nineteen hour drive to the back-of-nowhere Minnesota where we were punch-drunk and laughing? Nate thought darkly. *Yeah, I wanna go back there too.*

Not that that would do any good with the...thing rattling around in his chest. Nate's decently sure he'd lost his bearings with Grace before that.

Another strike for St Louis; stupid drivers and angst aside, it wasn't busy enough to keep him from thinking. He'd done way too much of that in the last four hours. Not even counting what he'd done between the phone call last night and when they'd left Curt's. He's relatively sure none of them actually slept last night. Grace didn't.

Extra houseful of people, there was no chance he'd have left her in her bedroom alone, even if Sam'd been willing to. She'd said she wasn't going to sleep probably and let Deke have her bed. Nate had known she'd intended to sleep downstairs, or kip on his floor.

Leaving her and Sam in a room together all night wasn't a great idea. They were too highly charged. Grace was too worried and she'd snap at him if he pushed. He'd been even more sure of that decision when she hadn't even muttered when he pushed his bed on her and kipped on his floor.

If the bad guy hadn't given them a schedule they'd probably wouldn't have even tried sleeping. But he had, and they all thought, Grace included, this was one of those situations where it was better to follow the directions. At least for now.

Now you're messin' with a son of a bitch...

Nate winced, digging his phone out. For half a second he was terrified it'd be his mother. *Guess what, I'm in St Louis and I can help!* Which would probably be about the most un-helpful thing ever actually, not that he doubted they'd have managed with the extra hand.

It was Deke.

"Hey." He glanced at Grace. "Plan?"

Deke sighed. "Go ahead and put me on speaker so we don't have to play telephone."

Nate hit the button. "Sure."

"Okay, so here's the thing..." Deke said, voice slightly tinny from the phone speaker. "Curt and I have been talking, and we think showing up early is probably a seriously bad idea."

Nate scoffed. "Seconded, or thirded, whatever."

Curt choked on a laugh.

"So we're going to get decently close, like a few blocks away." Deke huffed. "And then I think there's something to be said for a little surprise, so we'll leave the cars and walk the last couple of blocks."

"'Kay," Nate agreed. "So..."

"We'll work out the rest of the plan once we're there. For now, I sent you directions. We'll meet there, in case we lose you because you refuse to cede to the stupid."

"It's a matter of principle, Deke," Nate insisted. "They know how to drive. I know they do."

"Whatever. Good luck with that. We'll see you in half an hour."

"Will do." Nate turned the phone off, glancing at Grace, who hadn't stopped looking out the window through all of that. He looked back at Sam in the rear-view, catching his eye.

Sam shook his head minutely. He didn't have anything to say either.

~~~~~~~

Nate drove in silence for another half an hour. And normally he'd have made some crack about the possibility of leaving his precious car alone someplace like this. Or that he'd have wanted to put some C4 or something on it.

He didn't. Didn't know how to start it.

He crawled out of the car and went to the trunk, opening it up and shifting the weapons around. Started separating out the weapons he was going to keep with him, and the ones he assumed Grace wanted. He didn't ask. Generally he didn't need to. They didn't just work well together because they didn't get on each other's nerves. They meshed, and considering he'd never in his life felt like he meshed with anyone it wasn't surprising he didn't quite know where to put his lines with her.

Curt walked over next to him, checking a couple of guns. "So Sam's going to disappear. He says he can keep track of us this close, and if they don't know about him it's best to keep it that way."

Nate nodded.

"Is Grace with it enough to—"

"She'll do what she needs to do," Nate cut in, looking up at Curt. "She knows what she's doing."

Grace let out a quiet 'ha,' voice cracking softly as she stepped up next to them. "You have way too much faith in me."

"Not possible." Nate squeezed her shoulder. "Deep breath. It'll be fine."

"-ish," Grace said darkly. "Sure."

Sam pulled her into a tight hug. "I'll be there, even if you don't see me."

Grace hugged him back, before he stepped back and disappeared.

Curt slammed the trunk on the Charger for him, and stepped on to the curb as Sam popped away.

"Freaking weird," Curt muttered, cocking his gun. "Right. Much as it pains me to say it, ladies first."

Grace turned and started down the pavement toward the warehouse. Nate didn't let her get away from him, just fell in step with her.

She glanced at him, questioning.

"They didn't say you had to come in alone. They know about me, there's no way they'd believe I wasn't right here with you."

Deke grumbled behind him, and Nate threw him a look that practically screamed *shut up*.

The warehouse looked fun. Broken windows and darkened doorways. A giant symbol on the front in red spray paint that looked way too much like blood.

"That's the one," Deke said darkly.

Nate shook his head. "What gave it away?" he muttered. "Why didn't they just paint 'we're in here' on the door? Unless that means something?"

"We're in here?" Deke said wryly, re-shouldering his pack. He held a small, etched cloudy white coin out for Grace. "Put that in your pocket, please."

Grace took it, frowning and turning the little token over. The other side was more runes, with a form etched in the middle like a snowflake with weird arms. "What is it?"

"Since we can't track you right now, that'll help. It's a talisman, and obscure so I doubt they've covered that base. It means no one can move you while you're holding it. Not by magical means."

Grace turned it over again, and tucked it into her pocket.

"Might want to just start carrying it," Deke huffed.

Nate shifted, looking around them. "Grace and I'll go in first. I'm not sure there's much point in being stealthy."

"There's not," Curt said. "We're being watched now."

Nate didn't look because he knew better than that. "Ready Grace?"

"Nope," She bit it off, wiggling her fingers a bit to work some of her tension out. "Going anyway."

"I'm right here," Nate assured.

Grace looked at him, eyes serious and steady. "I know."

He watched her turn and open the warehouse door, walking in steadily with her head held high.

The door didn't even get a chance to shift away from it's opening arc before he was in behind her. The room was dark, inky black and large, except for one little pool of light in the corner, with a really unhappy looking Jamie sitting in its glow.

Nate had to give her credit. Grace didn't race across the room in the darkness to get to him. She stopped right inside the door, eyes locked on Jamie, but feet still right there three feet from Nate.

Deke swallowed. "I suppose I should try the lights, before I assume they're out." He shined a pen-light on the switch. "Doesn't look like there's anything hooked to it." Deke flipped the bank of switches, and the lights all over the warehouse hummed their way on, casting strange shadows around the empty interior.

Nate looked around, just to be sure, and checked with Curt— he got a stiff nod in return—before he gently shoved Grace forward.

She looked back at him, tense.

"Go ahead." He forced a smile. "I'm right behind you."

Grace still didn't run. She walked across carefully, watchful and quiet.

A door back in the corner swung open with a horrible grating. "You know," a voice cut through the darkness, the same cadence as the one he'd heard on the phone. "As connected as you two are, I'd sort of expected you to come running through the door and race right after him."

Curt cursed under his breath. "Richards."

"Hello there, Curt." He stepped into the light, tall and dark, a silver tipped cane held easy in one hand and a smooth smile on his face.

Nate frowned. "Richards?" He'd never worked a job with Richards, but he'd heard Curt bitch about him often enough.

Richards laughed darkly. "Where do you think Curt's been getting all those books on witchcraft from?" He grinned. "Surprise." He clicked his tongue. "Really, Deacon Hughes, you can't possibly have thought you were the only one who'd think hiding as a hunter was the best way not to get caught."

Deke cursed. "That's probably because I wasn't hiding."

Grace twitched, like she was about to move.

"Ah ah ah there, darling." Richards shifted focus back to her. "Don't go anywhere yet." He smiled darkly. "We've been looking for you for a long time."

Grace swallowed. "Me?"

"A First?" He stepped forward a bit. "I couldn't cover all the things we could do with you, never mind the raw power you've got. You know you set my wards off when you walked in here tonight? Light the world up like a candle little girl, that's a hard thing to hide."

Nate glared at Deke. "Forget to say something?"

Deke's jaw tensed. "It wouldn't have helped you to know, not right then."

Richards laughed darkly. "So. Grace Cleary," he said brightly and pulled a wand from behind his back. "I'm feeling altruistic tonight. I'll let you say goodbye to your friends."

"And what?" Grace crossed her arms. "I'm not going with you."

"I think you are," he answered. "Because I'll kill them and take you anyway." He grinned. "I know, life's unfair. I'm afraid this is what happens, poor little First, all alone in the world, unprotected."

He pointed his wand at Grace, clearly about to do something drastic. Nate pushed forward, to shove her out of the way, right as the spell formed on Richards' lips.

Chapter 20

Sam popped into being, between Grace and Richards, hand reaching out and stopping the spell. "I wouldn't say 'unprotected' exactly," he countered, face thunderous.

Richards screamed, eyes popping wide as Sam moved toward him. "No! The line has no Watcher!"

Sam cocked his head, moving forward slowly. "Technically it does not, as there is only Grace." He frowned. "I would be very interested in how you know that."

Richards shifted suddenly, laughing. "I know all sorts of things," he said, feinting to the side. "*Velns es jums pelevu, atbildi manus!*"

A stuttered flash lit the room behind them, and Sam turned on a dime, throwing something at the…thing taking up the rest of the room as Deke pulled he and Grace out of its way.

"What the hell is that!" Curt yelled, ducking away from a falling bit of pipe.

It was terrifying actually. Giant and horned, covered in coarse gray hair, with large curved claws and an unholy snarl of teeth.

"Ragveln!" Deke yelled over the noise.

It reached out a giant paw and slammed Sam back against the wall, knocking him down. He got up quickly, and hit it back solidly. The Ragveln stumbled, but didn't go down.

Deke pushed Grace over, handing her a knife. "Go get Jamie!" he yelled over the din. He looked at Nate. "What kind of bullets do you have in that thing?"

"In it? Holy water and salt."

"Perfect!" Deke shoved him out of the way of another piece of debris. "Shoot the damn thing. It won't kill it, but it'll get its attention."

Nate didn't pause, just lined up on it.

"Don't let it get near you!" Deke yelled, ruffling through his bag.

Nate rolled his eyes, and cracked off a shot at it, and it turned on him.

Sam grabbed it by the shoulder, throwing it head-first into a wall. "Keep Richards away from Grace!"

Nate could see her out of the corner of his eye. Richards had her pressed back against the wall, forearm pressed to her throat, pinning her there.

Deke pulled a packet of something out of his bag, and threw it at their new creature friend. It exploded, with dark yellow smoke that smelled like eggs and mustard. The Ragveln wheeled, clutching at what was on its back, just as Sam punched it hard in the head, knocking it to the ground. Nate tried to break across, to get to Grace.

But it started to crawl up again, and Nate was about get another shot in.

"Get him off Grace!" Sam yelled.

Nate turned, sighting along his gun, just as Richards grinned happily and pointed his wand at Curt, three feet away from him, lips pulled back in a sneer.

Nate watched in slow motion as Grace reached a hand out, fingers wrapping around the wand. "NO!" she screamed, word echoing around the warehouse as it erupted in light and fire.

269

The force blew Nate back, sliding across the warehouse floor before everything changed direction and sucked in, rolling him over. His ears rang in the sudden silence, ash raining from the ceiling. He blinked, trying to clear his eyes, aware that someone was moving and he needed to be.

Sam rushed past him, sliding to the floor next to Grace, tipping her head back.

Nate struggled up, trying to shake his laggard wits back into place, swallowing as the world suddenly sped back up like it was supposed to.

"What the *shit* was that," Deke said loudly, making them all jump.

"Shh…" Sam managed, voice shaking. "Calm yourself. Just breathe, everything is fine."

Nate looked around him, swallowing. Fine might have been overstating things. There creature friend was gone, and so was Richards.

"Where the hell did that thing go?" Curt managed quietly.

Deke swallowed. "She broke his wand, and that broke the binding." He looked uneasy. "The better question is, where did *he* go? And what exploded?"

Jamie shifted. "Someone want to cut me loose?"

Curt blinked at him, and walked over with a blade out. "Here."

Nate managed to stumble to his feet, and walk over to Grace, her eyes still pointed at the ceiling, breaths still slamming in to each other.

Sam swallowed, looking at him. "She should not be able to do that. She's— "

"Panicking," Nate said, leaning close and grabbing her shoulder. "Grace!" he shouted sharply.

She blinked once, swallowing.

"Jamie's fine, he's coming now." Nate knelt down in front of her. "We're all good, alright? Just breathe."

"Did I kill him?" Grace swallowed, face paling.

"Oh. Richards?" Sam blinked. "No. No, Grace. You did not kill him." He smiled slightly, grabbing a rag from somewhere and gently cleaning her face. "When you broke his wand I could move him. I sent him someplace he will not harm anyone and he will be dealt with."

Grace relaxed a bit, before she suddenly punched Nate in the arm, hard.

"Ow." Nate winced.

"You fucking…" She tackled him in a hug. "You were about to push me out of the way. Idiot."

Nate fell back on the floor, sprawling under her weight.

Sam grinned at him, eyes light. "Nate cares about you too much to trust me to continuously rescue you."

Deke sat down heavily. "You're all broken."

"Seconded," Jamie said suddenly, wrapping his arms around Grace and Nate. "Excuse me Nate, we're going to crush you for a second."

Nate choked out a laugh.

"What? You just tried to get yourself shot by a fucking dark wizard to save my best friend. That means group hug."

Grace hugged Nate tight, kissing his cheek. "I'm not done with you yet."

Nate had time to blink, and wonder what the hell that was about, before she turned and latched onto Jamie.

"Hey…I'm okay," Jamie said softly. "Occupational hazard, I guess. Everybody picks the college professor for their dastardly deeds."

~~~~~~

Nate rubbed the cloth over the back of his neck, slamming the hood on the Charger closed. Cold wind blew around him, winter finally starting to set in.

It'd been a crazy fall. Monsters and witches and fucking angels that weren't angels and…

Grace. Which was another matter entirely.

Once everything was over in St Louis they'd packed up and rolled back to Curt's. He picked through the regular bags of equipment he kept in the back, making sure they were all packed and ready to go. He didn't have a job in mind right then, but when all else failed he settled on being prepared. It made him feel better.

Noise sounded from the house and he looked up. Deke was still there. Because he'd decided closing the shop down for a week and just explaining things to Curt made more sense than getting phone calls every five minutes.

Sam was around too, off and on. Clearly he had things going on, but he was past the point where he just followed Grace around invisibly.

Grace was…Grace. Whatever he felt about her aside, sense wasn't always the first word he'd pick.

Things had been normal for them, since St Louis. Which was fine. Just not what he'd expected.

He turned around, to put the keys to the lock box back where they kept them, and sighed. "Now you're trying to sneak up on me."

Grace cursed, huffing. "It's no fun when you spoil it."

"You have a strange definition of fun." He glanced at her, out of the corner of his eye. Hair loose in the breeze, hands shoved deep in the pockets of her hoodie. "So…"

"You haven't asked what I meant."

Nate blinked, swallowing. That *I'm not done with you* she'd assured before. He thought about pretending he didn't know what she was talking about for half a second. "I…haven't." He grabbed the last bag from the edge of the car.

Grace nodded. "You aren't leaving without me?"

He froze, half-turned away. Did that mean… Fuck. There was some point here where he was going to have to grow a pair. "I wasn't sure you wanted to come."

She cocked her head at him. "Why?"

"You don't like it," he said, carefully. Because Grace was perfectly capable as a hunter, but she didn't like the life. Most of her itchy had been being crammed in with him and Curt, not about having to hold still.

"Well. No."

Nate pushed a hand through his hair. "Yeah. So…" He frowned. "Why would you want to?"

Grace trailed her hand carefully along the side of the Charger. "It's a shit job. You shouldn't have to do it alone."

He got that. It wasn't like he thought she hadn't noticed the job was easier with her.

"And also…" Grace bit her lip and looked up at him. "I don't like the job." She flushed, shrugging. "I like you."

Nate blinked.

She huffed. "Yes, I meant that exactly the way you're trying not to take it."

He swallowed, shifting uncomfortably. "O…okay. You know I…" Nate died off, not sure how to say the words.

"Yeah." Grace nodded. "So."

"Right." Nate rubbed the back of his neck. "Will Sam be okay with that? The hunting I mean, not…" He flushed. "Us. If there is an us, just…"

Grace choked out a laugh, and grabbed a handful of the front of his shirt, pulling him into a kiss. "We'll deal with it."

Epilogue

"Damn it, Deke." Nate cursed at his phone, rubbing a hand over the back of his neck. That was the twelfth time he'd called and it'd gone to voicemail.

Deke didn't fail to answer his phone. Ever. In the better part of six years of friendship, Nate thought he'd spoken to Deke's voicemail probably four times.

He looked out at the winter sky, through Curt's window, wondering if the snow was going to hold off as long as it was supposed to. It looked like it wanted to snow, but it wasn't supposed to blizzard until next week sometime.

Nate grabbed his phone and paced into the kitchen. The house was silent around him. He was alone. Freaking out, because Deke wasn't answering. But his only other option was to drive up to Chicago and look over the shop.

Now you're messin' with a son of a bitch...

He lunged for the phone on the counter, looking at the screen, heart squeezing painfully in his chest. He swallowed, pressing the button. "Hey, sugar."

"Hey," Grace answered. "Still no word?"

"No." He dropped his head against the fridge. "How is—"

"Job's fine." Grace cut in easily. "Curt seems to think we'll be done tomorrow, maybe the day after." She sighed darkly. "How are you?"

"I'm fine." Nate offered. Then felt the need to be honest and add "—ish. What about..." He winced. "Do you think Sam could do his thing?"

Grace puffed, the line crackling. "He said he had something to do for the council, and if I needed him in an emergency he'd be here." She swallowed. "And I get that you're worried and I'm not saying you shouldn't be. But it's only been twelve hours and he's an adult," Grace said. "But in your place I doubt I'd be able to make that, so if you want me to—"

"No." Nate rubbed his face, swallowing. "It's... You're right. If Sam's got something else on his plate we should wait a little longer." He looked around the empty house. "I think I might drive up there and make sure the shops...good."

"Alright." She paused. "Listen, I know you're gonna say no, but I feel like I should say it anyway. Curt's probably capable of doing this himself, if you want me to—"

"No." Nate shook his head, leaning back against the counter and staring at the ceiling. "No. I'm probably just..."

He couldn't manage to push out the words 'freaking out over nothing' for a whole host of reasons. Not the least of which being that he didn't believe it.

Grace swallowed. "Okay. Listen, I have to go. Curt's got some plan for convincing the ME to let us run tests on his mysterious corpse."

"Good luck." He smiled softly.

"Sure." Grace cleared her throat. "And call me the second you hear anything, okay? Or even if you don't."

"Will do," Nate agreed. "Miss you."

Grace chuckled. "I miss you too. Bye."

"Bye." He hung the phone up, staring at it for a moment. Before he dialed again, getting shuttled to voicemail.

"This is Deke. You know the drill."

Nate swallowed. "Deke, I'm coming up there. If I get to the store and you fucking lost your phone or something, fair warning, I'll probably kill you."

Nate grabbed his keys and headed out the door, stopping long enough to make sure the house was locked, before he was starting up the Charger and peeling out of the drive.

THE END

ABOUT THE AUTHOR

Lost and Found is J.M. Beal's second full length novel, and the first in a three part series about modern magic and monster hunters. Book 2, *Shelter in the Storm*, will be available from Golden Fleece Press in November 2015.

J.M. grew up in a small town in the Midwest, concocting elaborate ghost stories themed around the dilapidated Victorian mansions, abandoned zoological parks, and deserted frontier forts that populated her childhood.

She insists her childhood home was *not* haunted.

Most of the people who visited disagree.